Praise for Elleke Bohmer

Screens Against the Sky (Bloomsbury and Penguin, 1990)
Short-listed David Higham Prize

'A brilliant handling of an obsessional mother-daughter relationship. . . . Her descriptions are achingly acute.'
Financial Times

'An astonishing debut . . . swift, deft . . . expertly told . . . With a mordant wit, she shows how discrimination can become as natural as breathing, and as unselfconscious.'
Penny Perrick, *Sunday Times*

'Eloquently expressive'
The Guardian

'A beautifully authentic insight into a society turned in on itself in the face of black deprivation'
Wendy Woods

'Elegant, percipient writing'
Zoe Heller, *Observer*

An Immaculate Figure (Bloomsbury, 1993)

'remarkable restraint and subtlety'

West Africa

'a very clever book indeed. . . . It adopts the aesthetic appropriate to a culture in a politically hopeless age.'

Jenny Turner, *The Guardian*

Bloodlines (David Philip, 2000)
Short-listed SANLAM Prize

'an engrossing and intriguingly told chapter in anti-imperial history'

J.M. Coetzee

'a postcolonial fantasia . . . an imaginative exploration of the possibilities of connectedness. . . . The skilful tracing of bloodlines through several generations makes of a desperate act of violence a token of regeneration.'

Michiel Heyns, *Sunday Independent*

'a journey into the possible . . . an extremely good read'

Cape Argus

'*Bloodlines* is an engaging and compelling book binding a potent theme and memorable characters into a brisk narrative . . . the writing shows a controlled resonance, the sign of a talent that must not be ignored.'

Times Literary Supplement

Nile Baby (Ayebia, 2008)

A 'strange and often unsettling odyssey across England . . .
the novel asks us to consider the complex nature of race
and belonging in contemporary Britain.'

Patrick Flanery, *Times Literary Supplement*

'Boehmer's eye for domestic detail and ear for the nuances
of speech whisk the reader in and out of different ways
of being . . . Arnie gradually realizes that life is shaped in
unforeseen ways by history.'

Angela Smith, *The Independent*

'Elleke Boehmer's fourth novel is a remarkable change of
gear: after the complex weaving of South African historical
narratives in *Bloodlines* she has given us a focused,
mesmerizing, and an occasionally stomach-turning story of
two twelve-year-olds. . . . [The novel] grasps the enigmatic
depths of human, and continental, relations.'

Derek Attridge

'a moving portrayal of friendship'

Mariss Stevens, *NELM*

Sharmilla, and Other Portraits (Jacana, 2010)

'Elleke Boehmer brings to her stories two qualities that all too often are mutually exclusive: the lucidity of her intelligence and the passion of her engagement'.

André Brink

'Perceptive, new stories'.

Caryl Phillips

'The accurate simplicity is astonishing, especially because it is present in all her portraits'.

Tshepo Tshabalala, *Star Tonight*

Elleke Boehmer is the author of novels including *Screens Against the Sky* (short-listed David Hyam Prize, 1990), *Bloodlines* (shortlisted SANLAM prize), and *Nile Baby* (2008), and also the short story collection *Sharmilla, and Other Portraits* (2010). Her edition of Baden-Powell's Scouting for Boys was a 2004 summer bestseller. Her acclaimed biography of *Nelson Mandela* (2008) has been translated into Arabic, Malaysian, Thai, Kurdish, Portuguese and Brazilian Portuguese. She has published several other books including *Stories of Women* (2005), the anthology *Empire Writing* (1998), and *Indian Arrivals: Networks of British Empire* (2015). She is Professor of World Literature in English at the University of Oxford. She was born in Durban but now lives in England.

By the same author

Sharmilla, and Other Portraits
Nile Baby
Bloodlines
An Immaculate Figure
Screens Against The Sky

Indian Arrivals 1870–1915
Nelson Mandela
Stories of Women
Empire, the National, and the Postcolonial
Colonial and Postcolonial Literature: Migrant Metaphors
Empire Writing: An Anthology 1870–1918

The Shouting in the Dark

Elleke Boehmer

SANDSTONEPRESS
HIGHLAND | SCOTLAND

First published in Great Britain
and the United States of America 2015
Sandstone Press Ltd
Dochcarty Road
Dingwall
Ross-shire
IV15 9UG
Scotland.

www.sandstonepress.com

The publisher acknowledges subsidy from Creative Scotland
towards publication of this volume.

ISBN: 978-1-910124-29-1
ISBNe: 978-1-910124-30-7

Cover design by Mark Swan
Typeset by Iolaire Typesetting, Newtonmore
Printed and bound by Totem, Poland

For Thomas and Sam

Contents

Sheet

Ella pushes open the heavy wooden door to her mother's apartment block, and the weight presses back on her arm. She feels the hallway's chilly air wrap around her, the marble floor dewy with damp. It rained earlier. There were puddles out on the street. Deep inside the eight-storey building of the Dutch Ministry of Internal Affairs, though, she wasn't aware of the weather.

The door slams closed and the crash sparks in her memory an echo pattern of noises that has followed her across the day, doors upon doors falling to behind her.

Since nine this morning she has spent her time walking the neon-lit corridors of the Ministry, now on the sixth floor, now in the basement, each corridor blocked at intervals by heavy fire doors. All day she has been putting the flat of her hand to matte grey office doors on strong springs, and the heavy glass doors of waiting rooms, pushing and being pushed back. Today has been her last-ditch attempt to establish her right to residence in her parents' native land, now that a state of emergency in her own country has been declared and she received the tip-off: her after-hours work of hiding activists on the run has been exposed. But her efforts have been to no purpose, none at all.

Late this afternoon, a steel-haired official spelled it out in a nasal haute-Hague voice. *Mevrouw, there is no record of your birth in the* Volksregister. *Her pale blue eyes looked straight into Ella's, her manicured nail tapped the spot. See, beneath your parents' names? There is no name, no date, no details. I'm very sorry, but . . . you cannot be granted citizenship. We must ask you to leave the Netherlands as planned.*

Ella has a hand on the banister, a foot arrested on the first step of the hallway stairs. Take another step, she pushes herself, up to the second floor, her mother's apartment. She hasn't yet learned to think of the place as her own, the handsome one-bedroom apartment with the picture windows looking out onto the stately park over the road. A piece of property she must now leave behind, almost as soon as inherited. She takes another slow step, another. The blank she hit today, that white space in the Register, it's a towering wall. She's good at setting obstacles behind her, she's done it since she was a girl – but she has no idea how to get beyond this one. Her own father, as if from beyond the grave, put his hand to the door of this land that might have been her haven, and slammed it in her face.

Ella walks the length of her mother's living room, tidying and straightening things as she goes, as if readying the place for her departure. But, face it, there is no as if to the matter, she is readying the place. She should think about dust sheets and turning off the mains. It could be a year or more before she's here again, however long it takes to mount a fresh appeal for citizenship. She should try to think clearly, work out what to do next. She can't spend the whole time that is left pacing. She'll need her energy for later, the journey back to Africa, to Durban. From her bag she takes the sheets of paper that the steel-haired official handed her, the photocopy and the Department's formal letter imprinted with dents where her damp fingers have clenched it.

She sits in her mother's favourite armchair, still in its old position in the living room. It faces the large life-sized portrait of her aunt Ella, after whom she is named. The slanting late-afternoon light warms the pale bluish skin tones of the portrait.

You – you knew him better than anyone, she says quietly to the picture, then drops her eyes, can't hold its gaze. She looks again at the letter in her hand. Her bid for Dutch citizenship on the basis of ancestry has failed for 'one insurmountable reason': the place where her name should appear is blank. She, Ella, is not her father's child – not on paper, at least. And therefore, so the patrilineal logic of the Volksregister *runs, she is also not officially recognized as her mother's child. We regret to inform you ... Her life now lies elsewhere.*

How he must have despised her, she thinks, more so than even she suspected. He has annulled her existence, or no – it's more final even than that. To be annulled, an existence must first be acknowledged, which he refused to do. He could have taken steps, couldn't he? Popped down to the Dutch consulate in Durban to register her?

She gets up, walks to the nearest window, lays the letter on the sill. The sun has set behind the apartment building and the beech trees in the park make a deep green mass against the darkening sky. How well she knows those trees, that park. She could follow the network of its pathways with her eyes closed, draw out the sharp angles of the Second World War bunkers, overgrown now with rhododendron bushes, hunkering amongst the trees.

He hated me? He hated me not? – she gazes out. Her bookkeeper father who prided himself on his forward planning, his omission was an oversight? Not possible. There were simply other things on his mind than his daughter.

Once, years ago in Canada, she thought something was vouchsafed her about him, during the meeting with the Royal Navy veteran. He told her a story that seemed to explain her father's embittered fury. For a time it helped. She found the courage to change direction, stop running away. Her mistake. He might have forgotten about her but she could not be allowed to forget about him.

She turns, walks to the linen cupboard in the hallway, takes a single white cotton sheet from the pile there, the sheet tightly folded, still holding its starch though it hasn't been used in years. In front of the portrait of her aunt she shakes the sheet open, the thick cotton crackling as it concertinas loose. It's an unexpected convenience. The folds stay printed in the thick cotton like a grid of furrows and make the hanging easier. The topmost furrow lets her hook the sheet snugly over the portrait. She stands back from her handiwork, pats down a fold of the sheet. 'Take a rest, Ella,' she whispers, 'Just for tonight. Let me think this through.'

She's used to keeping watch at night, after all, staying awake though lying ramrod still, the fugitives' breathing under her bed telling the seconds. Before dawn she rouses them as agreed with a gentle shoulder-grip, a slice of buttered bread, then sends them on their way.

She goes back to the window, squints into the shadows between the dark green beeches. She makes believe she sees it, the big concrete sandpit she knows lies just beyond the trees, beside the duckpond. She pictures herself, years ago, a tall girl with a built-up shoe standing beside a sandpit in a Dutch park, huddled together with a group of other children watching something. A man and his talking puppet in a harlequin suit. The man's mouth silently opening and closing as the puppet chatters.

She swivels her mother's armchair towards the window, sits. She can see the reflection of her head in the black rectangle of the darkened window. She leans back, stretches, folds her arms; the reflection elongates and bunches also.

4

Sheet

She remembers her white-haired father holding a pair of binoculars, looking out to sea. She sees him sitting in a rattan chair on the verandah, chain-smoking and slapping at mosquitoes, shouting at the night air. 'Hold your tongue, idioot! Godverdomme. *Keep on, just keep on!*'

She sees herself peeping through the curtains, her eyes just reaching over her bedroom's windowsill. How she practised for hours at being a ventriloquist, mouthing her lips in synch with his. He talked more than anyone else she knew – about the war, his ships, the East, his friends. She remembers imagining an empty space in her middle, an echoey hollow through which to direct the flow of his speech.

Her fury is so strong it is almost exciting. It shakes her skull. She had so much reason to hate him, all those years – it's marvellous. Beyond the reflection in the black glass she sees a man with his mouth wide open. She closes her eyes. A girl runs past Ella's portrait swathed in shadow, out into the glittering garden.

African Shield

Here on the high rim of the African shield, on the shoulder of land that the great continent at its south-eastern edge hefts up from the deep-blue Indian Ocean, Ella has a garden that feels magical. The garden lies at the back of the square bungalow where she lives with her short father Har and tall mother Irene. Its centrepiece is a patch of kikuyu lawn surrounded by hydrangea bushes canopied in morning-glory creeper. The hydrangea bushes make a good shady hideaway and an excellent lookout. If Ella worms her way through the bushes to the perimeter fence, she can see down into the dark river gorge beyond, which is home to a tribe of grey monkeys. Some days the monkeys come up to peep through the wire fence. As soon as Ella sees their wet black eyes at the wire she runs to drag the washing off the line. The monkeys like to steal clothes, socks and underpants especially, to put on and wear as hats.

One Christmas holiday Ella uses broken bricks and two old blankets to convert the natural hidey-holes inside the hydrangea bushes into a secret den with two green cave-like rooms and a winding passage in-between. In the closeness of her den she talks out loud to her Dutch ragdoll Zeeboo. She also talks, but more softly, to the friend called Friend who lives in amongst the hydrangeas, whom no one can see but whose voice she can hear reply. To Friend she chants the funny half-Dutch, half-English rhymes that jump into her mouth from nowhere as she skips in the small yard beside the kitchen, beneath the sighing casuarina trees.

Under the bungalow is another hideaway, another level within the garden, a sandy cave dug out between the concrete support-struts to keep the rooms above cool. No one but Ella ventures into this breezy place, not even the gardener Charley, though his hoe and rake are stored here, the handles lying close to the grille gate so he can reach for them without entering. Charley says the area is bewitched though Ella doesn't think so. The one time he points, exclaims, 'Look, *ntombazane*, right there, that thing dancing!' she squints hard at the empty air but can see nothing.

Ella likes the space under the floorboards for how roomy it feels, how its dry sandy floor is good to sit on. She likes that whenever she plays here Charley keeps watch at the grille, making a tall shape against the light – just as if, she thinks, he was her big brother. She tells the Afrikaner children who play in the street she has an older brother called Charley, eighteen years old, but when they laugh and say that the only Charley they can see around is the Zulu boy, she clicks her tongue at them and walks away.

From the eastern edge of the garden is a clear view of the Indian Ocean. After work her father, still in his ink-stained bookkeeper's shirt and navy blue Lukes Lines tie, likes to stand here in the shadow of the casuarinas and follow through his binoculars the movements of the merchant ships and tankers from distant lands lying in the roadstead outside Port Natal harbour. He presses the binoculars right up against his black-rimmed glasses. Looking at the ships, trying to read their flags and signs, he feels freer and happier, Ella can tell. He's back in the days when he worked with ships in those same distant lands, so he says. And she, standing beside him, trying to make out with her naked eye the ships his binoculars are pointing at, feels freer also. The air around her father feels somehow lighter when he gets out his binoculars and looks at ships.

Her father has the same freed look on his wrinkled face when, on occasional Sundays, never often enough, he takes her down to the docks to see the ships at close quarters. Side by side they stand on wharves stained pearly with oil and watch the big square cranes silhouetted against the Bluff unloading their containers. They watch the tugs steaming out to dredge the sandbank and the trains rolling up to the very edge of the quays, the deckhands flinging ropes around the iron-ringed capstans as if lassoing them. He points out the different flags of the world flying from the ships, so she can learn them, the ones from the East especially, Japan, Malaysia, the Philippines, Singapore, Ceylon. His narrowed eyes behind his thick glasses trace the rows of containers stacked on the ships' decks, as if he were matching the loads against the figures in his blue-lined bookkeeping ledgers.

One day they see a group of stevedores shoulder a coffin made of packing-case slats down a gangplank. 'They'll be glad to get rid of that,' he shakes his head. 'Bad luck to have a stiff on board.'

On hot afternoons Ella sits in the shade of the gatepost with the mother's Ridgeback dog Rex. She has a boy's short haircut and freckles on her nose. She and Rex survey the goings-on in the street, the Zulu cleaners gossiping over their crochet work on the grass verge, the Afrikaner children kicking stones. Those children aren't of our standing, says Mam, so Ella isn't allowed to play with them. Listening hard, Ella tries to discover whether she can follow the cleaners' Zulu. When her father has visitors from the good old days in the East she also tries to follow the English that's mixed in with their Dutch. Zulu is as softly up and down as English, but English is more mumbling. Afrikaans is very mumbling, but the words are sometimes like Netherlands, so she gets it better than Zulu.

At home there are no opportunities to learn Zulu, only English from Dad. Because they are Dutch, that is, foreign and civilised, the mother and the father don't employ a black servant. Irene is fresh out of Holland, fresh off the boat, people say. She's all high colour, long arms, long gangly legs. In her few years in South Africa the foreign hasn't yet rubbed off her. She says she wants it to stay that way. Charley doesn't count as a servant, in her opinion, because he works outdoors.

The mother likes Charley. Some mornings she drinks her coffee with him out in the kitchen yard. Early on, she asked him questions about the ins and outs of gardening in this hot, sticky strip of coastal South Africa. Charley mostly advised her to avoid overwatering the flowers, especially down here within the rain-belt of the African shield. More recently, they've moved on to talking about his family, his hopes for the future. He often mentions his many aunts, his mother's sisters, how all of them are teachers. He confides that someday he aims to become a teacher like his aunts. As Charley and Mam talk, Ella hangs about behind the windy-drier listening, dangling her skipping rope.

One morning the father catches the mother in the act, the misjudgement, stupidity, trespass, he doesn't quite know how to put it— With Charley standing by, shuffling, still holding his coffee mug, the father spells out to the mother in Dutch, right here in the yard, that whites in Africa don't consort with natives, no, not even when they're good workers like Charley and aged just eighteen.

'In this country it isn't for blacks to aim high. That's the country's strength. It's for the white to aim high. Blacks can't aim high, they don't have the mental power. Charley is being plain *brutaal* drinking coffee with his Madam. Cheeky, Irene, *brutaal*, setting himself above his station. Don't encourage him.'

The mother puts her hands on her hips and puffs out her cheeks but makes no reply. Ella keeps out of sight behind the windy-drier.

At the end of the month, the father releases Charley from his employment. 'Self-respecting Europeans should avoid relying on black labour,' he says.

Ella pushes further into the hidden hydrangea passages in her garden. She finds a tiny den so deep inside the bushes not even the monkeys would be able to find it. Here she takes off the funny built-up shoe that's meant to correct her wonky left foot. Most of the time it doesn't bother her, but it gets sweaty in the heat. Though Charley's gone, she still wishes she had an older brother, tall and caring like he was, but she makes do chatting with Friend.

The next Christmas they move house. They go fifty miles inland from Durban to the dormitory town of Braemar. The father takes early retirement from Lukes Lines, the American shipping company he has worked for as a book-keeper without promotion for all of his fifteen years in South Africa. He says he's had enough of the sea. He doesn't want to keep living in the past. He'll set up now as a freelance bookkeeper, take part-work from some solid land-based companies, nothing as binding or soul-destroying as before. Durban reminds him wherever he looks of the days of his youth, the happy years spent on the lip of the Indian Ocean. Ella thinks of his face when they're down at the docks and doesn't believe him. How he can be tired of Durban when saying *lip of the Indian Ocean* makes his straight-line mouth turn up at the sides?

The first time Ella and her mother see the neat streets of Braemar and their new house is the day they move in.

The father settled for the town and then the house, a tidy bungalow on Ridge Road, after a single sighting during a Sunday drive on his own. He can't have stuck around long that first time, Ella thinks, or he might have noticed that, by way of waterways, Braemar has no more than a narrow ribbon of dry riverbed clotted with eucalyptus and poplars and, a few miles downstream, a shallow reservoir called Victory Dam.

But this is what I like, the father again assures them, the fact that Braemar with its well tarred streets lies a world away from ships and wharves.

'The grind at Lukes Lines was a living hell,' he says in his loud voice, as if to convince them, 'whereas here, from this verandah open to the sky, you've a picture of perfect freedom. In Durban, remember, the verandah was the size of a porch, low-eaved, dark. Here the wide world itself spreads out at the verandah's edge. See how the terraced lawn goes down the river valley, how the green fields stretch to meet the misty-blue horizon. Here you can gaze like a king upon miles of rolling Zululand hills. I worked myself to pieces for that view,' he adds, slapping his knee. 'The best highlands farmhouses on the continent would envy it. It's a verandah for a westerner, an Englishman – and mind you say verandah and not *stoep* like a Boer.'

But Ella's mother isn't convinced. Rural Zulu Braemar is too far from Durban's concert hall and shops for the lamps in her eyes to stay alight. 'I've lost everything coming here, Har,' she tells the father every day, handing him his morning coffee on the verandah, 'I've lost my life.'

'You think only of yourself, *mens*,' he mutters, scowling. 'How you go on. We lost the light of our lives long ago, the day our beloved Ella departed from us. For a change, spare a thought for parties other than yourself.'

As for Ella, ever since the house move she misses Friend.

Friend somehow knew the gardens up here on the African shield would have no bush, so she stayed put in Durban.

In Braemar, once night falls, strange wild cries leap from the father's mouth. Swaddled in a scarf of Rothman's Plain smoke, he sits on the verandah as if keeping watch, a tumbler of brown liquid on the rattan table beside him. The words he once spoke to the starry sky in his ordinary voice, back on the porch in Durban, now come out as shouts, raw noises that tear at his smoker's lungs. '*Idioot*,' he shouts, '*Klootzak*! Keep on, now, keep on!' The mother leaves him to it. After dinner she goes straight to their bedroom, tugs the door closed behind her with a click.

The father's noises pull Ella to the window. She can't help herself. She's seven now, almost eight, far taller than she was back in Durban. She can see over her bedroom windowsill. She likes to go over and watch as he keeps watch, to see how the hills fade into the dusty purple sky and the first white stars flare out like distant beacons. Then, at an invisible signal, the sounds begin to come from him, the groans and sudden ragged shouts, the swearing, choking, spitting.

Some nights, the sounds settle into the shape of stories, flashes of tall tales. When the friends from the East stay over, Ko Brink, Henk Vroom, Koen Zwemmer, Pim Faithfull, mostly one by one, sometimes in pairs, the mother long in the bedroom, the father calls up tales of their former days and doings. He tells of the roaring times they shared in the distant ports whose names Ella now knows – Singapore, Calcutta, Rangoon, Jakarta, Colombo. 'How hard we worked and played,' he says, passing round the Old Brown Sherry bottle. 'And never were the worse for it, were we, we sturdy cogs in the wheels of those great, continent-spanning European shipping companies that the war smashed into pieces?'

The listening friends know the stories well yet each time ask to have them again. 'Old chap,' they say, 'Remember that day?' 'Tell us again— ' And the father turns in their direction, towards Ella's bedroom window, his voice sliding into sharper focus. 'Well, yes,' he says, 'You remember, it was in the Great World Club and that crazy Commodore, trying out the foxtrot ...' He turns away and his voice dissolves into the dark, mixed with night-time noises, trucks droning on the highway to Durban, the sharp barks of distant dogs. The unfamiliar names burr in Ella's ears. 'Pfah, the cheeky fellow yelped, spinning my boater into the bay, Colonial Outfitters, Kalverstraat, Amsterdam – we don't wear that kind of thing out here!'

And the friend, Henk or Ko – mainly it is Ko – leans back in his chair, head to one side, a small smile sitting in the corner of his lips, as if trying to coax the story to step out from behind a screen and come forwards to greet him.

What a life you have out here in Africa, Har! the friends musingly say late at night, the father growing hoarse. What a terrific berth you've found after the many years of graft. Bah, the father rumbles back, Put your sunshine where it belongs, up your *gat*. Sunshine gives poor Irene migraines, reduces even lusty Zulus to zombies. Look, Ko, Henk, Africa is a shit-hole. It drives white people mad, even the Soviets. If they arrive sane, their senses all too soon go into reverse. I've survived in Africa because I've lived exclusively on this civilized southernmost edge. Here alone we old colonials can rebuild the white republic.

Most Braemar nights, though, the father is by himself, yet still talks out loud, beats his knee for emphasis, slaps the glass-topped rattan table with its chipped under-layer of mustard-yellow paint, walks to the verandah edge to heave gobs of mucus onto the lawn. He's a lipless mouth throwing out hoicking noises, only, when he's alone, Ella

13

notices, he doesn't speak so much about the good life strung
between the clubs, warehouses and docks of the Far East.
In these other stories he's not onshore but at sea and at war,
on a Royal Netherlands Navy N-class destroyer called the
Tjerk Hiddes, stalked by enemy frigates. Among the group
of old *makkers* he's the only one who doesn't return to the
Far Eastern haunts on Once-in-a-Lifetime tours. 'Who'd
want to see it? Whole place was shot to hell.' He's also the
only one who saw combat during the War. He alone, he
says, Ella listening, was fool enough to give ear to Queen
Wilhelmina's call, brace up for the beleaguered fatherland's
defence.

'People think the Royal Navy was all British,' he tells the
night sky. 'They forget the plucky ships of the Netherlands
and Norwegian navies, among others, how we mucked
in, made our way to Scapa Flow, skirted round the side
of the galvanized-steel lid Adolf Hitler had laid over the
Continent. How we, too, said *be buggered* to the Nazis.'

The father's war stories begin in the middle of nowhere,
break off suddenly, turn like boomerangs and hit Ella,
peeping, with surprises. Is it the war, she wonders, that
makes him shout like he does? Is he just a cross old seaman
missing the good days in the East? What presses him to hurl
those angry words at the night? Back in Durban, before she
began eavesdropping in earnest, she had no idea he was
in the war. Though he's old, fifty-nine last birthday, she
hadn't thought *that* old. The war, she'd thought, was ages
and ages ago. Hard a-port, he suddenly yells, clanging his
sherry tumbler on the table, Emergency front! That's the
ticket. *Ach waarom nou, waarom?* he sobs. *Verdomme,
Godverdomme*, those dear chaps and lovely girls, and the
storms and strafing and busy quays, and remember that
consignment of crazy Australian horses for the Sultan of
Johore, when they ran amok?

14

Some nights he calls out so loud that Ella thinks he must be hailing someone. He wouldn't sit and shout at nothing, would he? Could he be waiting for a secret visitor to arrive, she asks herself, someone to recognize at last all that he fought for? *We Europeans, we remade the world with our hard work*, he spits, *and then we gave it up again as if it cost us nothing.*

At first now and again, then by the time of her ninth birthday on most Braemar evenings, the father's night watches draw Ella from her bed to the window. She slips into the gap in the curtains, puts her ear to the glass, till he himself gets up, switches off the outside light and goes to bed. If she were ever to quit peeping and lie down, she wonders, would the long-expected secret visitor finally appear? Would he get the message at last that till now he's been refused?

International trunk calls come once in a blue moon to Braemar but Ella picks out their throaty pirrup as soon as the ring begins. So far, these trunk calls have always been for the mother, even the ones back in Durban. A relative is ill, or dead; Oma in Oegstgeest wants to talk to her only living daughter, mark some special occasion, the birth of a Royal baby of Orange.

Today, a Saturday, the pirrup breaks into her parents' coffee time on the verandah, so she is the first to the telephone, calling over her shoulder, *Trunk call, trunk call.* She hears the strange whirring in the background you get because of the undersea cables, very tinny and grinding, and then the click, *Hallo? Hallo? Wie is dat? Irene, Ella?*

'*Ja, ja, met Irene,*' her mother grabs the receiver from Ella's hand but immediately looks crestfallen. It's not her mother, not one of her cousins, but Har's brother. 'Jan,' she mouths at Ella. 'Call your father. *Quickly.*'

But the father, too, is already standing by. During trunk calls he comes to stand by, his watch held in his palm.

Ja . . . Ja, Jan? The brothers don't mince words, or rather Har doesn't. Jan has a few curt lines to report. *Ja, ja,* the father says again, nothing more than *Ja,* frowning hard, then thrusts the receiver back into his wife's hand. 'Can't make head nor tail,' he says, 'Can't actually hear a thing either. You talk to them.'

'*Hallo*, Jan,' the mother says pleasantly but loudly, pressing the receiver up against her mouth, 'Sorry, we must speak up, it's a bad connection. Could be our wires, storms somewhere. Har, *niet doen*, the connection will go totally.' The father has dropped to his knees at the skirting board. In his hands is a loop of white flex. 'Har's doing something, Jan, the loose wire – '

Ella hunkers down beside him. She sees his funny pad thing that her mother calls a truss bulging out at his side. She makes sure no part of her is touching it. 'Nothing doing, nothing doing,' the father murmurs, his glasses on the end of his nose, his callused thumbs massaging the loose wire loop, then suddenly gripping it tight, pressing it to the skirting board where the staples have come loose.

'*Ja, ja*,' the mother says excitedly, 'Yes, that's clearer, yes. Har's somehow playing aerial. Say that bit again, Jan.'

'Don't you people get it?' the father whispers at the wall. 'We're a long way away from one another, don't you see? The string of sound connecting us to Europe will always be snagging at some or other point . . .'

'Your mother's what-not, yes,' the mother repeats after Jan, 'In the attic, top drawer, small parcel with Har's name . . . Contains teaspoons, from the feel . . .? Left them for him when he was in Singapore . . . Send them out to us, or hold? What do you think, Har, *hold*?'

The father's fingers have begun to tremble, Ella sees, so

tightly is he holding the wire, pressing it hard and tight to the skirting board. She sees the whiteness of his knuckles, the bloom of his skin-warmth on the wall. Through the receiver, through the wire, her uncle Jan's voice still buzzes.

'*Ja*,' the mother is saying, 'I'll tell him, I know he missed . . .'

Hold? Jan hollers back again, *Hold*?

Ella imagines the round word *Hold* whirling over from her Uncle Jan's mouth to where they're crouched here on the floor. She sees it rolling along the thin black cable laid on the sandy seabed of the Bay of Biscay, the Gulf of Guinea, the Skeleton Coast . . .

Har! shrieks the mother, *Har!* He has dropped the wire and left the room, swearing something. Ella goes after him. She hears the mother return to the receiver, her murmured apology. From the door of the living room she sees the father standing at his desk, his hands arched on the desk-chair's back, the knuckles still dead-white.

She steps back quietly, lets herself out onto the verandah, the two untouched cups of coffee still standing there on the glass-topped table, her father's, her mother's. She sits on the verandah's edge, the sun like a burning hand on the back of her neck. A sound of hard breathing and the father is suddenly beside her. He hooks his insteps over the verandah's edge, as he likes to do, and begins to rock on his heels.

'Such a weasel whine on the face of Old Europe,' he snaps at the sky, rocking, 'So querulous, so snivelling. Oh, our long-lost Har – we're spending our precious money to tell you, by trunk call no less, our mother left you some old bric-à-brac. Why not just say it plain? That's all you get, brother, nearly forty years after the event. Guilt money, such a call, utter waste, costs twice as much as the *kut-*spoons are worth.'

17

Ella shifts her eyes carefully to the father's face. His eyes today are starey, far bluer than normal, as if emptied out. Is he drunk? she wonders. Even for him, it's very early in the day to be drunk.

'Why plague me with their links to their past, eh Ella, that's what I ask?' He uses her name but it's not her he's talking to, she doesn't think. 'That's not the past I want,' he says, rocking harder.

Ella moves away to the shade of the hawthorn bush beside the verandah, to where she can watch him between the branches without being seen. He stays put where she left him, glaring so hard he's almost squinting. He takes his glasses off, polishes both lenses on his shirt, then puts them back on and squints some more.

'Yes, my Ella' – again he surprises her – 'There are some I *would* like to speak to if I could. But not the most expensive trunk call nor the longest cable could get me a connection to them. Singapore 1940. All the friends. The happy ship, '44. Then Durban and you, Ella, *you*. The Singapore friends don't visit enough to tire of speaking of all that.'

His eyes sweep upwards, fix on the hilly horizon of his view. He tightens his tie – though he's freelancing, every day he still wears a tie. He takes his glasses off a second time, rubs his eyes.

'Of what use are those people in Nederland to me?' He squints quizzically into the distance through his rubbing fingers. 'Of what use for that matter, *verdomme*, is Nederland? Couldn't they have said all that in a letter? And I'd have said dump it in the bin. None of it's any use, not now, not ever. When the people one truly – Dead and gone, long forgotten.'

He shoots a sullen suspicious look over his shoulder. The mother, her face scarlet, has appeared in the frame of the French windows. In her hands is a wooden tray bearing two fresh cups of coffee, a sugar bowl with its mound of white

18

sugar, a silver spoon with the triple-X crest of Amsterdam on the handle.

'So you finished at last, bawling down that telephone wire?' The father again faces the hills.

'It was all over when you took your hands away.' The mother puts the tray on the rattan table, sits down. 'It just became noise. I had to apologise for you. You walked off.'

'They'd said plenty, it was enough. Enough of that useless past, that useless so-called fatherland. Who wants all that back? I don't. Never asked.' He thrusts an arm at the sky. 'This is the country I want.'

'But I do, Har, I haven't left all that behind.' The mother leans forward in her chair, smooths her crimplene slacks down her long thighs. Her expression has turned pleading. 'So rarely I get the chance nowadays, to speak to your *familie*, let alone my own *familie* . . . It's important to me, you know, our families, my country, a parcel left in the attic by your mother. Though it may not be important to you, it's important to me.'

'Important, my fat arse,' he sits down, looks at her. 'Some forgotten bits of junk turning up years after her death, what rot. When at the time, nothing was left me, remember? Not a letter or motherly billet-doux or perhaps, is it too much to ask, a few guilders? Out of sight, out of mind, that second son, disappeared somewhere in the Far East. Almost it makes me think they want something from me. Yes, no doubt about it, that's what they're thinking, let's get something from him, the white man in Africa, living like a king. Let's give him something to soften him up. Some silver teaspoons, how very Dutch! What a waste of time when, like I was just now telling Ella, real enterprising people, they look to the future, the good country that we're building right here in Africa, where only white men need apply.'

So he *was* talking to her? Ella finds a wider gap in the hawthorn bush to peer through. The twigs press into her face.

'As for my people in the East – all dead.' He thrusts his hands through his comb-over and the white hairs stand out from his head in tufts. 'If it weren't for the war I'd've stuck with them, the Chinese and the expats, the only Dutch worth knowing. Those in the so-called fatherland, bah, forget them. What did my fatherland give me after the war, when I most needed it? Nothing. Your beloved sister, our beloved, she was one of the few. She understood – how strangers can be friends like no others, the lotus smells sweeter than the rose . . .'

The mother scrapes back her chair. Her head is down, but, as she turns to the French windows, Ella sees her crinkling cheeks, her grimacing mouth.

'Even looked Chinese,' the father begins to stutter, 'That black hair, those gimlet eyes. Not the first but certainly the best beloved, eh Ella? Looked like the people I knew best – '

He may be using her name, Ella thinks, but he definitely isn't talking to her. He also isn't talking to the mother, who has vanished, leaving her tray on the table, the four coffee cups, the sugar bowl.

'No gift can make up for it,' still the ragged words come, 'Everything that disappeared . . . How can they ever understand? When they have their stupid lives . . .'

He begins to hiccup, then suddenly steps off the verandah, almost as if he stumbled. He looks up, straight at the hawthorn bush, at her face in the gap between the twigs. His eyes lock with hers and her heart begins to race.

'What are you staring at, *loeder*?' he calls out. 'Don't think I can't see you there, goggling like a moron. Step out, come on, show yourself.'

She steps out. Her fists are clutched so tight that she

20

cannot feel her hands and a tingling runs up her arms. The pounding in her skull makes her ears go blurry.

'Look at her,' he walks up closer. 'The un-daughterly thing. Never trust a person who stares like this,' he grabs her chin, his fingers clench, 'But who never looks another person in the eye. How often must I tell you? This stony face is *not welcome* in our house.'

He chucks her chin away from him, then bends over. A sound like a sob drops from his mouth. Ella takes a few steps back. She feels the hawthorn twigs again pressing into her skin. She wishes she could run away but can't trust the numbness in her arms, the strange softness in her legs. Before today, she thinks, she couldn't have imagined her father crying but here is a picture of a man bowed over, crying without words, only strange ragged breathings coming out of his mouth. Getting shot of shit, he tells his drinking friends. Sorry, Ko, here's another story for you, you know, the usual, just getting shot of shit.

This crying, Ella wonders, leaning hard into the hawthorn twigs, is it getting shot of shit? The sharp pricking of the twigs, she notices as if from a distance, dulls the tingling in her hands and arms.

Monsters

'Elly Belly, Jelly Belly!' the children in Braemar call in the street. Ella turns her face to the side. She hasn't yet met these children but somehow they've heard her name and what they're saying is no surprise. Up here on the African shield she has grown soft in front. Some days she's so puffy she can't see her feet over her belly. A little bit plump, the grown-ups say, but she knows better. Her belly has grown like a monster vegetable exhibit at the Midlands Royal Show.

Back when they lived in Durban, she had elbows and knees. She knows she did because she scraped them then. On kindergarten sports day she took off her built-up shoe and did the hurdles, outrunning some of the boys. But here, further up the African shield, closer to the sun, it's different. Things grow faster. They jut, thrust, push out strange shapes.

'Just puppy fat,' says Dr Fry, Braemar's favourite family doctor, 'Just a little bit squishy.' He sits beside her on the velvet upholstered couch, a chunk of her waist clamped in his hand, the mother opposite in the armchair, 'A good word for it, isn't it, Ella, *puppy* fat?'

He uses her name but Ella can tell the words are meant for her mother. She's the one who calls him Braemar's favourite family doctor. Together they look at the hank of flesh held between his finger and thumb. Ella shifts away from him. The movement is small but his fingers lose their grip. She goes over in her mind the fat dogs she has seen in the neighbourhood, as there are no fat *puppies* to speak of, just glossy, buttery-looking young dogs moving too fast to gather flesh – except maybe for Mrs Brickhill's ancient dog next door, a sedentary spaniel about as wobbly as his owner.

Over the fence Ella sometimes catches Mrs Brickhill at her habit, while gardening, of lifting her shirt as if without thinking about it and mopping herself with a tissue in the gulf between her belly and her breasts. When she's as old as Mrs Brickhill, she wonders, will she have to soak up the sweat caught between her fat rolls and pretend no one has seen?

The doctor looks the other way when he says she has puppy fat. The mother bends down to her dahlias when Mrs Brickhill uses her tissues. Mrs Brickhill is such a friendly lady, she murmurs in Dutch, as if to remind herself why she has to be civil to this red-faced South African woman whose uncultured breath even at nine in the morning – she says when they are behind doors – smells of whisky and bitters.

'Mrs Brickhill's a pillar of the community,' the father says warmly, 'She's a salt-of-the-earth English lady, and no mistake.'

Dr Fry's fingers give Ella's cushiony waist a final pinch. 'One day all this flesh'll disappear like magic,' he says. 'Believe me, she's retaining it only a little longer than most.'

The mother's gaze is fixed on the ceiling. Ella looks at her uplifted face, the high ridges of her cheekbones. She follows the line of her twig-thin legs in their pale-green crimplene slacks down to her toes, thin and bony in strappy leather sandals, daisy cut-outs stuck on the central strap. Till now she'd thought she was just like her mother, the same size, the same shape, an extension of her body, but now suddenly she sees it isn't so, not in the least. What's more, her mother doesn't think so either. In fact, she can't bear to look at her sitting here on the couch, her big white knickers spanned over her fat round belly.

Mam has chosen broad-shouldered Dr Fry as their doctor, Ella decides, because he's as thin and tall as she is, but made up of pure cheerfulness, the opposite to Mam's own heavy sadness. From the day of his very first home visit her mother and the doctor have settled into a talking game in which her role is to come up with new ailments for him to sort out.

Melancholic by nature, the mother tells him, stretching out her long legs, that's me. Droopy in stature, droopy in spirit. Expect the worst, hope for anything-but-the-worst, lie awake all night worrying about what might be around the corner.

Some things she tells only the father and the daughter, not Dr Fry, holding her forehead in interlaced hands. Every day she wakes feeling no higher than a worm, she tells them. By nightfall she is a mote of dust.

'Am I as useless to you as I feel?' she asks, moving her duster slowly over the furniture, 'Superfluous, in the way? I can't cook, my head's broken, my hair's falling out, I don't belong here. I live for the trips back home. My teeth are going black, aren't they? They wobble in my jaw. There's a bald patch on my crown, *kijk hier*, if you closely look. Yesterday the cashier in the supermarket was studying it. If all my hair falls out, if my teeth fall out, I can't go on living, I'd rather die.'

If ever the mother's body is briefly free of trouble then Ella's body is pressed into service. The defects that the mother likes to have inspected in herself crop up in her daughter also, mixed in of course with the father's defects. The ills of Dutch fathers and mothers are visited upon the children.

24

'These things lie in wait like fate,' Aunt Suus tells Ella on a Christmas visit home, chopping vegetables for winter soup in her Zuid-Holland kitchen. Not only our odd pigeon *voet* and towering height, she adds, but also the more hidden ailments – like the insomnia we all get, the migraines ... Even for an immigrant family like theirs, removed from their Dutch roots, seesawing between Europe and Africa, push-pulled by the mother's homesickness, the swelling or shrinking of Oma's trust fund, there's no difference. No matter how far from their Low Countries homeland they may wander, no matter how they seesaw, ills are carried deep in every family line. 'The kinks in our bloodlines are knotted inside us,' Tante Suus vigorously stirs smoked sausage in with her chopped greens.

It's true that Ella's left foot swings inwards when she walks and trips her up, a kink that has been passed down the mother's father's bloodline. 'In each generation there is at least one such wandering *voet*,' remarks Tante Suus conspiratorially. 'I myself have one, the sign of an adventuresome spirit, whereas your late Opa, my poor bronchial brother, he was spared.'

On the yellow velvet couch Ella shuffles another inch or so away from Dr Fry. 'Can I go now?' But the mother, reaching into her handbag, is not quite finished. 'There's one more thing, doctor,' her voice drops. 'Ella as you know is not quite ten but, well, between her legs there's often a sliminess, a whiteness that sticks to the inside of her knickers – ' She produces a used envelope resealed with Sellotape, something folded inside. 'Have a look when you have a minute,' she says, 'Let me know what you think. Is it that premature ripening you read about, you know, that happens to girls born in the tropics?'

Ella sits on her hands, stares at the opposite wall, tries to imagine she's invisible. Looking at how quickly Dr Fry slips the envelope into his bag, she thinks he probably wants to be invisible, too. He's in any case blushing as red as she is. Her father is nowhere to be seen. Hours ago, long before Dr Fry's arrival, he took himself off into the garden. 'Rake through the compost,' he muttered, 'long overdue.'

The father mostly keeps quiet on the subject of Ella's physical defects. Instead it's her character that concerns him. Is she strong enough to rise up and be counted, he wants to know, come forward as a citizen of the world's most disciplined republic? In the matter of her feet however he makes an exception, even considering the expense. 'Feet are about standing tall and getting a move on in the world,' he says, 'Pardon the pun. No child of mine should be shambling about like a loafer – and that's even when they're fat as a pancake and won't look their elders in the eye.'

On their visit to the podiatrist in a tall building in downtown Durban, the father stays in the waiting room holding his wallet on his knee. The mother watches as the podiatrist squeezes Ella's feet, then sets an infra-red lamp *to draw strength to the soles*. Ella looks through the non-opening window at the toy-sized cars in the street way down below.

The podiatrist prescribes special brown leather shoes, tells her to wear them for two, maybe three, years. The lace-up left shoe with the anklet and heavy sole will raise her instep, force the foot to point forwards. The right shoe has a matching anklet. An Indian cobbler in Victoria Market makes the shoes for a princely sum, so they have to be kept polished and nice-looking, yet every day thicker tidemarks of dried white sweat spread up the inner anklets, from the heel to the calf.

Ella plots cutting up the shoes with scissors, then burying them in the garden. With the built-up shoe on, she can't easily run and skip. Her belly puffs out bigger. If ever she does try to run, her left foot goes on hitting her right ankle just the same as before.

Everywhere in Braemar, in the shadows, around corners, behind the furniture, Ella finds ugly hunchbacked shapes skulking. She stares into the rectangular mirror the mother has hung in the hallway opposite the front door the same as in the old Durban house, so you cannot miss it as you come in. A larva thing, white and puffy, with a fat misshapen face, looks back at her. In the arum lily patch at the bottom of the garden, after rain, giant livid locusts cluster oddly together, noiselessly trembling. Almost she can't bear to look at them, yet can't tear her eyes away. But even they aren't as awful as the carbuncled toads that live down in the river valley below the house. Without warning, the toads blow out their throats, make brown balloons bigger than themselves that protrude slimily through the ferns. The Zulus who ruled over these hills and valleys long ago, the father says, used to curse the toads, but the toads cursed them back. The curse must be powerful, Ella thinks. Everywhere the land is scarred with the Zulus' losses, abandoned huts and hearth stones, red fissures that run through the earth like open sores.

In the native location on the perimeter of Braemar, between the poor white housing and the river, live survivors of the 1950s polio epidemic, withered Zulu children who come to the front door to beg. They stand on the step whining, hold up their small dangling arms for examination as if they were false appendages, hobble on withered legs that are asymmetrical like Ella's own, only more so.

'Tell the children to go away,' she asks her father, hating herself.

But before he can speak, they have slunk off through the garden gate like whipped dogs. Watching them go Ella is gripped by a sense of triumph. At least her limbs work, more or less. At least she is not as deformed as they.

Then she turns from the front door, catches sight of herself in the rectangular mirror, and the monster grub inside her opens its big scornful mouth and snickers.

She turns her back on the mirror, but out of the corner of her eye catches sight of herself anyway. Slabs of her puffy belly are reflected in shop windows, the sides of passing cars, even in the father's suppressed harrumph when by chance he catches sight of her, quickly looks away.

'That's our *meid*,' he says glancing towards her, glancing away, his cheeks flushed, 'Squeezed in the womb. A too-hugging mother. From the time I married her, the hugs in his family have never come to me.'

When they stood side by side at the Durban docks, he never made remarks like that.

In Braemar, cut off from the Dutch immigrant community in Durban, the mother's sighing grows more echoey. The days she spends sighing, the father's fits of fury come before the sun has set. To the clinking sounds of the Old Brown Sherry bottle, first in the garage beside his workbench, then on the verandah, he spits at degenerate Nazis, lily-livered Dutch, weasly Allies, everyone but the crew of his own trusty warship the *Tjerk Hiddes*. Ella alone seems to hear the clinking; no one remarks on it. The binoculars he used to watch the ships outside Durban harbour gather dust in a drawer.

Ella knows of only one truly lovely thing in Braemar, though it comes from Durban or in fact Holland: the oil painting of a lady in a midnight-blue evening gown, low-cut, that hangs on a wall by itself in the living room. It hung in the same place in their Durban living room, above the yellow velvet couch and to the left of the father's desk, except that down there Ella didn't notice it as much. In

Durban, there were other interesting things to look at; there was the hydrangea labyrinth to explore. But on early evenings in Braemar, the father already out on the verandah talking to himself, she comes to stand by his desk to gaze at the portrait and take in the pretty details, the pearly look of the lady's pale shoulders, her folded hands nestled in the soft folds of the blue gown. For a while, standing there gazing, Ella forgets the miserable things in Braemar, the toads, the polio children, the locusts, the squashed larva shape in the hallway mirror.

Ella doesn't think the woman in the picture is beautiful – she looks far too much like she does to be beautiful – but her eyes are amazing, shiny and big like planets. Though at night they look black, actually they match the blue gown. And they follow her around the room. Wherever she goes in the room, the eyes are on her. Wherever she moves the face calls for her attention – as if it were someone staring, making her look their way. Some days Ella avoids standing near the desk so that the eyes can't find her. Their gaze is too near, too close. What must it be like for her father, she wonders, when he sits here at his desk doing his freelance bookkeeping for the Memorial Order of Tin Hats, the Missions to Seamen, to have those eyes always on him?

She knows the picture is of her dead aunt Ella, but why, she'd like to hear, does it have this pride of place? 'What's it doing there, the picture of the lady?' she asks her mother, points. 'How's it so special?'

She says *lady* because she doesn't know the woman as *Tante* though the mother calls her sister and Dad says to Mam *your sister*. She died before her namesake, Ella herself, was born.

For a long time there's no answer to her question. When Ella asks it the mother only sighs and changes the subject. Once, her hands fidgeting, she says: 'My sister Ella had never laid eyes on him, you know, the artist, before he painted her portrait. One day in the tram he stopped her and asked her to sit for him.' Then she murmurs the word *décolletage. Décolletage*, she explains, is the word for all that open white skin.

The time comes for Ella to start school. In Dr Fry's opinion she is a Late Developer, in spite of her great size. He advises the mother to enter her in something called the Remedial Class instead of Class One. In the Remedial Class, he explains, children of all ages, both Afrikaans and English, are given extra help with their numbers and letters for however long they need it.

Though Ella doesn't know what *Late Developer* means, or *immigrant effects*, or *second-generation war-child*, or *outsider mentality*, or *second-language issues*, or *only-child introversion*, or any of the other put-together words Dr Fry uses when he talks about her, she is made to feel welcome in the Remedial Class. Standing outside her new classroom on her first day, she sees her name tag already stuck on one of the coat hooks by the door. At the moment she raises her hand to knock, the door opens and a small child with a dirty-blonde ponytail steps into the corridor, takes her by the hand and, without a word, leads her into the classroom.

From the first minute Ella decides she will like the Remedial Class. The classroom has tall sash windows for looking out of and a beautiful spreading loquat tree growing just outside. No one speaks much except to themselves – this Ella likes a lot. Even the teacher Mrs Woode mostly stays quiet, walks quietly in amongst the children trailing her long brown hair and soft cheesecloth smocks. A constant babble goes on, in Afrikaans, in English, but it's just the children talking to the fresh air in front of them. Though they may move about without asking Mrs Woode's permission, most of them like to stay put – stay put and pass the time swaying, sighing, occasionally singing. Ella enjoys staring. Mrs Woode lets Ella sit and stare with her mouth open for as long as she pleases.

In the Remedial Class each child has some feature that marks them out, a tic or habit, so by the end of the first day Ella has learned all their names. The eldest girl, Dawnie, who is eleven, sits facing the corner between the metal cupboard and the wall, and buzzes loudly in the back of her throat. Her buzz rings against the metal surface, an effect she likes because across the day she makes the buzz go louder and louder.

Dark Daan, whose cow's lick makes a slash across his forehead, rocks energetically back and forth, all the while whistling to himself. Daan is from a Reclassified family, Coloured in some or other proportion. Ella studies him out of the corner of her eye. If Coloured means flecked with different colours, Daan is no more Coloured than she is. In fact, she's more freckled. Coloured people are burdened by the sins of their fathers, her mother says. No more than I am, Ella thinks.

The two Down's Syndrome children in the group, Magda and Gretchen, are friends, the Mongoloid Mates Daan calls them, the M and Ms. They are quieter than most of the others, eager to please. Of the M and Ms Ella especially likes Gretchen. If ever Mrs Woode has a bad day and is cross, Gretchen reaches for her hand and gives it a squeeze.

And then there's tiny, silent Naomi Salome with her greasy ponytail and bruised-looking eyes, the child who first welcomed Ella, and always comes to sit beside her on the carpet. Now and again, quite suddenly, Naomi Salome puts her head tight between her knees and rubs her face from side to side till her cheeks go raw.

Ella is one of the youngest children so she has a place

on the carpet in the front row. In the Remedial Class there are no desks, no tables. She likes being here beside Naomi Salome and close to Daan because they keep to themselves and don't shout out loud.

It's a different story with Stuart, the very oldest Remedial pupil. Stuart has fiery red pimples and hairs on his chin. His habit is to interrupt what he's saying in his ordinary voice with other words like gobs of spit, short explosive sounds in both English and Afrikaans, *poes, pis, prick, piel, skyt, shit, shag*, and some words Ella has never heard before. It's a rare day that Stuart reaches home-time without a scolding from Mrs Woode for having got no better at controlling himself.

'I try, Miss, I try-try, but I can't help it,' Stuart hastens to reply without another *pis* or *poes* jumping from his mouth.

By and by though, Ella grows grateful to Stuart. Without meaning to he teaches her some important English words. She hears what the word is for the wobbly thing boys have between their legs and girls don't, the thing Stuart himself likes to hold in his fist through his clothes when he isn't shouting. She knows what to say to Mrs Woode when Naomi Salome has a bad stomach and dirties her pants, which often happens. Stuart's Afrikaans words aren't as useful but, still, she saves them up. They make her think of her father's talk on the verandah at night. How words can be shot out like bullets.

The Remedial group begins each day singing clap-along songs. After that, Ella is allowed to sit by herself and draw for as long as she likes, it doesn't matter what: a grille gate, a toad like a whale, a child with tiny limbs. Then, in the hour before lunch, Mrs Woode writes short English words like *Bat* and *Dog* or *Mat* and *Pot* on the blackboard. She invites the class to say the words along with her, clapping at the same time, *Bat*! *Dog*! *Dog*! *Bat*! – as if it was a game.

This is Ella's favourite lesson. She likes being the only one who can say all the words.

'Exactly the method the Rudolf Steiner school taught back home in Nederland, that you'll be taught when next we go and stay,' the mother says one afternoon from the kitchen door, catching Ella skipping to the chant, *Bat! Dog! Mat! Pot!* 'Do you remember, the Vrijeschool I pointed out to you, on the Scheveningseweg? That was my school, too.'

Ella lets her skipping rope hang, nods. She remembers the great mound of the dune behind the Vrijeschool that went almost as high as its top gable. She waits for Mam to say something more, something about the Remedial Class perhaps, now that she's mentioned school, but she retreats back into the kitchen. If the Remedial Class is to help children say the words Mrs Woode writes on the board, Ella wants to ask, what is she doing there, when she can say all the words? No one has yet said a thing to explain this – not Mrs Woode, not the mother or the father.

The problem can't be to do with her English, she tells herself. The father has dealt with her English. He's been her coach since the time they stood looking at ships in Durban. 'English! English!' he shouts if ever by mistake she slips into Dutch. English is the world's finest language, he says in his growly Dutch accent, mangling the English vowels. It's a world-conquering language, zesty with England's sea-power. I'll have you speak the Queen's English, Churchill's language. You speak anything else and I won't hear you. Consider yourself lucky to be growing up in this English province of Natal. Why else, after the war, did I choose to live in this one strip of South Africa where the Union Jack has always flown high?

At night the mother reads Ella stories from English books in her broken English. The father tells her to. Ella's eye races ahead. She is listening to her mother but at the same time she's reading the words she recognizes further down the page. Under her breath she tries out the longer English words, the ones with tricky swishing sounds her blunt tongue can't quite push to the front of her mouth, like *pars*ley, or *this*tle, or Li-*tull* Bo-*Peep*.

When she's been in the Remedial Class a month or so, Ella begins to rock in time with her classmates sitting on the carpet. She notices this off-hand, not minding. She especially likes rocking when they're chanting words. Rocking, she feels a part of the group. She feels so much part of the group that when she catches sight of herself in the hallway mirror at the end of the first term it's as if the widow's peak in the middle of her forehead, that she gets from her father's side, has stretched into a hound's-tooth wedge just the same as Daan's.

In the playground Ella and Naomi Salome go off by themselves. They coast up and down the corridor between the tennis courts holding hands. Like Naomi Salome, Ella keeps her eyes to the ground. Nothing can touch me, she murmurs to herself as they pace, Nothing, nothing, nothing at all. She's saying the English word *nothing*, with the tough *th*, not the easy Dutch *niets*. *Niets kan me raken, niets*, it sounds too sharp and piercing. *Nothing* is a proper magic chant to ward off evil. *Nothing, nothing, nothing can touch me*.

A week before the end of the winter term Mrs Woode catches Ella reading 'Goldilocks' from the *Golden Story Book* to Naomi Salome in class. They are in their usual place on the carpet. Naomi Salome has laid her head on her crooked knees. Bending down, her sharp nostrils distended, Mrs Woode asks Ella to explain in plain language what exactly she thinks she is doing.

'Reading, Mrs Woode.'

Mrs Woode straightaway flushes up but Ella can tell she isn't accusing her of anything.

'See, Naomi's listening, Mrs Woode. I'm reading a story to Naomi.'

'I do see that,' Mrs Woode says, and swishes her tasselled Indian skirt back over to her desk. 'Come here, Ella.'

Mrs Woode opens the *Picture Bible* on her desk to a random page, the opening of Exodus, the story of Moses. 'Try reading this.'

Ella reads, '*And when she could no longer hide him, she took for him an ark of bulrushes, and daubed it with slime and with pitch, and put the child therein.*'

She's word perfect, except for slurring *therein*. She knows she made no mistakes, though Mrs Woode says nothing. As Ella reads she directs her quiet thinking look out of the window, at the loquat tree.

At register the next day Mrs Woode touches Ella's shoulder, beckons her to her desk. 'Ella, this morning we're going to send you upstairs, up to Class One,' she tells her, then swivels her round to face the group. 'Time to say Good-Bye.'

'Good-Bye,' Ella says, repeating after Mrs Woode, 'Good-Bye Every-One.' Dawnie, Daan, Naomi Salome, Gretchen, all go on doing their usual things. No one bothers to look up.

'What's a Late Developer really, Dad?' Ella asks in her best English one early spring day in the car outside Ada's Hairdressing Salon. She and the father have dropped Mam off for her monthly perm. The mother pays for Ada's using Oma's trust fund so he drives her over in good spirit, remembers to bite back the usual remarks about cost.

It's been a while since Ella left the Remedial Class but still her father and mother have said not a word about it. At some point earlier they thought she needed Special help; Dr Fry thought she had *Effects*; but now they no longer think so: is that it? Ella's not certain. There's that glance of her father's, over in her direction and then off again, it gives him away, even now, there in the rear-view mirror when she asked her question, as if he can't ever quite get used to this skew-whiff creature that has cropped up somehow in the back seat of his car.

'What's a Late Developer, Dad?' she asks again.

'Late developer, early developer, who can say?' he eventually replies in English, reversing the Volkswagen Beetle out of the slantwise parking bay outside Ada's, his blue eyes in the rear-view mirror averted. 'If you're thinking of development late or otherwise, *meid*, if you want to be developed, to come forward and be counted as a good citizen, one thing you can do is drop that stupid look you wear, like now, that fixed face, it puts people off. A developed face is a pleasant, open face.'

Ella remembers how Mrs Woode in the Remedial Class let her sit and stare. From the hallway mirror she knows what happens to her face when she forgets herself and stares, when her mouth hangs open, her eyes go glassy.

'Cheer up, *schat*,' says Dad's Singapore friend Oom Ko on his visits, mussing her hair. 'No need to put on that glary look. I don't bite.'

'Underdeveloped, overdeveloped.' The father in the driver's seat warms to his theme. He takes a sudden detour from their homebound route, pulls into the big parking lot alongside the Wimpy Bar and lights up a cigarette from the Rothman's Plain packet in his pocket. 'Overdeveloped *and* underdeveloped,' he says, blowing out smoke. 'Both at once. Or maybe we can call it mis-development which is when you – and I mean you – act as silly as a young child but headstrong and obstreperous, too, talking to yourself, ignoring others, especially your mother, wilfully, like some American teenager. You make sure you don't turn into one of those, *een akelige brutale meid*, a truly miscast thing. Cheek is very ugly in a girl.'

Ella searches for his eyes in the rear-view mirror. His face is veiled in smoke. She's not familiar with some of his words, the English words, not the Netherlands. *Obstreperous*? Even *cheek*. *Cheeky* was what her father called Charley. She looks over at the oval Wimpy sign which is flashing though it's daytime. On, Off, it goes. Pause. On, Off. The Wimpy is new in town but she and Mam and Dad aren't likely to visit. They're not the kind of people who eat out, her mother says. If the Braemar white riff-raff go – what of it? They haven't been brought up to know what proper food is.

The father throws his cigarette butt out of the window and gives a harrumphing sound, like he does in his rattan chair, waking from a stolen nap. Without another word he turns the key in the ignition and drives the car out of the parking lot, in the direction of Ridge Road.

At home he heads to the verandah with his municipal library copy of *Winston Churchill: A Life* under his arm. It's one of the books he smuggles from the town library under his jacket and doesn't ever return. Taking a few extra books each visit, he says, cuts down on driving. A small economy when petrol prices are going through the roof.

Ella looks up *obstreperous* in his *Concise Oxford English Dictionary* and wonders if this was the word he wanted. For *obstreperous* she finds *turbulent*, *unruly*, *peevish*, also *fractious*, which she looks up too. *Fractious* means *brawling*, also *peevish*. What do these long, tough words have to do her? When Dr Fry directs her to the Remedial Class, she goes. The ugly shoes made for her, she wears. The short back-and-sides haircuts she gets at Dad's barber, she takes without complaint even though she'd love long hair like Naomi Salome's. Longer hair would fall into her susceptible eyes, her mother says, and damage them.

The flirty chatter Dawnie in the Remedial Class used to share with her dad when he picked her up from school, she doesn't share with her father, Ella knows this, too. She walks into a room where he's sitting and there's no glance up from his ledgers, no outstretched arm. But why should there be? She knows he doesn't like to look at her. She brings to mind things he doesn't want to see.

And then one day not long after, he does grab her to him, just the once, and it's horrible. In the bright spring light she darts into the main bedroom in her vest and knickers to fetch her school uniform off the laundry pile. He sits pulling on his socks in his armchair alongside, then suddenly stretches out his arms, links his hands around her. Every bristle in his early-morning stubble stands out silvery and clear.

'Make your mother jealous,' he says, dragging her onto his knee. 'Show your father how good and developed you are.'

Pinned to his lap she's a lump, squishy but solid. His kneecap is pressed in the soft place between her legs. She has to twist away. But in that second of twisting she brushes by accident against his truss, the dark-yellow pad on its twisted pink nylon belt, hanging in its usual place over the armchair back. She never meant to touch it, never, never. She'd thought he already had it on. That thing's private, he always says, it keeps me in.

Squirming on his kneecap, though, she can't miss it. There it is; the damage is done: it bulges out at her; it brushes against her. She catches just for an instant its sweaty, musty smell.

And as suddenly as he grabbed her, he pushes her away.

But she can't get down so fast as to miss just the flash of a possibility. How it feels for a little girl to be held close and made much of by her father.

Verandah

'Let me not bore you, dear Ko, with yet another tale of the warship on which I spent nearly three years.'

The two white-haired men sit in their proscenium of light. They have sat in the same position for every night of Ko's ten-day visit, the longest Ella can remember, the widower Ko on the left, the father on the right. Under the verandah's forty-watt bulb his yellow-white hair, already stained by nicotine, turns a deeper yellow at the crown.

'Bore me, old man. Pass the bottle and bore me. I miss your stories when I'm away from here, you know, they take me back. We didn't get away from Singapore in time. The *Kampen* got us . . .'

Ella stands at her night-watch spot between the curtains, her elbow on the sill. She is ten now, nearly eleven, but her father still has not let slip his secret. His expected visitor still does not arrive. There's only Ko, his old sidekick, grunting to order as he tells his stories.

The father is like an actor on a stage, she thinks. For years she has thought this. He lights his cigarettes with slow deliberate movements, he draws himself up in his chair. He takes a deep breath, slides the bottle over to Ko, then raises his head, throws his words at the darkness stretching beyond the verandah's earthenware tiles.

Night after night Ella stands and listens. She leans her shoulder against the glass, presses now one ear now the other against its coolness. When the visitor finally comes, she tells herself, she will sense it even before she sees him. She will know to open her eyes and discern his dark shape sliding like a hunter out of the night.

'Yes, we missed you chaps,' the father tells Ko. 'Missed the good life around Finlayson Green. Didn't know if you were dead or alive. When Churchill gave up Singapore it was over for our precious *Indisch* empire. It was left to our tiny allied navies, the Dutch and the Australian, the few Polish ships, to hold out against the mighty Japaner. Four hundred years it took to build our empire in the East, in less than forty days it was lost.'

'How those Japanese wanted to stamp their imperial face on the future,' Ko shakes his lowered head. 'Why no one else saw it I don't know.'

'There I was, caught high and dry, sent by the Company to attend the ship-chandlering course in Durban, just at that moment, '42, the East collapsing in my wake. Couldn't even get back to collect my things. Nancy Leong, yes, the very one, the lovely Nancy who went off with that bowlegged Englishman, what's his name, Dartmouth? – she eventually mailed them to me.'

'All pathways closed to us,' Ko still droops his head. 'Our Nazi-occupied *vaderland* closed to us— '

'At such low points,' the father presses on, as if building to a punch-line, 'Our thoughts of course turned to England, the true heart of the West. So, *listige* Nederlander that I was, nothing doing, I made my way to Scapa Flow, home of the British Grand Fleet. At Scapa Flow were the few warships of the Royal Netherlands Navy left intact after the Germans smashed into Rotterdam. The day I arrived, they were executing manoeuvres with the Australian warship *Nepal*. What a thing it was to join them, eh, those various motley others, some Nederlanders like myself, a handful of Flemings, a few Poles, the officers and ratings both now absorbed like the ships we served into the British Navy. Yet, despite all our losses, those ships of ours I saw were still deft, very deft. Dutch blood's seawater, it truly is.'

'It must be, Har, it worked for you. You had the luck. We in the *Kampen*— '

'Luck was to find a ship. On the *Oranje Nassau* at Holyhead, our motley band went for first training, gunnery practice. And then, back at Scapa Flow I stepped for the first time on board my beloved *Tjerk Hiddes*. What a ship she was, compact, quick, sound to the core, British-made naturally though named for our great 17th-century Frisian sea-fighter. On the *Tjerk Hiddes* we steamed through Suez back to the Indian Ocean, detouring via officer training in Madagascar to Trincomalee. I tell you, my friend, that was a boyhood dream come true.'

'I remember you always did want to go to sea. "My short sight relegated me to second-best, a job in shipping," you used to say. For me, shipping was always first-best. For the *Kampen* it taught some useful ropes— '

'Well, yes, dodging Japaner subs in the navy proper I wasn't going to waste a minute bothering about this eyesight of mine, was I? Rubbed my specs clean with spit every morning and got on with it. Couldn't believe my luck. Our first action of course was to help the aircraft-carrier *Illustrious* land troops on Madagascar, oust the occupying Germans. A true blooding. In Antanarivo that following evening we drank several kegs of genever, maybe more, to celebrate our success. Edith the English rose I'd met in Holyhead one Thursday and married five days later sent me a letter to say it was all over after just four months, she'd found someone else, just like Nancy Leong— '

Edith? Ella asks herself, stands up taller, Or was that name she heard *Ella*? An *English* rose? *Another* wife? Did she mishear something? She remembers that thing he told

41

her mother – strangers can be friends like no others, the lotus smells sweeter than the rose . . .

'I opened her letter that night,' the father says, 'But still I felt lucky. I had a ship and I had a victory, I was the luckiest man in the world.'

'Speaking of genever, Har,' says Ko. 'You wouldn't have another drop of that good South African fortified of yours? You've a terrific spot on this verandah here, I must say. No wonder it's a fixture for us boys. There I was only last month in Finlayson Green, a stone's throw from where our Seamen's Institute once stood, spending my pension on *pahits* like there was no tomorrow. But there's no point trying to rediscover the old atmosphere, you're right, the spirit's gone out of the place. It was nothing like what we have here on your verandah, though the drink there, I must say, wasn't quite so, ahm— ,' he makes a wry face, 'Cheap on the tongue.'

The father's hand is raised in the air. Enough, he shakes his head, enough. He doesn't want to hear about the old haunts, unrecognisable now, rebuilt from the ground up, laminated in dirty modern paint. He's seen photographs of the new Singapore in the *Elsevier*. The bustling entrepôt they knew so well, it's changed beyond all recognition. The war wiped it out, the teak-panelled clubs, the ferns in pots on the verandahs, the tall merchant houses with their Victorian turrets and curlicues, the Great World where they danced the night away, they have all been flattened, he knows.

'Life's too long nowadays, eh Ko?' The father stares down at his planted feet. Both men's crowns are ringed with light. 'Sometimes, I don't know, I think it might have been better if one of those sharp-eyed Japaner dive-bombers had sought me out. I've lived too long, I've seen enough . . .'

'My feeling, Har,' Ko nods and shakes his head at once,

'My feeling exactly. Our generation – we were always out of time. Children of one war, young men in another, old before our time. The world we fought for, it was gone before the war was over. We've seen too much, done too much, for too few returns.'

'We've done too much? Who can tell? I remember what our Captain the good Klaas Sluijter used to say after heavy action at sea, to lift the men. It's better to do a wrong thing than to do nothing at all. It was a Chinese motto, Lin Yze Tang. *It is better to have lived and lost than not to have lived at all.* How much we all lost, Sluijter too. He was a man of the East, our captain.'

Condensation sticks Ella's cheek to the window. She peers out through eyelids grainy with sleep. The verandah lies in darkness. So she must in fact have slept. The men have gone to bed and she missed their going. This is something guards must learn on sentry duty, she thinks, something her father will have learned keeping watch on the bridge of his blessed *Tjerk Hiddes*, the name he always says with a choke, not only because of the strangled sound of the Frisian. It must be possible to sleep for minutes at a stretch while standing fully upright, leaning your head against the cool surface of the window, or the steel side of your ship.

In the queue at the butcher's the father makes a new acquaintance, a retired army major called Tom Watt. Tom invites Har to the monthly meetings of the local ratepayers' association, introduces him there to a friend of his, another steel-haired retired man, a former town planner, Nobby Clark. 'Don't want to stand outside this community like some foreigner,' the father says, punching his knee. 'Got to meet the leading citizens, the men of worth. Pitch in, share views. That's how we build the New West here in the Deep South.'

When her father talks about the West, Ella is puzzled. The verandah faces west. Does he mean the distant hills of his view? On winter evenings just after sunset, the horizon is golden with illuminated dust. The west beyond the horizon is far-off though, not here on the doorstep, here where the father is beating his fist.

One night Har treats Ko to a verandah meeting with his new friends. 'They're relatively young men, *makker*,' he explains at dinner with a snort, 'if you see what I mean. Nobby wasn't ever tested by war. Tom saw action only in Italy in '45. But they're both good men, worth talking to. They know what we mean when we talk about the war, how it broke our ideals instead of mending them. How it's up to us to refashion law and order here in the only country in the world where the natural rulers stand apart from the ruled.'

Both Tom and Nobby, Har says, are long-time members of the United Party, a weasely outfit, though not entirely misguided. Tom stood for election to the Provincial Assembly once, but was defeated by a sugar farmer with an Afrikaans name. Like Nobby, Tom believes that South Africa should be ruled exclusively by white people, just as the Afrikaner nationalists do. However, he doesn't hate black people in the same way. He'd consider giving them some form of vote, nothing important, to keep them smiling. 'I switch off when he talks about blacks, Ko, and I'm happy for you to do so too,' the father says. 'I try not to think about blacks, those hewers of wood, drawers of water. I'm with the Dutch-born Verwoerd, the architect of this great state. Blacks are here to make sure the white republic runs from day to day. They're not members, not citizens. They're after all not western. They don't belong.'

That night Ella moves early to her post at the window. Will her father's stories be different in front of a bigger audience, she wonders, less angry? The men at first are quiet, she notices. They drink quickly, offer the expected praise of Har's view, this incredible tranquillity that no ratepayers' association could begin to pin a price on. Ko talks about his travels, the gaudy new shopping centre in downtown Singapore. Before too long the men are drunk. Their heads hang in unison. Three empty bottles of South African sherry stand on the table between them. The father is the only one still vocal.

'I sit here often, you know, my friends, looking out,' he says in English. 'I sit here considering the wreck of the world we knew, how hard we fought to prevent it, how little of what we believed in remains.

'I remember the final years of the war,' 43 to '44, the North Atlantic, that most vital theatre, as the great Churchill said, the true battle for the west. In '43 my *Tjerk Hiddes* and the other N-class destroyers were called from the south to help safeguard the supply routes to Britain. I close my eyes even now and it's like yesterday. The silhouettes of the big German destroyers just visible through the North Atlantic haze, dogging us. Those great merchant ship convoys cutting through the freezing sea, the ships piled high with tanks, trucks, grain. Their speed was incredible, some thirty, thirty-two knots. And then the noise of the Luftwaffe that you heard approaching long before you saw them: the screaming Stukas, the Heinkel bombers' growl, and then the yelling of our turbines as we switched to full speed ahead, anti-aircraft guns thudding. Tom, you won't ever have heard this roar in Italy. The Germans were in full retreat by then.

'It was my vision of the end of the West, Nobby, Ko, Brother European bent to destroy Brother European, fighting to the death. How do we go on from here? I thought to myself watching those Stukas, frost nipping my fingers. This vital theatre is the death-throe of all we have believed in. And I was right. The last of the West's here on this rim of the African shield. What you see from this *stoep*. At the time of course we carried on, our visions of damnation regardless. We sang to ourselves the refrain of the great English navy song.' He begins to whinny in his throat. Tom beats a languid hand on his armrest. '*Ours is not to reason why. Ours is but to do or die*. It kept our spirits up when we most needed it.'

The father breaks the seal on a fourth bottle of Old Brown Sherry. The men raise their heads, hold out their glasses. Ella's cheek has grown cold against the window. She takes her head away from the glass, uses the hem of the curtain to prop her other cheek, a vertical pillow. The father's chin goes up. She sees he's gathering himself for a second wind. Even with more than one listener present, she notices, yawning, he talks over their heads, still addresses his invisible audience arrayed on the dark lawn.

'Let me tell you about Trincomalee in Ceylon,' he says, 'the base of that Do-It-Yourself operation I once was part of, the British Eastern Fleet. After Singapore fell, that place became our paradise, our strategic paradise. It has the most beautiful natural harbour you ever saw, all green and blue, shaped like a human hand. The Brits could've packed a whole fleet in there and the enemy would've been none the wiser. The first morning we were there, I see it like yesterday, the HMS *Adamant* slid out from behind a headland like a shark with gloved fins.

'We called our arrival in Trinco the Return of the Nederlanders. Wherever around the harbour you were, you saw impregnable old Fort Frederick, built by our seventeenth-century forefathers, standing on that great massif that rises up from the sea. No matter what we were doing we took comfort just from knowing it was there. Every one of the tiny nugget bricks that went into its building had been transported from the Netherlands in VOC sailing ships as ballast. Traders to the bone, we Dutch, eh Ko? We men of the sea, westerners to the core, competitors to the last. Marching into the Fort for our daily training drill felt like coming home.'

Ko gives a nod, makes a tired gesture with his hand. Har has the floor, he seems to say, he has the best stories.

'There were four of us up for naval officer training that time and it took four months to knock us into shape. Tom, you'll know what I mean. Chris Donker, Wim Vermeer, Hans van Alphen and I, we worked like devils till finally we were sent over to Colombo to be assigned to our positions. Chris the big fellow, built like a tank, he went to the great minelayer *Willem van der Zaan*. Tall Wim Vermeer found a temporary calling in the machine room of the *Van Galen*, our sister ship, but within no time he was back, joined us under our Frisian banner. Hans stayed quayside. I, glasses or no, became deck-officer on my beloved *Tjerk Hiddes*, as I'd hoped from day one. And I certainly slaved from day one, attached to artillery officer Crommelin who, due to some sickness, panic attack or bowel complaint, stayed often in his cabin when we were on missions. So I made myself handy in his stead.

'By this stage the Grand Oriental Hotel on Colombo harbour had turned into a sort of Allied Navy HQ, known among the men as the Great Old Hoer. We abused language, us lusty young fellows in Singapore' – Ko nods again – 'But it was nothing to touch the seafaring folk I now got to know. They called a *hoer* a *hoer* where they saw one, no translation needed, gentlemen. In those days, if you were unable to find a mate around Colombo, then he was sure to be in the courtyard bar of the hotel, knocking them back, arguing the toss. Hans, disappointed at his new land-hugging position, was bar prop number one. They loved the Hoer, the men, especially after our out-of-the-way life at Trinco. Especially after that accidental oil spill put a stop to water sports in the bay.

'You never heard about that, the oil spill?' The father cocks his head at Tom's raised eyebrow. 'A visiting dignitary, we never were told who, some know-it-all *idioot* from London or The Hague, he one day experimentally pulled the pin on a torpedo, sped the missile straight into an oil tanker. Pandemonium. For a while we thought a Japanese sub had got into the bay.

'As for me, well, maybe losing my heart in Singapore had given me due warning about staking too much in Colombo, who knows? Ko has some idea. The sloe-dark eyes of Nancy Leong. I'd worked hard for my placement with our Frisian hero Tjerk. While we were at anchor I stuck on deck, avoided the Great Old Hoer. My task in any case was cut out. There was a massive back-log in our correspondence with British High Command, due to the fall of Singapore. None of us Dutch were great stars in the English language, but I was the best of a bad bunch. I bombed myself into the position of secretary and worked in my spare hours. No sacrifice. I took to your good old English language, Nobby, Tom. I enjoyed being on the side of the English. From the very first day I felt grateful to be on that ship and call it home, to be able to do something in return. I wouldn't have exchanged my place there for the world.'

'You tempt me yet again to say you fellows were lucky.' Ko blows a smoke-ring and watches it dissolve into the night air. Tom looks up, seems for a moment to listen more closely. 'Lost generation or no. Bar prop or no. There you were, with your free training, your good berth, in the company of friends. No crawling up the Italian boot for you, Har, as for Tom. Not a detention centre in sight, not a *kamp*, as for me. That's lucky.'

'Yes, that's lucky,' echoes Tom. 'The luck of you seafaring Dutch.'

'Well, we were happy, at least at the time,' Har continues. 'We were sometimes even lucky. Certainly we were lucky with Klaas Sluijter at the helm. How could we not be happy? The *Tjerk Hiddes* was from the word go a *happy ship*. There's no equivalent for this in our language. She was a plucky trusty ship with a happy crew, and made from top-mast to rudder of good solid steel. Her turbines, navigating equipment, weaponry, all of it was reliable and lethal – the six 12.5 cm dual-purpose cannons set in crafty double formation to welcome enemy planes, the Tommy guns and hydraulic torpedo launchers stuffed into every available corner to deal with attacks from the sea. She was a fighter all right, the *Tjerk Hiddes*. Your people the English knew what they were doing when they built her, Tom. They also knew what they were doing when, after Rotterdam, they transferred her and the *Van Galen*, the other two-tonner, to the Royal Dutch Navy, to give us the extra clout at sea we so desperately needed. Not for the Brits the building of so-called economy ships, second-rate cruisers like the Dutch disgrace the *Sumatra*. She was the ship that very nearly capsized on the Java Sea when she tried to fire her cannons from port and then starboard in rapid succession. Or the Dutch training cruiser *Tromp* – '

'The *Tromp*? Didn't you once go minesweeping on the *Tromp*?'

'Once and once only, in the Gulf of Bengal,' The father casts a searching look at Ko, 'And never again. That day of minesweeping, a couple of Japaner fighter planes crossed the *Tromp*'s path and she tried Emergency Full Ahead. Result, her so-called solid steel mast split in two. What a trough our once-great seafaring nation there faced. The Dutch marines were all good fellows, still are, but our ships this century ailed. Yet to this day the people's representatives in The Hague's Inner Court, restored to their offices, their forelock-tugging Nazi insignia neatly tidied away, do not smoke one cigar the less in consequence . . .'

The father's voice descends to a sour rumble at the base of his throat. Nobby, the one non-smoker, bats at the ceiling of cigarette smoke floating above their heads.

'So your *Tjerk Hiddes* was a *happy ship*, you say, Har,' Nobby says, squinting, 'but even with everything you've told us, I don't quite see how. Excuse me for saying, but I'm a planner. After the German occupation she will have been the last ship of any size you Dutch were in a position to staff. Prisons must have been swept out to find those ratings you had. Pure criminals – '

The father clears his throat, knocks back his sherry, straightens up still higher. The sound of the words *Tjerk Hiddes* in an English-speaker's mouth is enough to restore his humour. 'See, Nobby, any prison sentence you might think of, any crime, theft, manslaughter, it's no hindrance to waging war at sea, not for white men. Any scoundrel can be used in the marine service and turn into a good mate. We two hundred heads, our captain and his merry men, including forty fellows from the British Royal Navy, we all got on despite our motley make-up, maybe because of it. Within six months the excellent Captain Klaas Sluijter had transformed us into a beautiful unity simply by working us hard, all together. There's a moral for us in that, right here in South Africa today.

'Take my friend, the ordinary seaman Schilperoort. He'd been a bouncer and petty thief back in Rotterdam, or so he often told us. He'd had a starring role in the drinks heist the crew once carried out in Fort Frederick, the time when the sub-captain received a DSO. But he was a firm friend. He remained my friend throughout. He taught me about loyalty. Humour, too. Resourcefulness. Whenever Theo Verwerda and I came down at midnight after our watch on the bridge, wet and tired, Schilperoort always had mugs of *kaai* ready for us, thick, bitter chocolate with a shot of rum. God, I can sometimes still long for that stuff. You could rely on Schilperoort. At full alarm I always forgot my helmet. "Without this pisspot on your head you don't look the part," he used to say, coming up after me, the helmet in his fist.'

Nobby puts out a hand, wants to say more, but Har talks on regardless. Nobby thuds back in his chair, steals a look at Tom.

'He was a born leader, Klaas Sluijter, *onze Kapitein*,' says Har, 'cool-headed in an emergency, a fine seaman, too. On one of the first outings the *Tjerk Hiddes* ever undertook in the Indian Ocean, I'll never forget, we'd been detailed to evacuate three hundred Australian commando-troops from Flores, in the Banda Sea. It was there he first made his name. The night-time evacuation itself proceeded well, but at dawn, moments after the ship set out to sea, the cloud cover broke and a pair of Japaner reconnaissance planes spotted us. For two solid hours they attacked, remorselessly, and for two solid hours, high up in the three-prong mast, holding to a stay, his eyes fixed on the heavens, Klaas Sluijter stood calling out his orders. It was thanks only to his ingenious zigzag course that the ship evaded everything the Japaners chucked down at us. And the only visible effect on Klaas was a bad case of sunburn.

'After the Flores excursion, for ever after, whenever something serious was the matter, the cry went up: *Klaas zal ons redden!* Klaas will drag us through it!' The father, Ella suddenly notices, has switched into Dutch. The friends look unconcerned. Nobby's eyes are closed. Tom squints at his wrist watch, tips a wink in Ko's direction. 'And he did, my friends,' Har shouts. 'Klaas did drag us through it, even when we were once in the direst straits with even fiercer opposition, fiercer even than at Flores. Or as old Schilperoort put it in his usual meaty Nederlands, when Ma's bosoms get caught in the mangle, the Captain'll sort it out.'

The men do not laugh. Perhaps they weren't expected to. Nobby and Tom scrape back their chairs. 'I'll see them out,' Ko mumbles, rising also. He does not return. Har sits with his head bowed. Ella turns away, her jaw sore with yawning, then looks back one last time. She sees her father suddenly flailing his arms like a madman, as if hitting at a swarm of mosquitoes. He's like Captain Sluijter on his zigzag course, Ella thinks, only her father— she can't see him straight, he tacks erratically across obscure waters.

It is the last night of Ko's stay, a cool evening. A bolster of mist lies in the river valley. The two friends keep to their seats till after midnight, restored to the solace of their Singapore brotherhood. They both wear short scarves knotted around their necks, the ends sticking out horizontally like giant bow ties. Ella puts her cheek to the window.

'Can't let you leave us without my best story, can I Ko?' the father says late on. He pulls a fresh bottle of Old Brown Sherry out of its cardboard sleeve. Now that his audience is reduced back to one he's not as loud as before. 'Pity that our English friends aren't here to hear it. Concerning how I briefly became an honorary Englishman.'

Ko holds out his tumbler. His yawn, bitten-back, creases his lips into a half-smile. The father seems not to notice. Ko's tumbler stays dry.

'It was the time when the *Tjerk Hiddes* accompanied the

52

damaged battleship *Valiant* back to England for repairs. When the portable dry dock in Bombay failed and we didn't have anything to fix her in Trinco. Up until that time I'd thought, when it came to ships, I'd seen it all. Like the double-rigged *Silindoeng*, for example – the time we relieved her of a thousand-ton load of coal and in just eight hours replaced it with the purest sugar for our men in Burma. But that Rumpelstiltskin story's for another occasion, for Tom and Nobby. Till that day with the *Valiant*, though, I'd not seen a ship in disguise before. It was then I discovered that war at sea was a different can of Bully Beef altogether.'

Revolving the sherry in his tumbler the father faces Ko, yet seems to be talking to himself. Ko puts his own dry tumbler on the table, lets his head sink back onto the rattan headrest.

'A big convoy accompanied the *Valiant* that day, including a huge Navy tanker for fuel and four of our N-class destroyers, Britain as ever propped by the Dutch. The better to evade our Brother the Japaner's subs, the ensemble proceeded fast-slow, now at thirty knots, now at fifteen. And, sure enough, on the third day out of Bombay, the *Quebec* wiped out one of their circling evil genies. On the fifth day, a beautiful clear morning, the Indian Ocean like a mirror, it was the turn of the *Tjerk Hiddes*.

'Theo Verwerda and I had just assumed the 0800 watch on the bridge when the *Valiant*'s Commodore called us. The radar had spotted at twenty-five miles a lone ship, direction 010. Interesting, far from routine, very far off the beaten track for merchant convoys. Proceed and Investigate, came the Captain's order. In my best schoolboy English I gave the usual answer, Acknowledged. You had to use English when a quarter or so of the crew knew nothing else.

'Gathering speed the *Tjerk Hiddes* began to stamp two pure-white arrows on that mirror-like blue sea, the bow wave in front, the wake behind. We'd set off on what would become the most memorable day of my life, bar one – but that's for another day.

'After a half-hour the blip of the lone ship appeared on our radar screens also. The *Valiant* and her entourage had long since disappeared from view. In about ten minutes, binoculars to the horizon, we also could see it, a regular merchant ship, loaded with red containers. But appearances can be deceptive, especially in wartime. Our Commodore called a full alarm. At a distance of three miles he instructed our Yeoman of Signals to use the Aldis lamp to ask the standard questions. In response the merchant ship raised the blue-and-white Greek flag. And then I spotted it. My shipping know-how clicked on. Captain, I said in my best English, though Sluijter was of course Dutch, Look, unless I'm mistaken, I deem that to be the goalpost silhouette of a Japaner ship.

'A shot across the bows and the order to stop. The answer came at once. The ship raised the Japanese war flag. On deck the so-called containers fell open, turned out to be camouflage for a set of four 15 cm cannons. We were faced at close range with a Japanese auxiliary cruiser, a provisioning vessel for submarines in the Arabian Sea.

'Almost instantly four projectiles came from her, two plunging into the sea in front, two behind. Ace work – a straddle with the first salvo. But Captain Sluijter, too, wasted no time. Already he'd given his orders. "Hard a-port. Emergency front. X-guns open fire."

'A quick destroyer can turn on its ass like a gymnast. Without warning, the *Tjerk Hiddes* showed the Japaner her stern. My mouth fell open. Were we running away? Never ever, says the Marine Catechism, turn your back on the foe. Never ever.' The father emphatically shakes his head. Ko, as if in a dream, slowly follows suit. 'But Sluijter was one pace ahead of the game. He hadn't forgotten his Flores tricks. "Steer zigzag seven," he cried. So every seven minutes we changed direction by fifteen degrees. The ship became a pair of pinking scissors. Imagine the speed, the churning of that ship through its own bow wave, our wake arrow a white zigzag, the dexterity of our fire command that minute-by-minute had to adapt its bearings. At that range only the 12.5 cm cannons in the X-formation where I was positioned could be used.

'The second strike like the first was the Japanese cruiser's. Our starboard sustained a hit from a 15 cm projectile. Six of the English service staff, poor chaps, lay stretched on deck. At last my X-cannons responded, twelve salvos a minute ploughing into the enemy's side. We'd reached a distance of five miles from him, our maximum range, when our Captain threw the ship into a 180 degree turn, whisked our bow towards the enemy's face. A new strategy, I saw. Klaas Sluijter had the Japaner where he wanted him.

'Built for speed, a destroyer is not a tank. This is what you non-Navy men don't know. Its steel sides are only about as thick as an arm, so it chooses never to fight broadsides. A direct hit broadsides is fatal for the sardine-tin construction. What you do is you show the enemy your bow or stern while at the same time forcing him into repeatedly exposing *his* broadside. The Japaner caught in our sights in just this way, we surged forward to make good our threat, forty-eight high explosives a minute coming from all three chief gun installations. The noise nearly exploded my ears.

'The Japaner's bridge was destroyed and fire broke out on deck. We could see the dark figures of the crew running silhouetted against the flames. Then suddenly the ship's aim went wild and almost as suddenly her cannons fell silent. Our torpedoes finally took their turn. Two wing-torpedos working together with the movement of the ship launched from starboard at two thousand meters. All that remained for us to do was to count. One . . . two . . . three . . . it didn't take long. Both were direct hits. The auxiliary cruiser broke in two, the waves quickly closed over her. We didn't stick around to look for survivors.

'What a terrible shame it was though, those six young fellows of ours, blown to bits. Just ordinary fellows, liked a spot of roulette after hours with the set I'd bought at Crawford Market, Bombay. I remember a couple of the names. Alan Jones. Dirk Kan. Someone Smith who got on well with Schilperoort. It was left to the Boatswain and his mates to ready them for their final rest. Within the hour the Commodore granted us permission.

'But now there was a potential difficulty. Admiralty instructions are clear about the order of service for burial at sea: a reading from the Book of Job, the fourteenth chapter, followed by the Prayer for the Dead. Thomas Overbury, however, the only British Officer on board, had a heavy cold. And though Klaas Sluijter might have his wizard way with steering, the clotted English of the King James Bible was a whole different challenge again. Was there not among the Nederlands officers on board one with a big enough voice to attempt a reading? Sluijter asked. There was. And there would be again every time we lost any of our chaps. In my cabin I laid matchsticks in the correct places in both books and at the appointed hour followed the Captain on deck.

'There the six were, sewn up in sailcloth, bound at the feet, each laid on a plank on deck, covered with the White Ensign. The turbines stopped, the ship lost speed. The flag came down to half-mast. There was just the ping-ping-ping of the submarine surveillance apparatus and the wash of the Polish battleship *Pidulski* circling us for protection.

"Ship's company, attention!" the First Officer gave the

command. Everyone came into position. "Caps off. Stand at ease."

'Cap under my left arm I began to work my way through the Bible verses that so many others have pieced out across almost three and a half centuries.

'"Caps on, attention, general salute!"

'The dead slid *over the wall*, as the English say, as Tom would agree if he were here, the planks and flags well lashed together so that they stayed fixed, retained for future use.

'"Ship's company, stand at ease, dismiss!" The flag went up again. The officer on duty called the machine-room telegraphist. Full services were resumed.'

The father falls suddenly silent, stares at his feet. Ella cranes forward at the window. Ko's chin long ago fell on his chest. His rib-cage rhythmically rises and falls, saliva glistens in a corner of his open lips. The father pays him no heed. He slumps lower, then suddenly jolts. A cry rips from his mouth, a torn, hollow sound of shock and abandonment.

'*God, O Godverdomme,*' he cries – the same cry, Ella thinks, as on the nights when he believes he's alone on the verandah. 'Can you credit it, Ko? How fucked we've been, *gesodomierterd* by the lot of them, the bosses, the Admiralty. We gave everything, everything, and in exchange— '

Ella steps back and closes the gap in the curtains. She doesn't want to hear more. What the father's invisible listener waiting out there in the darkness makes of these cries, she doesn't want to think.

She lies down in bed, puts her pillow over her head. Enough, it's been enough. She hears Ko stagger upright and a few minutes later the click shut of the guest room door. Out in the darkness there still are noises, hoarse and ragged. She presses the pillow harder to her ears. As many times as Ella has heard the noises, it still is terrible,

57

the wordless snarling, spitting and gasping, the father no longer the English-speaking deck-officer at the centre of the action, no longer the level-headed artillery man managing the guns when Crommelin's taken ill. She sees him instead, a poor frantic fellow, stumbling about on deck in the thick of enemy fire, his X-installation abandoned, squeezing his head in his hands.

Sleep

'Sleep, *schat*, sleep,' the mother begs, standing beside Ella's bed. She wrings her hands and sighs, 'You lay your head on the pillow, Ella, you go to sleep. You *will* go to sleep. Without sleep a young person will go insane.'

But sleep in up-country Braemar, Ella already knows, though it's often commanded, is easier said than done.

Her Mam and Dad, each after their own fashion, believe in sleep. Her father believes in short sleep, intense and economical, two hours for the price of one. He says that less sleep is required with increasing age. He cuts down his sleep at the start of the night by following the stars that shine through the crack in the curtains, as he used to do on board his plucky Netherlands destroyer the *Tjerk Hiddes*.

'What about robbers, Dad?' Ella asks, 'People who might come in the night?'

'There are worse things that come to you in the night than robbers, *meid*,' he says, casting a look at the mother through his black-rimmed glasses. 'Besides which, this great country South Africa looks after its own. Robbers and other miscreants are put where they belong.'

The mother craves sleep but cannot easily find it, same as her daughter. Sins of the fathers and the mothers. In bed at night, she says, her thoughts will not drift off, a great heaviness presses on her heart. Sometimes she doesn't have the breath even to stretch out for the Catherine Cooksons on her bedside table.

'I was awake last night for hours,' the mother tells her husband and daughter at breakfast, cradling her forehead in woven-together fingers. 'I had to get up and walk about. The birds were already singing. This lack of sleep will boil my brain, I know. It will end up breaking my skull in two.'

Like an eggshell, Ella thinks, a head cracked by sleeplessness. She knows what her mother means. The thin Braemar air here on the high Zululand escarpment doesn't weigh her head down on the pillow either. With the father's night-time talking added in, sleep is tough to find. As soon as he starts his noises, she must get up, check on things, catch what he will say, the stories of the *Silindoeng*, the *Oranje Nassau*, the *Tromp*. She must make sure he eventually comes inside, especially on nights when he is raging, see that he gets to bed.

Lately, though, her wakeful mother has discovered what she's up to. Ella hears her in the passage just outside her door, creaking about, listening out for her listening. If ever by mistake she makes a sound, the bedroom door opens, the mother peers into the darkness. 'You go to sleep, Ella,' she says, night-time breath spitting, 'I don't want to find you up. Go on, go to sleep.'

One sweaty summer's night, the father long in bed, the mother's footsteps in the passage are louder than usual, much louder. There's something about those footsteps that wants to be heard. Ella pushes up from her rock-hard pillow to listen. She slips out of bed, into the passage.

In the living room a side-lamp is on. The mother in her pink nightgown is perched on an arm of the yellow velvet couch, as close as to the portrait of Aunt Ella as she can get without actually touching it, framed by its rectangle of darkness. 'Are you – ?' Ella begins to say, but the rush of her mother's arms snuffs her voice.

'I didn't mean to wake you,' she grips her shoulders.

'Sorry. You sounded asleep – for once. But there are nights, Ella, you know, I can't stand it, I must come to her. I shouldn't say this really, you're wakeful enough yourself, but the words well up. I feel she needs me, especially now. See here, this crack in the oil-painting, around the skirt of the dress. Our dry winters. I can't stand to think of her portrait breaking up, flaking away – when we've already had to lose her once. Look at her, staring down at us. Don't leave me here, she's telling me. Oh, it's sometimes too much, Ella, all this, living this life she should've been living.'

Ella sits down on the couch. 'But why, Mam?' she says, 'I don't see . . .? Even if it's your sister's picture. A crack can be fixed.'

The mother's profile is white against the portrait's dark blue dress. A quick hand goes through her hair.

'Well,' she says suddenly, and sighs, 'Maybe the portrait's extra-special because my sister Ella was also at one time married to your father. Before me. And after the Englishwoman called Edith who left him. And then, not long after her marriage, she, Ella, died. Cancer. So, yes, you can work it out, if she hadn't died, you'd not have been born.' She puts the heel of her hand to the portrait frame, as if to steady herself. 'She was different from me, Ella, *baldadig*, cheekier, a proper big sister. Wouldn't let him push her around.' She sighs again. 'She wasn't musical like I am. Her soul didn't need music and gentleness like mine does. She didn't care about raising her voice. I can only imagine how she yelled at him. The two of them met after the war, back in Nederland. Your father was home from the Navy, from England. Friends paired them up. He was lonely and rootless with no job and they got on. She liked adventure, Ella, she grabbed opportunities with both hands. I'll always try something once, she used to say. She even took to Africa. For her, Africa was a place where you

61

could try things out. She wanted to set up a trading store in some *dorpje*, sell things like blankets to the blacks – '

But Ella can't stand to see how the mother's face is working, her forehead stretching and wrinkling, black shadows darting over her cheeks. She looks away.

'Oh, she was remarkable, Ella, unforgettable,' the mother's voice pulls her back. 'Everyone said so. It was a way she had, she burrowed under your skin, saw the world from your point of view. You felt you couldn't do without her. So that, when she died, you thought your life would end. I did, when she died. I think your father did, too. Who could replace such a person? Not a sister, no; certainly not me. When I was hollow inside for missing her.'

She stoops forward. In the muted light it's as if she's leaning against the painting, pressing her front to its breast, speaking into its face. 'They had their big plans.' She coughs, swallows, presses on. 'After the war, it was thought, places like this, South Africa, Australia, remote places, they offered opportunities to Dutch people down on their luck, reduced by all that had happened. The Far East by then was no more. They couldn't go there. And your father knew about Africa. His Singapore shipping company had seconded him out to Dar es Salaam, then Durban. He knew it was green and prosperous here. It wasn't a bad idea of Ella's to establish a trading store somewhere in the Lowveld where lush gardens can be coaxed out of the bush. Ella, your Tante Ella, she loved peonies and magnolia and such like, flowers that grow well in humid places . . .' She pauses. 'Her skin was the colour of creamy-white peonies,' she adds, '*Peon-rozen*. The painter captured it almost exactly. He painted the portrait around the time she met your father.'

Ella has stopped listening. *Tante Ella*? It was then that she stopped. The more the mother talks, the more distant the lady in the portrait becomes. Her aunt, her father's *wife*, second wife, the wife after the Englishwoman – she doesn't want to hear more. It sounds a scandal, this story. She wants to walk away from it. She herself, named for Mam's sister Ella, looking like her – like some version of her returned from the dead? Mad. As for the business about her father setting up a home in the African bush, selling blankets and buckets in a place far from proper roads or a library with books by Winston Churchill – it's crazy. The father says he hates Africa *in his gut*.

'I couldn't bear it if the painting began to crumble.' The mother scrubs at her glistening cheeks. 'What would I do without it? Here in the half-light I like to sit and imagine her alive, what she could be telling me. She was always ordering me about, her baby sister, telling me what to do. God knows I needed it. Still do. But I never imagine her reproachful, when, after all, we're alive and she's a portrait. See, he wanted someone after his loss, Ella, and not just anyone. Loving her as I did, I was happy to stand in. How could I have known it would be like this, a lifelong walk in her shadow?'

Ella goes over to the window and looks out. Squinting at the stars through her lashes, she merges the Milky Way into a shimmering scarf of light. 'What happened to the trading store plan?' she says. 'Did it get off the ground?'

''Course not.' The mother dabs a finger to the portrait's face, as if it, too, were weeping. 'They had no capital, knew nothing about trading. They rented something for a week, perhaps, who knows – then they backed out. There were too many natives in the bush, natives without pay packets. Durban's good life sidetracked them, I imagine, the bridge clubs, the golf club. Ella got ill . . . Hodgkin's, the cancer was called. She had to be sent home to Europe for treatment.'

The mother walks over to the piano. Her eyes move silently over the music on the stand, Chopin's *Nocturnes*. She lays her hands on the white keys without depressing them. Here in Braemar, miles from Durban's City Hall, she often says, unless she plays her beloved music herself, she doesn't get to hear it. Ella makes her way to the door but her mother doesn't look round.

Ella's wakefulness begins to come unprompted. Before the conversation beneath the portrait, she went to bed when her father's vigils ended. Sometimes she slept. Sometimes she heard her mother pace. Now, she's mainly just awake. She tries to make no movement but still tiny sounds escape her. Her hair rasps on the pillow. Her book thumps across a fold in the sheets. At once the door cracks open, and her heart sinks.

'Sleep, Ella, sleep,' the mother stoops over her, eye sockets pooled in shadow. '*Please*, just sleep. Don't worry about the things I said that night. I said too much. I'll get a painting restorer to come up from Durban, see about the crack. So sleep. We must sleep to live. Go to sleep, Ella, go to sleep.'

But Ella does not sleep. She lies as still as she can and wishes her mother wouldn't mention the portrait. She doesn't want to hear more about it. The picture of her *Tante Ella* is different to her now. Before, she thought it the prettiest thing she knew, but it was the portrait of a stranger. Now, it knows everything about her. Its gaze follows her round the room with tenderness, maybe curiosity. Some days, when she's alone, she sits and lets it stare at her. But these sessions leave her feeling drained, wrung-out, as if something inside her had been sucked away.

The mother telephones Mrs Garth. Rosy-cheeked Adam Garth, a year above Ella at Braemar School, is One of Our

Bright Kids, so hearsay has it. The mother has never before laid eyes on Mrs Garth. She looks up the number in the telephone book. Ella sits on the floor beside the phone table, her hands over her ears.

'Please, Mam, do you want everyone to know?'

The mother's finger slips determinedly into the first round hole in the dial.

Invisible Mrs Garth is helpful, however – helpful and matter-of-fact. Yes, she says, the bright ones think they can survive on less sleep. Adam takes a while falling asleep. To pass the time, she says, he reads *Encyclopaedia Britannica*.

'The thought,' says the mother, putting down the receiver. '*Bright ones*, what does that mean? All children are bright. As for giving a wakeful child books to read, big heavy books! *Wat een nonsens!*'

She brings into use the bed-strapping contraption she bought at a radical health *Reformhuis* on one of their trips to the Netherlands. In temperate Braemar, she explains to the father, the contraption will keep the girl tucked up warm at night. It will fasten her into her bed clothes like a passenger is belted into an aeroplane seat, only tighter. Back in Holland, lots of people use them.

'*Kind in zijn kooi,*' she says, yanking at the straps each night to tighten them. 'Bug in a rug. You'll learn to sleep again. Nature's sweet way will teach you.'

Ella doesn't feel taught. She's fond of her strapping contraption. She looks forward to the mother hugging her, then belting her in, the round clicking sounds the fasteners make as they latch onto the bedclothes. She likes lying snug and straight as a board as the mother pulls at the straps, snaps the six metal fasteners into their plastic holding cups. The straps tie her down so firmly she can barely turn over. There's no way she can get up, go to stand at the window, meet the mother crying in the living room. She likes it very much this way. Strapped down, unable to move her arms, sleep strikes her like a concussion.

Some days she wriggles in under the bed to take a look at the contraption. The spinal cord of the thing, a leather thong with branching straps, hangs beneath the mattress like a hammock, filled with a soothing quiet force, a patient spirit of hiding and waiting. This space under her bed is the safest place in the world, she decides. It's a hidey-hole almost the same as her hydrangea den, tucked away and invisible.

The contraption's straps remind her of something different, however. The straps are made of the same stretchy woven nylon from Holland as the fittings on the father's pinky-brown hernia truss. It, too, was purchased over there, though its straps are much thicker.

After six months or so, the contraption begins to lose its tightness. The stockingette starts to fray, the fasteners grow slack. Once again Ella is free to move about at night. Once again she hears the mother's creaking, opens her eyes and finds her pleading beside her bed. 'Sleep, Ella, sleep, *please go to sleep.*'

'I cannot stand it another day, Har,' the mother begs at breakfast, 'Help me find a solution. We must find a way to sleep.'

Dr Fry prescribes Valium pills. The mother resists the idea, but only for a while. From the magazines she reads she knows that Valium is a new wonder medicine, especially for women. It fixes matters to do with nerves, upsets both big and small. Yes, she knows, she should rather be trying holistic therapies, yoga and breathing and so on. Her family back home is devoted to an organic lifestyle. For generations they've been *Reformhuis* pioneers. But her family back home has backbone, staying power. They also have each other, whereas she, here in Africa, of those

66

alive, is all alone. By herself, the mother says, she doesn't have patience for natural remedies, farmhouse vegetables, eurhythmics, reading auras, finding her astral body. Her sleepless nights have driven her over the limits she may once have had.

'I'd go for the quick-fire solution, Irene,' the father says in English, crisply, as though the doctor were present, 'Whatever feels best for you.'

He's agreeing with a decision she has already taken, he knows, and Ella knows. Already she's heard her halving her Valium pills with a nail file in the bathroom, the broken dragees pinging. Half a pill, she must think, is 50% less damaging for one's soul than a whole.

Late one winter's night her mother's spit is suddenly wet and cold on Ella's cheek, 'Sleep, Ella, sleep. I heard you stirring again.' Ella squints blearily into the darkness. Was she really awake? The mother is crouched on the floor, at work with her nail file. Thump, goes her hand, then her head rears up. 'Never mind,' she says, and presses a whole pill into Ella's palm. She sees its pale yellow triangle as trim as a sweet's, a neat *v* like an arrow stamped on each flat face. 'Take a whole one. It's only your first time. It'll definitely help you sleep.'

Ella swallows the thing without water, lies back down. She barely has the chance to pull the blanket tight around her shoulders. One minute she's stretched on her back as she was before, with her contraption in place; the next minute, snap, she's asleep.

She wakes dreaming of a button, her finger on the snooze button of her alarm clock. The button, she sees squinting, is embossed with an arrow sign, another *v*.

Ella hears the father in the kitchen rattling the carousel toaster with its four turning flaps. 'Where's Ella? *Waar is ze?*' he mutters loudly to himself, using English strung together with Dutch, a comfortable mix he wouldn't try talking to her directly. 'Already it's very late.'

There's no sound from the mother.

Ella creeps to the window, draws open the curtains. The winter sunlight smacks her in the face. It plants a streak of neon-green in the centre of her field of vision, slightly to the left. She cannot look at this streak. She knows that, should she look at it, her brain will shrink to a single point.

If the mother is feeling anything like this, she thinks, then she will still be fast asleep in bed.

That whole school day she keeps her head down, protects her raw eyes from the sun. She has followed her mother's directions to the letter, she has done nothing wrong, but still she feels ashamed, deeply ashamed; *vernederd* is the Dutch word, lowered, brought low. Never again, she knows, will she be able to raise her head or peel her eyes off the ground. Some mean thing has been let into her skull that she herself allowed to get in.

At break-time she stands as usual with her classmates, Linda, Jerri, Mandy, on the edge of the playing field, scuffing the grass and chatting. Except today she's not chatting. Today, her brain wants it to be night-time. Why's the sky so very bright? she wonders. How come she didn't notice before how hard the sun beats down? Don't look at the neon-green streak, she tells herself. It will draw her in if she looks at it. It will crush her head into pieces.

Behind her fringe she steals glances at her classmates. There's something different about them, she suddenly sees. They're from another world, a normal world, not like hers – a world divided into day and night, sleep and not sleep.

'My mother gave me a sleeping pill,' she wants to tell them, Linda especially, who has smiling eyes. 'It was stronger than I needed. It has ground my brain into a mash.' But she's too proud to admit to these dark things: to confess that she can't do the natural thing, sleep, on her own; that her father's night-time rants have stolen away her rest; that her mother, too, has killed her sleep.

So she adopts a new nocturnal life and a new secret, the secret of how many of her nights are topped with a round dot, her pill. This new secret is heavier than the secret of her mother talking to the portrait; heavier even than the secret of how much she wishes, when her father's rages possess him, when he's shouting in the dark, spitting *rakker* and *schepsel* – that she could put a hand over his mouth and squeeze his face somehow, squeeze so hard that he'd never shout again.

Now almost every night before bedtime her mother comes to stand at her bedside.

'Ella, are you asleep?' she whispers. 'Please, be asleep.' In her hand is the bottle of Valium pills clicking quietly together.

But Ella is rarely asleep. Most times when the mother comes in she has just jumped back into bed, her skin clammy from leaning against the window.

Then, across the next few hours, their waiting game unfolds. Ella lies still on her pillow. In the bedroom or in the passage the mother from time to time sighs loudly, signalling she's awake. Ella could have a pill just by making a small noise.

To help pass the time, Ella tells her way through her favourite lists, the capitals of the world, the names of the stars within the Zodiac and the Southern Cross. Then, when these run out, the best saved till last, she memorizes her favourite thing – the paintings she has seen on their visits to the Netherlands, to the Rijksmuseum in Amsterdam. She pieces the paintings together, the blocks of colour and then the tiny details, the turned-over glass tumbler, the bowl of oysters, the twisted ribbon looking as if someone had dropped it in a rush.

It's a good exercise, hardly difficult. She sees versions of the pictures close-up every day. Her mother has fixed postcard reproductions of the Rijksmuseum's most famous paintings to the inside of the toilet door. Why not dream, she says, make-believe these beautiful things lie somewhere close to this godforsaken Africa?

Rembrandt's painting *The Night Watch* is Ella's favourite of the postcards. She herself observes after all a kind of night watch, a *nacht wacht*. In bed she remembers each one of the faces in the *Night Watch* crowd, the man on the edge of the painting beating his drum, the witchy girl in yellow. A buttery golden colour bathes them all. Rembrandt must've known that night watchers get cold, she thinks, that their blood runs slower in their veins, that they'd appreciate the fire burning here in front of them. She likes how the man with the extended arm is holding his hand towards the blaze.

Some nights she's exhausted enough to slip off to sleep in the middle of her lists. But these nights aren't routine. Worst is when the Dutch clock in the hallway strikes twelve and still she's lying open-eyed. Now she must take a gamble. Either she makes a noise and receives her pill, which means she'll be clumsy in the morning but not too drowsy. Or she waits till later, still hoping to drop to sleep but failing, till at last she must give up, signal for her pill, invite in another dazed day.

Three nights out of four she settles for Valium around midnight. Now and again, if she's very wide-awake, there's also temazepam, a new kind of pill Dr Fry gives her mother to alternate with the Valium, for her more agitated nights.

'There,' her mother says, lightly touching her shoulder as she swallows her pill, 'Sleep now, you will go to sleep.'

And so Ella does, each and every time. Her mother can spend all the hours she likes with the portrait and she'd be none the wiser. Her father can shout and cry on the verandah and there'll be no one at all to watch him.

The temazepam however is a different story. The temazepam brings waking dreams etched in silver. On mornings after a temazepam, impish creatures with elongated faces dance in the corners of Ella's eyes, but, when she turns to look at them face-on, they break up like mercury droplets and dissolve away.

Ella learns to manage the new regime of pills. Some nights she pretends to swallow her pill but instead saves it under her tongue till her mother has left the room. She stores the pill in her pencil case for another night, a worse night, when she might need two pills. Other times she succeeds in lying awake till three or four in the morning, without inviting a visit. She falls asleep just as dawn is breaking. To her surprise she can better cope on two hours of unassisted sleep than after six hours on Valium.

But the regime lasts a month or so only. One night the Valiums she stored in her pencil case have gone. The pill she once slipped into her tissue box has disappeared also. It's as if a giant fist has punched the air from her lungs. Till daybreak she lies staring dry-eyed at the ceiling.

At breakfast, the mother stares dumbly at her empty plate. The father is seized by an unusual lightness. Browning the toast well on both sides with the carousel toaster, he raises an eyebrow at Ella, glances in the mother's direction. 'No one at home, it looks like?'

Ella drops her eyes, won't rise to the invitation.

But she cannot look at her mother either. She knows that mask-like expression too well, the hanging jaw, the sudden jerks of the neck. She, too, has performed those whiplash head-turns following the impish temazepam ghost.

Now Ella discovers that, if her brain felt crushed before, it was a dummy run only. This dull-red pain that throbs all day inside her head, breaks up her thoughts, forces her to speak slowly – this is the real thing. She thinks about taking a day off school – but no, it's beyond imagining. She must not be weak, she must not give way.

In bed she contrives a way of binding her arms to her sides with her skipping rope to give the old feeling of being strapped down. Getting this right requires a bout of wriggling and rope winding, for which she uses her elbows and teeth. At the end of the process she's tired enough at least to want to lie still. She stuffs tissue into her ears so as not to hear her mother's creaking. Well swaddled, she runs through her list of star names till, suddenly, it's morning, she has slept. She sleeps four hours at a stretch, then five, six, seven. She no longer nods off in class.

One effect that doesn't wear off is that the world seems louder than it was before. Sounds have a sharper edge. An unexpected noise slices like a razor blade into her ear. For the first time she's aware of how loud they are together, their small family of three, how *big* their voices, especially the father's. The tidy streets of Braemar feel too puny to contain his loudness. No matter how hard her father tries to sound English and soft-spoken, he booms like a Dutchman. Every word he says sounds furious. The librarians at the town library hear his voice coming from a distance and disappear up ladders to re-shelve books.

Frith Fouché, whose mother is a librarian, tells the story at school.

'Poor lady,' Frith says the librarians whisper amongst themselves. 'To have Himself around all day to deal with. No wonder Mrs is a bit wound up.'

Ella wishes she could make common cause with the librarians and disappear up a ladder. Because if her father's loud at large in the world, how much louder isn't he boxed inside the four walls of their house?

Sleep

One morning the father's new friend Major Tom Watt gives him a frosty reception in the queue at the butcher's. That evening he stands behind his chair at the dinner table glowering, his white-knuckle hands arched on the table's edge, his breath dark-yellow with cigarette smoke and bile.

'Couldn't get him to talk to me about a thing,' he frowns at the leathery chop the mother lifts onto his plate. 'No matter how I tried. This man who has enjoyed my hospitality, my Old Brown. I asked what he made of our Prime Minister Balthazar Johannes Vorster as a successor to state architect Verwoerd. Was he sufficiently firm? A worthy custodian of our dream of a white republic? He kept looking away. Finally, at the till, he asked me to "tone it down". Be more measured, he said. Measured! Was the burden of history too heavy for him? I asked. He scooped his change into his pocket and made off. These English, I tell you, they may be the pillars of this society, but when they decide to dodge an issue, they're weasels like the rest of them, slippery as hell.'

He bends down to his plate, discerns for the first time a fine charred line running along the length of his pork-chop.

'What's this? Burnt again!' he drops heavily into his chair. 'When will you women ever get it right? Irene? So little I ask. Fresh chops purchased this very morning at the butcher's, and now look!'

He stabs at the chop with his knife and it skids off his plate onto the table, trailing grease. The mother picks up her napkin, leaves the room. '*Moeder*,' she whimpers to herself as she goes, '*Mijn Ella. Mijn moeder.*'

'*Idioot*,' the father bellows at her back. 'What earthly use do you people have? You give me nothing, you two, only take. Just like the rest of them, those Dutch, succubi all of you, sucking the lifeblood from my veins.'

Ella quietly puts down her knife and fork, yet still

73

catches his attention. 'You keep quiet, you dumb staring *idioot* no better than your mother,' he roars, white spittle gathering in the corners of his mouth. 'It beats me utterly. That you women can't get right even the few things you're good for. Like homemaking maybe. Like maybe giving a man an embrace.'

In the reflection in the dining room window Ella sees herself seated between her parents' places, the father's on the left, the mother's on the right. The window has no curtains because her father likes to follow the last of the sun sinking behind the rolling western hills of his view. From her seat she can read the titles of the books in the bookcase behind her mother's empty place. *A Town Called Alice* in a battered cream cover to the left of a blue *Plain English Grammar* and beside that the green *The Cruel Sea*. One title in particular always catches her eye – the biography of a famous soprano Oma once gave her mother. The title is printed on the bottle-green binding in silver. *Am I Too Loud?*

You are too loud, Ella wants to tell her father, her mother; we are too loud. Except no one could hear her for the noise he is making, and the blood pounding in her head.

Not long after, the skipping rope Ella leaves coiled at the foot of her bed inside the covers disappears as silently as did the pills, but nothing is said. Undeterred, she finds another way of binding herself in bed. She hoards clothes she has outgrown, that corset her tight, wears them under her pyjamas. In the morning her tourniquets have left red welts on her skin.

She takes two precautions. First, she binds only those parts of her body covered by her school uniform. Second, she hides the tight clothes each morning at the back of her cupboard.

The mother pays another night-time visit to her bedroom.

'Ella, *hier zijn wij eerder geweest*, we've been here before,' the mother whispers, her breath mint-scented with mouthwash. 'We thought you'd got over it. But still I hear you, every night, moving about. What's it this time? You know we can't live this way.'

Sweat pools in Ella's tightly bound armpits.

'Dad, he's so loud,' she moans, instantly wanting to kick herself. Her father talking on the verandah – it's something she looks out for every day.

'*Nonsens*, he's been doing what he does out there since we moved here. He likes a late smoke. No, *meid*, whatever the problem is, it's inside you, it's unbalanced. You'll end up killing us all. So, try to remember, if you can't improve this night-time situation on your own, there are other things we can do, tougher ways of looking after you.'

Other things we can do? Tougher ways? Ella brings her finger down on the bedside lamp switch and faces the mother in the light.

'There are sleep clinics, Ella,' the mother says, unflinching. 'Places to help sufferers like you. There's one in Durban, very quiet, I've found out all about it. They give you an injection, a big dose of anaesthetic, the same as when you have an operation, so you sleep for twenty-four hours, forty-eight, whatever's necessary. Your sleep cycle's put back into a normal rhythm. Your overworked head is made to rest.'

Like Rex, Ella thinks, the Durban dog she sat with at the gatepost, put to sleep a year or so after they moved to Braemar. The father said he was old and in the way. She remembers his warm firm neck under her arm. The sweat in her armpits is suddenly freezing cold.

She walks to the window, separates the curtains, presses her forehead to the cool glass. The father tonight is in his rattan chair but quiet. The lamp overhead makes a still mustard pool on the chipped table beside him. At the verandah's edges the light fades into the surrounding brown darkness. Funny, she hadn't noticed before, how the colours out there are the same as in *The Night Watch*.

An anaesthetic to force her to sleep though, she thinks, that would tax her to her limits. It would be like loading a strapping contraption right inside her head.

She remembers the black and white photograph in the father's *Winkler Prins* encyclopaedia, an asylum ward full of mad people in their pyjamas. *During the First World War mental illness among ex-combatants in Britain soared. Bed rest was prescribed.*

'Make the drug strong,' Ella imagines the mother saying on the phone, 'Mix it up well. She must be trained to sleep.'

To emerge intact from such bed rest, she will have to find a hidey-hole deep as a Durban river gorge; she will have to set her mind into a granite groove. She puts a hand to her cold forehead. To her surprise she finds her whole face is wet, as if it were possible for tears to fall upwards as well as down.

Bear

The Netherlands, as far as Ella is concerned, is the best place in the world to visit. These northern Low Countries are her other home, her home from home. She may not have visited many places, true, but Artis is in the Netherlands, this is one of the reasons why it's the best place. The two-yearly treks with the mother all the way from their edge of the south-east African plateau to the misty flatlands where her parents were born are wonderful because they have this one main destination – *Natura Artis Magistra*, the Amsterdam zoo.

They make the long journey to Oegstgeest, Zuid-Holland, to help look after her grandmother, Oma, her only grandparent. Oma is suffering from old age and lives in a two-storey home for the elderly on the edge of the town. They make the journey also because the mother misses the Netherlands and the home she left behind. 'Only daughter as I now am,' she says, 'My mother needs me and I need her.'

Ella doesn't mind the journey. If it was up to her they could make the journey every year instead of every two. She doesn't mind the long days they spend in the home sitting beside Oma's chair, not talking much, nibbling Sun-Maid raisins from California. She doesn't mind Oma's warm powdery old lady's smell sifting down to her and the startled look of her eyes behind her thick bifocals don't bother

her either. Oma here in Holland is at home, so Ella sitting beside her feels at home, too.

In fact, there's nothing about Oegstgeest or the old age home Ella minds, but still she's happy to accept the treats and outings Mam offers as a compensation for having interrupted their other life back in Braemar. When the treat is Artis Zoo she's more than happy to accept.

She begins her reminders about the zoo just as soon as they have set foot on the smooth walkways of Schiphol airport, once her mother has had a chance to comb her hair and calm down after their long flight from Durban. Knotted inside the hugging arms of cousins and second cousins who smell of wet wool, Ella pitches her voice high to make sure everyone hears her request. 'Mam, Mam, Tante Suus, when are we going to Artis, Tante Suus, Mam? You said soon, very soon.'

No arrival in the drizzly geometry of the Netherlands is complete without the promise that tomorrow, or, yes, very soon, she will be taken by Mam or Tante or Cousins Ineke or Lieke, to visit Artis.

Ella thinks often of her mother's story about Artis and its wolves: how their yowling kept Mam awake at night when as a child she went to stay with *her* oma in Amsterdam, whose house lay a few streets away from the zoo. The awful feeling she had listening, Mam says, was that she herself, there in her safe bed in the big city, was the creature out of place, not the wolves. The city by night belonged to their yowling.

Ella thinks that, on the contrary, she would've liked hearing the wolves, the yipping barks cutting through the cold night air. Wouldn't that be incredible, to lie in bed surrounded by wolf noise, as if you were in a snow-covered hut in Siberia, safe in bed though circled by blazing eyes?

As far as she can tell, all the world's wild animals great

and small are collected together in Artis's long rectangle stretched across three city blocks close to the grey-brown Amstel River. No matter how often they visit, every time she walks through the gateposts each mounted with their large gold-painted eagle; every time she sets foot on the moist brick walkways; turns left to her first port of call, the reptile house; sees again the slowly shifting hieroglyphs of the snakes in their glass tanks – her breath catches in her throat.

Where they live on the African shield there are no zoos. In Africa many marvellous animals are to be found in the game reserves: white rhinos, lions, herds of shaggy wilde-beest, all roaming free – or so the ads in the KLM brochures she reads on the plane say. However, game reserves are out of bounds for her family. If ever she mentions the two words *game reserve* together the father has his answer ready. 'What do those dumps offer but daylight robbery? A moronic drive through a worn-out old bit of African savannah where most of the animals are asleep, bah, what's the point of that? When you have an excellent view of the African landscape here from your own verandah.'

So there are the caged animals of Artis instead, but Ella isn't complaining. There is as a matter of fact nothing to complain about on their four- or six-month-long visits to the Netherlands packed full of treats she never gets back in South Africa. There is Zippo's circus where the lions Harris and Tieras jump through flaming hoops without getting scorched. Ella loves Harris and Tieras. She draws pictures of them at her new Dutch school, the Steiner Vrijeschool, where the mother has registered her. They take outings to see the old familiar pictures at the Rijksmuseum, though this time set in their fancy gold frames, not postcard-size. They go to afternoon shows at the Oegstgeest puppet theatre, famous for its child-high puppets. For breakfast Mam gives her sugar waffles, and then as much blood sausage with every meal as she can stomach.

Even the ordinary everyday things in Holland are good, like the evenings they spend at Tante Suus's house with her teenage cousins Ineke and Lieke, doing nail-painting, making popcorn and watching television. Television is a special new treat as South Africa does not have television. There are also the times sitting with Oma. Oma is so still a person, so unlike the mother and the father. The space around her is very soft and quiet.

But above all the other enjoyable things is Artis. In Artis, once they are past the opening exhibits, the reptile house, the dromedary enclosure, the African rock rabbits, the mother's strong middle finger inserts itself between her shoulder blades. Ella leans back into it and goes more slowly. She likes to stop everywhere, at each and every animal's precinct. She won't be hurried. Where the cages look empty she kneels and peers in amongst the leaves till she finds a sign of life: a moving tail, a stirring horn. She knows there will always be one.

No visit to the zoo passes without some new sight to see. The elephant with the star-branding on both haunches, who one afternoon breaks into a shuffle dance a circus trainer must once have taught him. The tiger's sudden leap from one rock to another, his burning stripes creasing and stretching. The moulting wallabies with mood swings that on each visit look different, now curious, now scornful, now enormously amused.

The polar bear cage is on the final turn of the circular walk through the zoo, beyond the seals and the penguins. The first time Ella sees him, just like every other time she will see him, he is standing swaying on his hind legs, the zoo's one bear, shifting his weight from one leg to the other. Reared up as he is, he could be scary – but he looks more than anything bewildered, as if something had hit him in the face.

Seeing the bear Ella immediately bursts into tears. Her eyes move up across the yellow-white belly, the mighty forepaws dangling like a puppet's hands, then meet his small dull eyes. But she cannot go on looking. She stands stock-still on the brick pathway, buries her face in her hands and sobs.

She cannot look again at that huge hopeless swaying bear yet she still feels him moving. Through her wet fingers she sees his shadow shift. The winter sun is setting behind him so his shadow touches her red wellington boot, then moves away again. She stands rooted, her chest aching, her chin jammed into her chest, till the mother takes her by the hands and drags her away.

But no sooner have they left than she is begging to go back. She must see again the bear. She *will* see again the bear, *zij wil, zij wil*. They must go to Artis, they must see the bear.

So, within the first few days of each visit to the Netherlands, a weekly pattern is set. As Friday approaches Ella clamours to go again to the zoo, tomorrow, this weekend, as soon as possible. Her mother coughs a little, suggests something closer to Oegstgeest, the *kermis* in the town square? But by Saturday breakfast she has given way.

Again they walk through the tall gateposts. Ella can feel her breath coming faster. They seek out her favourite animals, the tiger, the llamas, the curious-and-scornful wallabies. They detour via the antbears; they loop back to the African rock rabbits. And then, at the very end of the route, they reach the polar bear swaying in his cage, his great paws dangling, and she is inconsolable.

The second or third time they see the bear, the mother, prepared, produces tissues, leads her away to buy ice-cream.

It is a cold day, the vanilla cones smoke. Perched on an icy concrete bench the mother tells Ella that the zoo prides itself on being a humane zoo, it takes the welfare of all its animals seriously.

'Look around, *kind*, at the size of the big cats' pits and length of the wolf run,' she says. 'See how well everyone is looked after. Perhaps your *ijsbeer* likes to stand up, that's why his cage isn't so big? Perhaps he's taking his exercise by swaying. Wasn't he a dear beast though, didn't you think, *een lieve dier*, like a huge white teddy?'

Ella moves her head slightly but says nothing. She doesn't think her polar bear looks like a teddy at all.

The third or fourth time Ella and her mother see the bear, there is the hurrying away after a short period, there are the tears, but this time no ice-cream, no reassurance, only, once again, a short talk about the big white teddy, *het lieve dier*. 'Why should a big white teddy make you cry, Ella? It makes me think of curling up in an armchair with a soft toy and a hot chocolate. It doesn't make me want to cry.'

Ella puts her hands on her knees, raises her shoulders and puffs out air.

The fifth or sixth time, the mother is fed up. 'We won't go again if this *tendency* persists,' she tells Oma when Ella is present, raising an eyebrow. Oma remarks that Ella has the nose of her third cousin Jeroen on her father's side, lucky for her, avoiding the family conk.

But by the next time, a week or so later, the mother has forgotten about Ella's *tendency*. Most mornings in the Netherlands she forgets to prod her as she does back in Braemar, like a pawpaw, to measure her height and peer at her tonsils. She declares herself willing, yet again, just this once, to indulge Ella's *quite sweet* interest in her polar bear. She buys a monthly Artis pass. They get their route through the zoo down pat. The rock rabbits, big cats, et cetera, at double-quick pace, and then, the silent agreement is, the mother lingers at the seals while Ella goes on ahead on her own. She turns the corner in the brick pathway, her eyes to the ground, her nails digging into her palms. Finally, when she is ready, she looks up. She comes face to face with the polar bear standing swaying on his hind legs.

She doesn't think of the bear as *her* bear, though the mother calls him that. She sees him as – what? A bored, penned-in beast. Her tears make no difference to him, she knows, but still, whenever she first sees him, she can't help sobbing. There's no father around to say the usual. 'Stop that womanish mewling; how I hate to hear a female cry. Women's hearts are blocks of ice. Their tears mean zip.'

Across the weeks of their Netherlands visits, Ella inches a little closer to the polar bear's cage, though never onto the gravel semicircle in front of it. Her crying shouldn't disturb the bear. He shouldn't see how sad her thoughts about him are.

Once, she tries looking up into his eyes, to see if he's as bored as he looks from a distance. Though bears can't tell the time, she doesn't think, still he sees his shadow move, doesn't he? He sees it shifting to and fro in front of his bars like a pendulum.

But the thought of the bear marking the minutes of his endless days in the cage is too much. The idea of him swaying there tomorrow and the next day and the day after that, seeing his shadow going to and fro with no change in sight, day after day – it's worse even than the first time she came face to face with him. She tries to put the thought somewhere else in her head but it's too late. A hole full of black fluid opens in her chest. The fluid rises and flows up her throat and out of her eyes though she tries as hard as she can to swallow it down.

It's always winter in the Netherlands, a gentle dove-grey winter, because the mother plans their months here to coincide with the scorching Zululand summers. On cold mornings Ella likes tracing the ferny frost patterns on the windows with her finger and making smoky breath when she goes outdoors. She likes the tureens of primary-colour paints she's given at her school, the Vrijeschool, and mixing green, purple and orange on the newspaper spread across the floor. The schools here are conveniently open, because it's winter, while the schools in South Africa at the other side of the world are closed.

Even if the Vrijeschool involved less play and more work Ella wouldn't mind going to school here just as she doesn't mind being away from Braemar. She knows that their months in Oegstgeest are not a holiday. Her family doesn't go on holiday and, even if they did, the father would insist it must not be to the Netherlands. They are never here in the company of the father and they never call him while here. Calling would mean an expense, yet another waste of money and time.

'You won't catch me stooping so low as to creep back into that tight yellow arsehole of the country of my birth,' the father says when he lets them out in the drop-off zone at Louis Botha airport in Durban. Every time they leave to see Oma, as he hefts their suitcases out of the car boot, he seems to feel pressed to make the same speech. 'No, not even if you paid me,' he says, his hand in the air for silence, though no one is contradicting him. The mother starts breathing audibly, as if to drown him out. 'Certainly not for months at a time, no, you won't catch me creeping,' he goes on, his voice rising. 'Currying favour with those lily-livered toadies, and that includes our relatives who've never so much as left the place, except for the occasional holiday – it's insupportable as well as unaffordable, yes indeed, *ja zeker*. Some people have to work for their *kuch*. You go with my blessing but that arsehole isn't for me.'

The mother holds her cheek up for a kiss.

'Hippy hippy shake Holland,' he says, pursing dry lips in the general direction of her face, 'Just look at it, your Dam encrusted with drug addicts, can't you see how the country has gone to rack and ruin? The minute the Nazis were allowed to march in, the country's game was up. First the Nederlanders let those Moffen walk all over them, and then, beaten and abject as they were, they fell into the embrace of drug-crazed American hippies, let them piss on the remaining achievements of the past. A once-robust body politic reduced to pure flab, oppressed by the freedom the War so dearly bought. Whereas this country, well, look around you, the place is run like a tight ship. The good strong laws of the land make the European truly free – free to work, free to succeed. In the very year the child was born they clapped those terrorists who were threatening to undermine the place in gaol for life, and rightly so, that tall schemer Mandela and his sidekicks – *bah!* – trying and failing to use their brains.

'As for spending *one last time* with my mother-in-law, as you, Irene, suggest,' he raises his voice over the noise of an ascending plane, 'Sorry, it's beyond me. In respect of your family, I've had enough of *one last time*. They can't stop, your family, pushing things to their limits, begging just *one last time*. How many pleas of *one last time* has it now been, going over to see Oma? So typical it is, so Dutch, *trying it on*, like trying on neutrality versus Hitler because you're too yellow in fact to *take him on*. All Dutchmen are shirkers, mark my words – Dutchmen, Dutchwomen too.'

He briefly puts his leathery cheek against Ella's forehead. 'Trying it on, begging *one last time*,' he walks round to the driver's side of the Volkswagen, 'It's not for me,' he says, and casts a strange, haunted look at the mother. She checks the travel documents in her bag, doesn't again look at him. The prospect of the trip gives her courage.

'Like that other one before her, when she got sick, she begged to go on one last furlough home,' he tosses over his shoulder, getting into the car. The mother pulls at Ella's hand. 'And your family, that precious Oma, my two-times mother-in-law, falsely promised all the while to send her back.'

So the journey by air across Africa every two years is covered by the trust fund Oma has set up in the mother's name. And, once here, they stay on as Oma's guests to make the long trek worthwhile, to give the mother time to recover from its horrors, hating flying as she does, in fact hating it like death. For the mother, the distance of South Africa from the Netherlands is a personal insult inflicted by fate, so she says – the fact that these days the KLM jumbo jet and not the Union Castle Line is the quickest way to go.

If it was up to Ella, they could stay even longer in the Netherlands than they do. They could stay as much as a year. In the Netherlands she doesn't miss South Africa. She definitely doesn't miss Braemar, except maybe one or two things, like the nights keeping watch at her window, some of them, listening out, picking up stories, watching that her father stays upright in his chair. Come to think of it, her father's stories on the Braemar verandah are the nearest thing to television she has in South Africa.

At the Vrijeschool, as far as she can see, she slots in. Every time she's back, she slots in. Her voice, her clothes, even her built-up shoe, everything more or less fits. All the children wear shoes. Three of them even live in the same tall apartment block as Ella and her mother, a rental arranged by Oma's second cousin's daughter, Loes. Ella and her Vrijeschool neighbours make up a small gang. In the afternoons after school they gather at the tall mound of sand on the building site behind the apartment block to kick stones and make sandcastles. They hook up in chains and chant the marching songs they learn in class, '*Witte zwanen, zwarte zwanen*', '*T'is plicht dan ied're jongen*', a song about fighting for your fatherland's independence. Ella shouts out the songs the loudest of all.

In Oegstgeest Ella feels her mother is contented, or so it looks. She shops at the grocer on the ground floor of the apartment block without complaining as she does in Braemar that there's nothing to buy in darkest Africa and no money to buy it with. She sits with Oma by the hour talking about all kinds of things, family doings, local house prices, knitting patterns, the Vrijeschool, how little it has changed since the mother herself was a pupil.

Sometimes they look at old photograph albums and play 'Do you remember?'. 'Oh, look, see, behind Tante Han's head, that *Jugendstil* clock we had, remember, that lost two minutes every twenty-four hours?' 'And here you are, Irene, on the old swing in the back-garden of the Hasselsestraat behind the red currant bushes. How I loved that swing, the dry sweet smell of the dunes that wafted up as you swung high.'

Now and then they mention the mother's sister. They point to her face in the photograph albums, say *Ella* and sigh. Though Ella sitting pressed against Oma enjoys the game, she avoids looking at dead Ella's face.

'Too generous always,' the mother mysteriously whispers. 'If she hadn't given everything up and gone out there,

I wouldn't have had to follow, would I? I always ended up walking in her wake.'

She puts her hand over the studio photograph of Ella's portrait that's in one of the albums. It takes up a whole page. 'At least certain parties now have her to themselves,' she says, 'For a limited time anyway.'

'I don't like it,' Oma shakes her head. 'That portrait captures her exactly. I don't like to think of her left out there without her family, alone.'

The mother and Oma don't talk about the wider world. They never talk about South Africa and they don't talk about the father. Ella sees that these things somehow go together.

One afternoon though, when the mother's in a meeting with the home's dietician, Oma does mention the father to Ella, the father and his two wives, her daughters: first dead Ella, then our young Irene.

The photo album is lying open on the side table. Oma lets her finger fall on a small square photo: the two sisters, Ella and Irene, stand in short-sleeved summer dresses and stout walking shoes in a meadow lane, their arms draped over each other's shoulders. Ella is sturdy and smiling; Irene's eyes are averted to avoid the bright sunlight.

'It might just about have been tolerable losing one daughter to that bad-tempered Navy man, old before his time,' Oma says, looking askance at Ella stacking empty raisin boxes on the floor. 'Two, however, is harsh. I know it's harsh for her, too, for Irene, though she doesn't ever say a thing. She did what she did and she's sticking to it. Maybe I shouldn't say anything either, but still, I have my thoughts.' Oma rears back in her chair. Ella peers up into her face but can't find her eyes behind her glasses.

'My older one, Ella, she was heedless,' Oma continues, sighing. 'Yes, he's short, grey and half-blind, mama, she

88

once said to me, but after a war, can unmarried girls be choosy? I never thought the virginal younger one would think so too. That she'd so want a husband as to take her dead sister's. After her death, I remember, they started writing to each other. Those pale blue air letters like missives from the underworld. How quickly she darted to the letter box when they arrived. A pact of the living against the mourned. But a pact forged in sorrow, is that likely ever to bring happiness— ?'

Oma tosses her head, her bifocals flash. '*Ach, lieverd,* look at you, staring at your Oma as if she was some silly person, babbling. I'm forgetting myself. Come, give me your hand. Shall we go to the kitchenette to see if there are more raisins?'

On Friday nights in Holland Ella's mother puts on the smart Loden winter coat she bought with her first pay cheque at eighteen and never takes out of the country. All by herself she attends recitals and string quartets in various *zalen* in Den Haag, the *Concertgebouw* in Amsterdam. She leaves Ella on the sofa in front of the television with Cousin Lieke as babysitter. Lieke sits side by side with Ella and wraps a big cosy quilt around their legs.

When the mother returns late at night she half-carries Ella, drowsy and blundering, from the sofa to her bed. Ella puts a hand up to her mother's rosy cheeks.

'Just the cold, *lieverd,*' the mother says. 'The lovely brisk cold.'

One evening in front of the television, Lieke puts the finishing touches to a geography project on South Africa she has done at school. She traces a map, sticks in pictures. Ella helps by cutting photographs of zebras and lions out of a travel brochure. Colouring the sea around Durban with a royal-blue pencil, Lieke asks Ella, quite abruptly, what it's like living in a police state. Are there lots of rules to follow?

'A police state?' Ella stops cutting and looks at Lieke. 'What's that? I don't know what that is.'

'Our teacher's told us,' Lieke says, 'In South Africa you must do as the authorities say and if you don't you're punished.'

Ella shakes her head, No, she doesn't know about that.

Later that evening she watches a programme about the Anne Frank House in Amsterdam, where the secret stairway behind the bookcase is being restored. Dutch actresses reading extracts from Anne Frank's *Diary* intercut with footage showing the restoration team at work. Lieke by now is curled up at the sofa's end, dozing. Ella watches Anne Frank's sad story to its end. She can't believe that Anne and her family spent all that time during the war hidden in an attic. Imagine, the bookcase door clicking closed behind them. The footsteps of their minders walking away, receding into silence. She sees Anne lying in bed, maybe even under her bed for better protection, listening out for suspicious noises . . .

Then, as Ella watches, Lieke's question begins to gnaw, that thing she said about punishment. Anne Frank and her family were terribly punished, the programme tells her, once they were discovered in their *Achterhuis*. They had disobeyed the rules about being Jews so the occupying Nazis rounded them up and put them on trains headed for concentration camps over the border in Germany.

Ella glances over at her cousin, her peaceful face and closed eyes. She wonders what Lieke would say if she, Ella, told her about the strange things back home in Braemar: the Remedial Class and the visits from Dr Fry; the father shouting on the verandah? But she wouldn't know where or how to begin telling her about these things. She wouldn't have the words. Loyalty in their family, she knows, is an iron band. Her mother Irene went to South Africa to marry her father out of loyalty to her late sister's memory, Oma herself said this. Irene booked her passage on the Union Castle Line because her late sister Ella had been Har's wife before her and now he was left all alone. If she, Ella, said anything funny about the father and the mother to Lieke, wouldn't it be she herself, named for that sister, who would look bad?

Outdoors, the Netherlands is made up of horizontal planes painted in primary colours, like a stage set made for the sole purpose of entertaining children. Wherever Ella and her mother go there are more playgrounds filled with red and blue climbing frames than she has time to play in. Once a fortnight, the park beside the old age home is visited by a ventriloquist and his red-haired man-sized puppet dressed in a harlequin suit. Oma saw his poster in the hallway. The ventriloquist stands and performs beside the big sunken sandpit and Ella is allowed to run out on her own to watch him. Huddled together with the other children she listens in wonder as a chirrupy voice springs from the puppet's mouth. The ventriloquist barely moves his lips.

On her way back to Oma's room Ella practices lowering her voice till it rumbles deep inside her chest. With time, she wonders, if she had a life-sized doll like the ventriloquist's, would she be able to jump her voice from her chest like he does? Throw it straight into the doll's mouth without stirring her lips? She'd like to practise, she thinks, to watch and listen till she learns how to fill up a puppet's chest with words.

One morning on a walk in the park Ella asks the mother what the father could be doing today, right now. There's a pause. They circle the pond. The mother inspects the last husks of withered white roses still clinging to the bushes in the small rose-garden. Her voice when it finally comes is curt. 'I'm sure he finds things to do,' she says. 'He'll have no trouble entertaining himself.'

But what things does he find to do? Ella puzzles. How does he entertain himself? Does he tell himself stuff out on the verandah just as if they were home? Does he keep himself amused that way? Not ever knowing that he has an audience, does he shout his stories just as energetically when she's not around as when she is?

Sitting with Oma one afternoon during her nap, Ella finds in the knitting bag beside her chair a blank postcard of a beach scene slipped in alongside the fifty or so other bits of scrap paper she likes to keep there.

Dear Dad, she writes on the postcard, then doesn't know what to say. She tries, *It is misty today*. She wants to tell him about the *ven-trill-o-quist* in the park but she can't spell the word. She draws a picture of the doll in its harlequin suit instead. The doll has a bubble in its chest. *Buikspreker*, stomach-talker, is the Dutch word for ventriloquist.

She gives the postcard to the mother to post. Weeks later, a few days before they are due to fly back to South Africa, the blue-sky edge of the postcard is still there in the document wallet the mother carries in her coat pocket. The mother sees Ella catch sight of it.

'Look, we'll give it to him when we see him,' she says, patting her pocket. 'Too late to send it now.'

At the Vrijeschool Ella paints on a big sheet of jotter paper an outline of Africa shaped like a huge human ear, a right ear. The outline is in red. Inside the ear outline she paints whorl shapes, bulgy swirls encircling smaller loops. Then she paints in brown the names of the towns where they have landed on their air trips up and down Africa, words full of round *a* sounds, Abidjan, Accra, Brazzaville, Luanda along the outer whorl of the ear; on the inside, within the smaller loops, Lumbumbashi, Nairobi, Cairo.

Bear

In some places the letters fuse together. They look like shadowy knots of cartilage within her great red African ear. *Mevrouw* Kramer, her teacher, offers to pin the picture to the wall. It's very dramatic, she says kindly. Ella shakes her head, grabs the edge of the paper. She wants rather to store it in her folder.

Flights

It is terrible to return to Africa from the Netherlands. But then, Ella thinks, staring out of the aeroplane window, it's terrible also to leave Africa. The terrible thing is the travelling, flying up or down the continent in a blue-and-silver liveried DC-8 in the company of her mother. The first hour or so of every flight Mam spends screaming, until her pills finally take hold and she falls asleep. For her, there's nothing more terrible than flying – the whole appalling *nachtmerrie* of it, the deafening whoosh of the take-off, the shrieking of the brakes on landing, the awful distance away of the safe earth, being caught like some Soviet test monkey in a capsule in the sky.

But the problem with travelling up or down the African continent isn't only the flying. For the mother the flying is made worse by the regular stops they must make so that the plane can refuel. Sleek and modern though it looks, the aeroplane cannot complete the journey from far South to high North without one or two touchdowns to take on more fuel. It must go in stages, hurdling its way from one African country to another, each time plunging down through the storm clouds into the forest or savannah, then straining back into the bumpy sky, the engines yelling and the mother along with them.

From where Ella sits in her window seat looking out, Africa high up is all green gauze and grey cloud. Conical mountains point through the clouds to the sky. Closer to the ground, Africa becomes a broken ribbon, a narrow laterite airstrip bordered by red earth, unfurling in pieces of irregular length. The ribbon spreads to receive them as they land, peters away into the surrounding green when once again they lift up into the sky. At night Africa's darkness is dusted with silver lights the plane trustingly dives down to meet.

'Look, Mam, see, the airstrip down there, how lit-up it is.' She taps the plane window.

'Be quiet please, *kind*.' In her lap the mother kneads her knuckles till they go red. 'Talking makes things worse. My only wish right now is that the whole of that landmass down there would just sink into the sea.'

The airstrips across Africa look a lot like one another on the ground as well as from the sky. When they disembark for fuelling to take place, oily silver mirages everywhere ripple across the tarmac. In the various transit lounges, plastic chairs are arranged in rows. They sit down and wait. Sometimes, paper cups of lukewarm water have been set out on plastic tables. The film of dust gathered on the water glistens under the neon lights. But if there's a war on in the country where they've landed, there are no paper cups and no tables, just a plastic container of water with a tap, though often not even that.

At a coastal airport late one night, maybe in Ghana, Ella notices that the place name over the main entrance to the transit lounge hall has been painted over in black. A new name is not yet in evidence, except for where someone has chalked *Viva!* on the wall in red. Another time, the town in Congo where they stop and wait has a completely different name from before. The pilot announces it before they land. Still, Lubumbashi airfield looks more or less like she remembers Elisabethville. The arrivals hall is the same hangar-like shed though this time it's crowded with soldiers.

Wherever in Africa a conflict is on the go, a steaming energy comes to meet them the minute they step onto the tarmac. Huge-shouldered men in battle fatigues escort them on their sticky walk into the transit hall. One by one the soldiers check their travel documents at the entrance: the taciturn white businessmen; the Dutch tourists in safari outfits, looking tense; the yawning fathers and mothers holding their grumpy children's hands. The soldiers direct the air stewards to join the queue. The humid air seethes.

The first time Ella sees soldiers on their cross-Africa journey is in Luanda, where a tank is parked beside the airport buildings. The soldiers standing around it look full of themselves, their automatic rifles held close to their sides, belts of bullets spanned across their chests. Without saying a word they make it known that here, on land, they and not KLM are in charge. If things got difficult, no airline would have the least leverage over them. In the transit lounge a soldier stands guard over the water dispenser and frowns if ever a thirsty passenger approaches it. When those who do approach take too long drinking, he flicks the tap to upright in front of their mouths.

The wars in Africa nowadays, the father back in Braemar says, are either civil wars or wars of independence, struggles for so-called freedom, but who's to tell the difference? Either way, Ella thinks, these Luanda soldiers look like they've just taken over the country. They walk about like men in command.

Later, after Luanda, on other journeys, there are more soldiers corseted with arms and ammunition, in Lubumbashi and also Accra, and these men, too, look full of themselves and in command. If freedom is what these soldiers have got hold of with their frowning and posing, Ella decides, it must suit them. She has never seen black people looking this tall and big-chested in South Africa; nor, for that matter, white people in Europe.

In the transit lounges they visit across the African continent, time passes slowly. The fuelling process seems to take hours, sometimes a whole night. The hands of the broken clock on the wall don't move. The passengers sit in their plastic chairs with their cups of water placed on the floor in front of them. Their heads loll and mouths fall open. Some people sleep by crouching forwards. A courageous few lie down on the ground to sleep but, with the soldiers patrolling, are soon roused. Sit back down, the soldiers motion with their rifles.

The mother sleeps with her head held upright, her eyes squeezed shut. Ella tries to stay awake. She thinks about all that Africa out there, the huge, unsinkable bulk of the continent. What goes on beyond these baking buildings, that skinny airstrip? She measures herself against the feeling of danger pushed out by the frowning soldiers. Is she bigger than this feeling? Is she brave enough to look them in the eye? So far, she has only glanced at them aslant, making as if to stare out of the window.

From far away she hears the sound of singing and drumming, the same as she can hear in Braemar on weekend nights, from the direction of the African township. Or maybe she's making it up, maybe it's no more than the whining of the neon lights overhead, the bristling insects bombarding them. She watches the chins of the other passengers drop slowly onto their chests.

Late at night, when even the soldiers standing guard seem to let their eyes sink closed, she stands up, pretends to stretch and yawn. No one takes any notice. Keeping the corner of her eye trained on the soldiers, she goes over to the window, peers out into the darkness. It's an ordinary darkness, lit with a few points of light. A roar of frogs and insects bears down from all sides. If it has rained, the fresh smell of vegetation seeps through the locked doors. Once, from far away, comes the sound of sporadic machine-gunfire, a burst, a short pause, another burst.

Ella can sense whenever the time has come to leave the Netherlands. Nothing's said, but under her skin she knows it's time. The mother is suddenly jumpy, just like she is back in Braemar. When she opens her mouth small gobbling sounds pop from the back of her throat.

Ella feels she is a bird, a swallow maybe, tossed on a great wind that blows now north, from South Africa to the Netherlands, and now south again, away from Europe. When it's time for her direction to change she senses the atmosphere begin to fibrillate around her. A moment ago she was faced north, now there's a strong force shifting in the opposite direction. She hears doors shut behind her with firm closing clicks, the Vrijeschool's cheerful red door, the sliding doors to Oma's old age home, finally the door to the rented apartment. Mam parcels up *stroopwafels*, spicy biscuits, Vitamin E face cream, out-of-date magazines she hasn't yet had time to read – a pile of lumpy necessaries to sweeten their life in Africa.

In the cousins' living room Lieke ceremonially invites Ella to switch off the television for the last time. Ella listens to it crackle into stillness. She will miss the television – the television, and Artis and the polar bear, and all the other favourite things, the ventriloquist in the park, evenings with Lieke, the frost patterns on the window, the gang and the building-site playground, Oma's Sun-Maid raisins.

The mother spends a last afternoon with Oma. She is meant to be saying goodbye but when she picks Ella up from her cousins', she tells Tante Suus with fixed, reddened eyes that her mother was impossible. All she, Irene, was allowed to do was tidy the room yet again, for the hundredth time. Her mother responded to nothing she said.

But it's not like Oma to be troublesome, Ella knows. Probably she just didn't want to say goodbye. Yesterday she and Oma agreed not to say goodbye, only *Tot ziens*, see you later.

'*Moedertje, moedertje,*' Ella later hears her mother cry into the telephone but there seems to be no one talking back to her. '*Ik kom terug, hoor,*' she sobs, 'I will return.'

Then, at last, it is as if the lights dim around them and everything gradually goes quiet. They begin their walk down the shimmering tubular tunnel that is Schiphol airport. At one end of the tunnel, far behind them, as if suspended inside the wrong end of a telescope, stand Tante Suus and the cousins waving. In front, Schiphol's polished walkways and smooth conveyor belts weld into a long continuous passageway that leads at the very end into the jet bridge into the plane. The mother clutches Ella's hand till it goes dead.

They interrupt the smooth walk just once, in the Ladies beyond Customs. It is time for the mother to take her pills. No pill can properly crush her difficulty, they both know, but still she taps several of the triangular tablets into her shaking palm and swallows down the lot without water. Ella makes a screen of her body so that the queue of women waiting for the toilets, already looking away, cannot see Mam crouching down here in the corner, her arms around her knees, whimpering.

Their journeys are always like this. There is always this time of preparation. At the other end of the journey, leaving South Africa, it's no different. When a flight is imminent nothing but a palm-full of pills can help the mother, and then only just. There the same as here she cowers in the corner of the Ladies pressing her temples. There, too, Ella stands over her holding their hand luggage, her eyes trained on the ceiling.

'It'll soon be over,' Ella says carefully. 'When the plane refuels, there'll be time to get some air.'

But the mother has ears only for the sounds coming from her own tight throat. 'Not yet, please, Ella,' she moans, 'Help me, not yet. I can't breathe.' Ella raises her hand to the *Push* plate on the toilet door. Her mother struggles upright, braces herself between the wall and the sink, grabs her wrist. 'No, Ella, no. God, let me breathe. Before I reach the plane I'll fall over, I know it, my lungs will shut down. I'd rather die than disgrace myself.'

Ella gives her fingers to her mother to be crushed. Like a drowning dog, she can't help thinking, a drowning dog in a tank, Mam's nails scraping the walls.

Holding hands, they edge step by step out of the Ladies' door. Ella makes a rough calculation based on the numbers of wrongs of the Dutch fathers and the Dutch mothers that have already passed down to her. The off-kilter foot. The towering height. The widow's peak. A lot of wrongs. Considering the law of averages, she might just about be safe from inheriting the mother's terrible fear also.

The truth is, she doesn't mind flying. She likes being swept up high while feeling safely strapped in. She thinks of the plane boring through the starry sky like a rocket and tries to ignore her mother completely.

But it's never for long. Within moments of take-off, sometimes when the plane is just ascending, often without warning, the mother undoes her seat belt, pushes herself upright and starts yelling. Ella can't then blank her, not easily. When air stewards come running to force her back into her seat she can't pretend they don't belong together.

'Yes,' she nods when they ask, 'Yes, I'll hold my mother's

arm, I'll try to help her stay in her seat. I'll ask her to keep her seat belt fastened.'

Hardest is when the plane meets with tropical storms. Around the equator the turbulence is often bad but for noise and bumpiness the thunderstorms over West Africa take first prize. Hurdling its way north or south over the bulge of the continent the plane is tossed like a rubber ball from thunderhead to thunderhead. Lightning bounces off the plane wings in broken zigzags. The mother crouches by the emergency exit retching, beating the door with her hands.

'*Moeder, O moeder*,' she cries, her mouth making a dark circle, '*O mijn moedertje, mijn lief*. O Ella!'

The passengers adjust their eye masks, light up a fresh cigarette. Ella sits on her hands and chews her lips hard. She fixes her eyes on the slow blue spiral rising from the passenger smoking in the row ahead. She wishes she might watch the lightning but the mother long ago pushed the window shutter down. For all that she believes her mother will now really die, just as she has long threatened to do, she doesn't want to reach down to her. If she did reach down she might want to shut her up. She might want to clap her hand over her mouth and make her stop her dreadful yelling. More than anything she wants to stop that noise.

One night, about an hour out of Accra, flying south over the Gulf of Guinea, there is a violent electrical storm, even by West African standards. The white-lit turbulence shocks the mother from her tranquillized slumber. She shudders upright, then falls suddenly to the ground. As she drops she strikes with her strong Dutch forearm the head of a passenger in the aisle seat opposite. She doesn't mean to; her arm, her whole body, drops down out of control. But the passenger, jolted, cries out in shock. Within seconds a bump appears on her forehead. Her husband beside her leans on the call button.

Ella watches from her seat as two air stewards hold her mother down in the aisle, scold her like a child. Do they hold something against her arm, a syringe of fluid, a compress? She thinks they do. 'When a passenger becomes a danger to others – ' one of the air stewards says, glances over at Ella. 'Sorry,' he says uncomfortably, 'She must be very frightened.'

Ella looks away, raises the shutter. Out in the night the clouds are on fire.

That moment she looks away, something in her heart hardens and turns sharp. The woman lying semi-conscious on the floor, her open mouth gasping, doesn't belong to her, she decides. They don't belong together. She wants to block her nose at the meaty smell of fear rising from her mother's body.

As if they have read her thoughts, the air stewards draw the mother's arms over their necks and half-drag, half-walk her to a seat behind a curtain at the front of the plane.

Ella pulls out the drawing pad the air stewardess serving dinner gave her. The pad comes along with a pencil cunningly tucked into the spiral binding of the pad. On the first page she writes in English:

Either we fall out of the sky or we don't. Either way, no amount of crying will help.

She reads what she has written. She likes it: it makes sense and sounds wise. She has a picture of their plane up high in the sky, above the clouds, as if balanced on a pinnacle of thin air.

Something about this thought gives her perspective.

She writes a few more things.

Up in the air, she writes. *Middle of a storm. Inside a bubble.*

The effect is wonderful. Anything she writes down, whatever it is, one word after another, turns things quiet.

What was noisy evens out, looks suddenly level and smooth. *Mam lying there like a beast,* she writes, *a dumb beast.* The disgust she felt at seeing her restrained ebbs away. Writing, she is both separate from herself and steady within herself. There, over on that side of herself, the part of her that is being written about still feels what, a moment ago, the rest of her was feeling. Here, over on this side, she is writing what happens. Here everything is at a distance but everything at the same time is under her control.

She so much likes the effect of the writing that for the next couple of hours she goes on putting down words with her pencil, words like *zoo* and *beast* and *hate*. Until long after the overhead lights have been switched off, she makes up sentences. *I hate to see her lying there like a zoo beast.* She wonders about the word *hate*. It comes without thinking about it. Maybe she doesn't mean it. But as she puts down the letters *h-a-t-e* it gives relief.

By the end of the Gulf of Guinea storm something new has started. Landing in Luanda the next day Ella stores the colouring book inside her travel belt. The mother is back in her seat, her face pale, her purple eyelids pressed closed.

Later, at home, Ella uses her pocket money to buy a fresh writing pad at *Pentops*, Braemar's stationery shop. She tears her notes from the colouring book and staples the pages into the front of the writing pad so that the pad becomes her notebook. Writing down words in her notebook she knows she will each time feel airborne once again, flying above the world in a jet in the clouds, balanced on a pinnacle of air, as if nothing down there on the ground could hurt her.

Things are not very happy right now, she will write, many times she will write this, always in English. *In fact things are quite bad. Anything I do, I don't do it right.*

103

The Shouting in the Dark

There is a lot of noise. There is shouting from Dad, there is crying from Mam. Since we got back from Holland she cries more than ever before. How can I tell other people these things, Linda or my other school friends? I wouldn't know how to begin. I don't invite my friends home. They wouldn't be welcome. So I write things down. I write also to remember. If I was reading all this about another person, you see, I wouldn't believe it was true.

Some days, as she goes about, walks to and from school, lines and word-pictures come to her so fast she must tear strips from whatever paper she can find around to write them down – tissues, bits of newspaper, even the father's old ledgers. She doesn't have time to run for the notebook in her bedroom. *Soft shedding shales of shadow*, she writes. *Leaves spattered against the sky.* And lines done by others, for their rhythm. *She left the web, she left the loom, She made three paces through the room. I wandered lonely as a cloud. Sorry I could not travel both, and be one traveller.*

In a poetry book at school she discovers a poem called 'Romance' by W J Turner that sings out to her from its first line. She learns the poem off by heart and writes the best verses into her notebook.

When I was but thirteen or so
I went into a golden land;
Chimborazo, Cotopaxi
Took me by the hand.

My father died, my mother too,
They passed like fleeting dreams.
I stood where Popocatapetl
In the sunlight gleams.

The houses, people, traffic seemed
Thin fading dreams by day,
Chimborazo, Cotopaxi,
They had stolen my soul away.

She doesn't know where the names *Cotopaxi* or *Popocatapetl* come from but she likes how the words sound strong and difficult. Whenever she recites the poem to herself, walking to and from school, she changes other things to suit her, like *thirteen* to whatever age is right at the time. She can see herself as the orphan-traveller in the golden land, the one without father and mother, the waif-child whom Chimborazo will, no two ways about it, steal very soon away. Chimborazo, she imagines, has Durban Charley's handsome face and long head, as she saw it from under the house, etched against the light. Cotopaxi looks like the ventriloquist in Oegstgeest, but stands as tall as Charley and is equally as dark.

At school in Braemar, the annual poetry recitation exercise that draws groans from the rest of the class becomes Ella's favourite day of the year. In her recitation she gets to say out loud some of the best, most rhythmic lines from her notebook. Even some of the groaning classmates get her excitement and cheer her on.

'Go on, Ella,' they call as she plants her legs at the front of the classroom and waits for silence. 'Do your thing. Eat the *Oxford English*.'

Their encouragement makes her happy, though she'd never admit it. She knows English well now but still can't get enough of shifting the curious shapes of English words around her mouth. She cherishes old-fashioned *hath* and *doth* in the King James Bible they read in assembly for their softness. She feels loyal to *brick* and *block* because they have hard edges like the playthings they point to. *Brick* and *block* click together. *Box*, too. *Quench*, *Wiltshire*, *tooth* are wedge-shaped; green on top, blue underneath. Dutch words by contrast are shapeless and spongy, beige all over. No one would dream of cherishing them.

Every year her recitation from Hopkins, Hardy, Frost, ensures her nomination as Braemar School's representative to the annual provincial Eisteddfod down in Durban's City Hall. She stands in two categories, Poetic Recitation and Speaking One's Own Poetry. For the Own Poetry category each year she weaves her scattered lines of verse into two stanzas in her notebook, a collage that is always about nature but set in a world nothing like the warty lands around Braemar. *A country lane fringed with trees. A towering indigo mountain. An ocean wave churned to cream.*

It's good to go down to Durban in a teacher's car, to suck in the humid air and see the big white sky suspended like a lamp over the Indian Ocean. She gives her parents a vague excuse about litter picking at school, doing homework at Linda's house. What the father might say about her recitation hobby, no matter the prizes, she hasn't wanted to imagine. Total rubbish, he'd probably bellow, *je reinste flauwekul*, a waste of the teachers' time. What good can possibly come from that unruly mouth?

Each year for five years she brings home the gold certificate in both categories of the competition. The certificates she stuffs behind the books in her bookcase. The thrill is in the competition alone, the speaking and then the winning.

The sixth year that she participates, a Durban boy reciting Mark Antony's speech from *Julius Caesar* wins the gold certificate and she the silver, for Coleridge's 'Kubla Khan'. Her Eisteddfod career comes to an immediate end. That's it, she decides, it's over. Never again will she try so hard for such poor returns.

The night she fails to win the Eisteddfod she creeps as usual between her curtains, looks hard at her father talking to the invisible audience on the lawn. Does he have word shapes in his head like she does when she chants poetry? she wonders. Seeing how he loves the English language and reads his *Roget's Thesaurus* for pleasure? Peering, she tries to make believe she can see the sounds that come from his lips, the dark brown Dutch curses, the silvery chains of English sound, the jagged blood-red and purple bursts of his late-night sobbing.

On Sunday mornings the family takes the mother's new dog Bogey for walks in the pine plantations that cover the hills above Braemar. The pine plantations give the mother the same sublime sensations as the Veluwe in the Netherlands, her favourite woods. 'Can't you feel it?' she carols to the husband and daughter already trailing in her path, 'These resiny smells, how they brace the lungs?'

The mother acquired Bogey from a dog rescue with the aim of bringing him up as a walking companion, to replace dead Rex. An eager-to-please spaniel mix, Bogey will help her feel safe in the woods. So far however, though she's had him several months, she hasn't yet gone out on her own walking the dog. The pine plantations may be resiny and bracing, but they aren't exactly the Veluwe. The Veluwe doesn't have, for example, that ravine that cuts through the middle of the forest here, an alarming cleft plunging for several zigzag miles through the uplands, or the dense indigenous forest that flourishes in the shadowy depths of the ravine. At Ada's she has heard there are Bushman paintings in the depths, writhing ochre and white shapes that lour from the overhanging rocks.

On the family's walks Bogey from time to time gets wind of stirrings in the ravine's depths and sets off over its rocky edge, kicking up dust. But his barking gives the wildlife, if any, early warning. All too soon he returns empty-jawed, scrambling crestfallen through the undergrowth. The mother dusts him down, tells him to behave, stick to the pine-covered uplands. Not for them the *oerwoud*, that ancient forest down there, all its horrid, coagulated primitive life.

One Sunday, on the final lap of their walk, within sight of their parked car, Bogey disappears. They hear him sliding and crashing in the undergrowth at the lip of the ravine, where there's a dry waterfall bed. Then there's stillness, just the sound of the pines. Even the cicadas suddenly fall silent.

For a while the three stand listening to the silence, the pines. Then the wind changes direction and they hear Bogey's thin whimper. Ella picks her way over the rocks to the lip of the dry waterfall bed. The mother follows, the father a step behind her.

Ella cranes into the ravine and sees it, perched on a needle of rock rising out of the depths, a great bird of prey with a yellow eye and a grey hooked beak. On a sandy ledge some metres below the bird crouches Bogey. The two look frozen into place, the whimpering dog and the bird of prey on its ledge.

Ella recognizes the bird. It is a lammergeyer, one of the endangered predators, big as a young baboon. They can lift whole lambs high into the air, she knows, and crash them onto the rocks below, then swoop in to feed on the animal's remains. The bird lives only here and far away in the Himalayas.

Bogey's whimpers die away. As he falls silent, the mother starts sobbing. 'Bogey, O Bogey,' she cries, 'O, *mijn lieve hondje. O moeder*, Ella, *moeder!*'

Ella's nails cut into her palms. From the mother's aeroplane frenzies she knows how fast the volume of her anguish can build.

The bird leaves its perch. Ella, the mother and the father fall as one to their stomachs. With a metallic whisper of its wings, the bird makes a lazy swoop in the air, over the ravine and back again, to a rock just above where the dog cowers. The mother yells. The father rams his balled hand into her mouth.

For a moment the air is still. A second swoop, lower this time, just overhead, and once again out over the valley. Ella looks across and sees stamped on the blue sky above the ravine's lip the bird's feathered gauntlets, the talons beneath.

The mother grunts, gagged by the father's hand. '*Hou op Irene, hou op*,' he mutters in Dutch, 'Stop your noise.' A dark stain spreads across the seat of her skirt.

Ella wriggles away from them, as far away from the mother's wetness as she can go. From her new position there's a clearer view down into the ravine. The lammergeyer has returned to its rocky needle; Bogey is still squashed flat on the ledge.

'O, O,' cries the mother in her throat, more softly. '*O Ella, moeder*.'

The lammergeyer waits, the sunlight glitters on its eye.

'Never really bargained for the life of an African bush-whacker,' the father whispers, crawling up beside Ella.

She doesn't reply, doesn't want to. She keeps her eyes fixed on the bird.

Moments later there's a skittering sound on the rocks, Bogey's paws scrambling for traction. Powered by some overwhelming force, the dog comes driving up the ravine slope. His dash brings him along the dry waterfall path, up over its lip, his tongue lolling, foam on his muzzle. He falls upon the mother, covering her face with the pink handker-chief of his tongue.

The mother is the first to scramble upright. Crouching

low to the ground, her hand on her dog's collar, she sprints to the car, jams the key into the lock, throws the door open, bundles them both inside. Next the father rises creakily. Keeping his back bent, he takes a moment to rub at his dusty knees. He plucks at Ella's sleeve, 'Come,' but she pulls back, shakes her head. Then he runs.

Ella stays on her stomach. The lammergeyer is still perched on its needle of rock. In the dust in front of her nose she sees one of the strange overgrown insects that infest the surrounding hunchbacked hills. *Goggas*, the Bushmen called them. This one's something between a beetle and a locust. She watches as it lurches over the small stones in its path. From where she's lying, it is as if it's crawling towards the horizon of the ravine edge, straight to where the hooked beak of the lammergeyer is etched against the air.

Ella feels suddenly dizzy, disoriented, as if her parents and the dog in the car had been transported a distance away, to the other side of the ravine. They're smalled by the distance and she's here on her own, flush with the dust, lined up in a straight row with the lammergeyer and the *gogga*, both African natives, hardy and unkillable, just the same as she.

The lammergeyer's talons grip the rock. Ella slowly stands up. The bird disappears. It's not in the ravine below. It's nowhere in the sky. Then her parents begin to yell from behind the closed windows of the car.

'What kind of *idioot* are you?' the father roars as she opens the car door. He grabs her arm and pulls her into the back seat. 'Why didn't you come? We called you. You weren't watching out. That beast could've taken you off, in place of Bogey. It swooped that low over you before it went off.'

'Drive, Har, just drive,' says the mother, Bogey curled in her lap. 'Let's never come to this horrible place again.'

110

But the father is set in his rage. '*Idioot*, stupid *idioot*,' he continues as he steps on the accelerator, jumps the car into reverse.

Ella presses her hands over her ears. She doesn't want to hear him. She doesn't want to smell the strong smell of her mother's pee. She thinks of mouthing *We are too loud, so very, very loud.* She wishes she could place her hand across the father's mouth and choke up his voice, the same as he did back then to her mother. Where to escape from here? she asks herself. There must be an escape better than lying flush in the dust with a *gogga*, or being swept away by a lammergeyer? For years there has been the Netherlands, with its zoo and puppet theatre. But after the recent flight through the storm, its dove-grey refuge feels suddenly out of reach. As for the rhymes in her notebook, right now, her father's shouts clanging in her ears, she can't even bring them to mind.

Homeland

Television is a new arrival in Ella's house as well as every-where else in the country. Till now, to get the news, the father has switched on the dark-veneer Philips radiogram in the dining room six times a day like clockwork, beginning at zero six hundred hours, ending at twenty-two hundred. The family's meals fit around these news bulletins. But now they have television. Its coming coincides almost exactly with Ella's thirteenth birthday. Our local buffoons, the father says, decided in the end it was better to control white people's view of the wider world than to block it completely. *Local buffoons* is his pet name for the Afrikaner nationalist government when he thinks they're getting their job more or less right. He's concerned they get their job more or less right. Didn't he, after all, choose to live in this happiest police state in the world, to quote Prime Minister B J Vorster, this orderly white republic that, after the war, South Africans both English and Afrikaans promised to forge together?

So far, South African televisions come in black and white only. European South Africans, the joke at Ella's school is, can only see in black and white. The joke's lost on the mother. She's against television whatever the colour. TV, she tells Ella, fries the young imagination. She doesn't like Ella watching it, not at any time, no, certainly not in the daytime, she can protest all she wants, not even if it's Wimbledon and that Arthur Ashe she so likes once again

112

going for the title ... The mother switches off the set. Almost immediately the father switches it on again.

The father loves television. If electricity were free he'd have it on all the time, especially during the news programmes. As soon as he finishes his dinner, he walks over to the set and stands close by watching, haranguing the screen. Can't deny it, he tells the mother and Ella, there's something about the sick saga of African politics that drags me in.

'Yes, it's a God-forsaken rubbish pile, this bloody continent,' he turns and spits at the news-reader, 'Why d'ye look that dismayed? If Europe's a heap of ruins, Africa's a dump, we all knew that. The Cold War has shifted here only because Europe is laid low, the West's appetite for war is exhausted, its dream of a free world trashed. Here in Africa, all around, are the creeping worms upon which the world's remaining predators can feed. South Africa, in my view' – he plants a fist on the set and it hisses sympathetically – 'South Africa is a success story *in spite of* Africa. South Africa is like an isthmus attached to the mainland by a thin thread.'

When yet another African coup or arms heist or civil outburst is announced, he shouts his excitement out loud: 'What a pity we can't hire a team of strong Zulus to dig a moat all the way around the country! Cut ourselves off from that useless hinterland to the north.'

On winter nights, when it's too chilly to sit out on the verandah, the father watches the history programmes that come after the late news, flickering newsreel footage of the World Wars, of Vietnam bombers landing and taking off, wrecked cities, clouds of billowing smoke, cannons juddering. For no reason Ella can see, he invites her to join him. They also follow a more contemporary documentary series. It runs for several weeks. In it, the Union Jack

113

repeatedly makes a limp descent down a grainy flagpole. The flag runs down, the flag runs down, though each time the backdrop, the sports field or stadium, is different.

'Mark my words,' the father says, watching from his armchair, fists planted on his stubby knees. 'When our B J Vorster and his police boys outdo the blacks at African buffoonery, they keep hold of their cunning. They have the cunning of the lion. They'll never let the flag run down the mast here. What I say to them is, don't forget who the Puppet-master is, who really wants to be Big Boss.'

They haven't had the television long before he shifts the set into the dining area, pushed up against the Philips radiogram, to be able to watch it at mealtimes. When the news is lively, with several hotspots around the continent flaring up, he has both the television and the radio on at the same time, the volume high.

In response to the mother's protests, he holds up his hand. 'So what about the cost? It's nothing compared to your pathetic European pilgrimages. This is something I want and for a change I'm going to get it.'

He turns to the screen, begins to bellow, 'Don't you just adore it, this puppet show of African politics black *and* white? Yes, I really do mean white politics too, those white Afrikaner politicians imitating the crazy moves of the black ghouls and then bettering them, excelling at the dictatorship of one tribe by another. Especially now, with these jumped-up countries trying to survive their so-called independence – and by that,' he smashes his fist into his thigh, his face bright red, his nose purple, 'I include that pig-headed Ian Smith in Rhodesia. Our men in power know what to do, Irene. They know law and order, the iron fist in the gauntlet of steel.'

Ella trains herself to lay the table blind, watching the news. She and her father look out for similar things on television, she can tell, though they have different words for what they see. To her, far from being an old rubbish heap, Africa is teeming with goings-on, as she knows for a fact from her cross-continent trips. If there were any doubt in the matter, see this report on Soviet insurgents and Cuban saboteurs popping up somewhere soon in South African cities, infiltrating markets and department stores in their battle fatigues, places where people would least expect them. 'South Africa is a Cold War front line,' the newsreader is saying. The Prime Minister B J Vorster sagely nods in agreement: 'This country is leading the free world in the struggle against the Soviet threat. We have the Terrorism Act my government implemented that safeguards our law and order – puts saboteurs in prison for sixty days, renewable.'

At the end of the six o'clock news every evening the newsreader works through a roll-call of the soldiers who have recently fallen in the wars South Africa is heroically helping to fight on distant borders: the Caprivi strip, the Rhodesian low lands, wherever the Cold War is riding piggyback on local wars.

'Michael Darling, 19 years of age; Graham Jones, 19 years of age; Simon Marais, 20; Angus Rathbone, 18; Nigel Raubenheimer . . .' The roll-call is accompanied by a picture of a grainy grey sunset and the flag fluttering in silhouette.

As the reading of the list begins, the father goes to stand in his place in front of the television. He pushes his glasses up his nose as if to see more clearly. The mother leaves the room, murmurs about the washing-up.

What if, Ella wonders to herself, stacking plates, those communist saboteurs might ever pop up closer to home? She tidies onto the Philips radiogram the crystal butter dish, silver knife rests, glass coasters, all the European

115

accoutrements of her mother's table. As Africa is on the front line of the Cold War, she thinks, it's not so crazy to imagine the front line erupting soon right here in their town. What if a soldier, a live soldier, a dark-haired Cuban maybe, were to parachute into Braemar one afternoon? She sees him landing in a neat crouch position on that bank of dirt ground at the end of their garden, then standing up, stretching, checking his kit . . .

Ella discovers a new sensation pricking her in the ribs, a proper grown-up sensation, is how it feels, to suit a nearly grown-up girl, tall as she'll ever be (or so she hopes). She likes the thought of the wide world bursting into Braemar, that's the nub of it. She begins to read the father's news-papers, at first surreptitiously. She fishes them out of his waste-paper bin when he's in the toilet. He spends a great deal of time reading the newspaper in the toilet. But then to her surprise he takes to leaving the paper in obvious places, spread on his armchair or the Philips radiogram, open to articles with an African focus, about the threat of the Russian Bear creeping south or Mobuto Sese Seko's 'fabulous and criminal' wealth or – this one he pores over before leaving it for her – 'Prime Minister Baltazar John Vorster's clear-sighted *realpolitik*. Worthy son of our late state architect Verwoerd.'

Lying on the moss-green carpet under the dining table, Ella reads that B J Vorster is meeting his Zambian counter-part Kenneth Kaunda to talk about the problem of Rhodesia, on the railway bridge at Victoria Falls. She's aware of the father standing in the doorway but doesn't shove the paper under her belly as she would if it was the mother, seeing as he's left it out for her at exactly this article.

'The two leaders are playing for time.' She pats the photograph of the train suspended in its no-man's-land in the sky. Just reading the words aloud gives her a sense of importance. 'Why part with power when you've fought hard for it?' she asks.

Privately she thinks that Mr B J Vorster is the ugliest man she's ever seen. Even her father's not so ugly. His nose isn't quite so shapeless, his hair not as thin.

Her father harrumphs, half to himself. Was that a sound of approval? It may have been. He pulls out a chair and sits down, scrapes at his stubble.

'Politics is not just about getting power,' he talks to the wall. 'It's about holding onto power once you have it, it's about the wheeling, dealing and scheming. It's about looking like a buffoon, if you have to, or a tightrope artiste, like our B J here, or even Uncle Kenneth, but then reasoning like a Russian as you do so. Reasoning like Kasparov.'

Ella thinks of the Cuban spy who will drop into their garden by parachute. She imagines him crawling out of the hiding place he will make for himself in the hydrangea bushes at the gate, stooping his way out of his den just as she's setting out for school. Brushing off the dead leaves clinging to his uniform, he will step into her path to ask for her help, his musky Spanish mixed with halting English. She feels her legs jolting to a halt. The sunshine glances off his copper-smooth forehead.

Would she be able at that moment to rise to her responsibilities? she asks herself. Stand tall and call calmly over her shoulder, 'Dad, we have an intruder. Please phone the police.'

She glances up at the father but his speech is at an end. His eyes rest on the photograph of the train under her elbows.

Or would something different happen? she wonders. Isn't that the effect dangerous spies and saboteurs have? When she sees the Cuban's gallant bow, his gentlemanly stance there by the hydrangea bushes, legs at ease but arms stiffly by his sides, won't her voice falter and her breath drain away, her hands descend helplessly to her satchel? She imagines giving him her lunch box, her juice bottle, everything useful she has – supplies to get him onto the highway to Johannesburg. Johannesburg, everyone knows, teems with communist insurgents.

In the black and white photo-comics Ella and her classmates swap at school, hunky Cubans and Russians are forever teaming up with low-browed black terrorists in battle fatigues, to the point where Ella wonders what they see in the Africans, square-shouldered though they may be. The communist leader Mr Brezhnev – the mop-haired history teacher Mr Donovan McDonald tells the class – has built his country's strategic nuclear arsenal so that it exceeds that of the United States in its number of weapons. The Cold War foe has power in spades.

In Ella's picture of the gallant Cuban standing beside the hydrangea bushes, his sign language is clear though his English is halting. She gets his meaning perfectly. Assist me or I die, he'll say, and she will feel her insides cave in. She won't be able to hold back. She'll give him what he needs. Kindness will have nothing to do with it.

In her picture she gives in to the Cuban totally because the dark power inside him reaches out its octopus tentacles to grasp the badness inside her. Like copies like, Mr McDonald says: it's a rule of nature, in politics as in life.

Ella doesn't betray her communist susceptibilities to a soul. In fact she enjoys hugging them close. But then she stumbles on a surprise fellow-thinker. One hot summer's day the father announces from the dining-room door that he's been pondering things, this damned mess in the world, these *kut* politicians everywhere. Ella under the table looks up from her photo-comic. He has come to an important conclusion he'd like his daughter to hear, he says, which is this – his regard for South Africa notwithstanding, he nowadays has time for the Soviet Union. He wipes the sweat off his shapeless purple nose so like B J Vorster's. Yes, though he resents how the Russian Bear is the Puppet-master in Africa, he admires the cunning way they go about pulling the strings. In truth, it's his regard for South Africa that leads him to embrace the Soviets.

Ella watches the father's polished shoes march across the floor and come to stand beside her head, planted on either side of her photo-comic.

'Things have come to a limit, *meid*, a bloody limit,' he says, a high-pitched note whistling through his loose front teeth. Usually, when he finds her photo-comics lying around the house, he puts them in the bin. Today he takes no notice of what's at his feet.

'That slime Henry Kissinger, that insect-faced David Owen,' he goes on. 'They're coming over here yet again to slap B J Vorster's wrists, bloody boss us about, the cunts, tell us how to run the place. I just read it in the paper. I say, let's show them what we're made of. Let's be the strongmen of the world for a change, the real strongmen who bring about real solid effects. Let's stand up to them. I'd as soon as support Brezhnev's Russia as the rotten West, as long as it enforced law and order, which it does. What do you say we write direct to the Russians, appeal to Mr Brezhnev the Soviet leader, ask him to give us a hand?'

Write to Mr Brezhnev . . . ? Ella has to twist her neck round to look up at him. Can he be serious? Has he peeped into her thoughts and found the picture of the Cuban insurgent lurking there?

For the first time in years he holds her gaze.

'Yes, *meid*, you've got it – you and me, we write to Brezhnev. He's bound to have a better idea of how to proceed than these interfering do-gooders. Like our Nat buffoons here, he talks tough but also acts tough. He knows how to keep hold of power by whatever clever means short of cruelty and perhaps not even then.'

Early that Saturday Ella and the father sit down to write their letter to Mr Brezhnev at the glass-topped table on the verandah, a Croxley Cambric writing pad open between them, a fresh piece of sticky carbon paper slid under the top page. Their unfamiliar solidarity makes her skin prickle. Out of the corner of her eye she sees him scrub at the sweat on his forehead with his hanky. She averts her eyes. She doesn't like to think about the sweat droplets running like abacus beads along his Brylcreme-polished hair.

The mother brings the father his morning coffee, iced for the heat, then retreats indoors. 'Told you to switch that television . . .' she murmurs in Dutch, as if to herself, lips pursed in disapproval.

'Come,' the father draws his Bic from his pocket and hands it to Ella. 'You're quick with your pen, good at English. Write now, *Dear Mr Brezhnev*, and make sure the carbon paper's taking. We must do a copy for Mr Vorster. We've nothing to hide. We're proposing only what's good for the nation and will make us stronger. Everywhere but in South Africa and the Soviet Union and its allies, the world's going down the pan. South Africa must learn from the strong-arm example of the Soviets, like the Cubans do, rather than yammering about insurgents on the border.'

Ella takes the pen. Most days the look of the father's Bic grates on her. Its chunky shape reminds her, she doesn't know why, of his gnarled middle fingers. Today she just takes the pen, there are no grating feelings. She watches as he checks the carbon, squares it up.

'Come,' he says again, pushes the pad closer. 'The point we must make is that the Soviets' communism isn't an obstacle for us. You watch, the moment communism becomes unviable for the Soviets and drains the state coffers, they'll drop it. Politics works like this. It means making up a more difficult crossword when the one you're doing is no longer challenging your brain.'

Beside the writing pad he spreads open a recent copy of the *Elsevier* with the closed trapdoor face of Mr Brezhnev on the cover. Though the *Elsevier* subscription was a gift from his mother-in-law in lily-livered Holland, the father looks forward every month to its arrival. Unlike Dutch politicians, he says, the *Elsevier* doesn't mince its words.

'He looks like Mr Vorster, Dad, don't you think, though his nose isn't so puffy?'

'Forget his looks,' says the father, 'Looks is for girls. Think of joint strategy. Think of what the Leader of All the Soviets wants that we also want. Here in the *Elsevier* is an article, just here, look. It says that the Soviet Union has built new counter-insurgency weaponry, for street fighting and the like, hardware that many countries quelling terrorism would find useful. I suggest we propose a secret arms deal to Mr Brezhnev, where we give some of our heaps of gold in exchange for his smart new armaments. We say that we hope such a deal will provide building blocks for deals in the future.'

Ella tries to pull the magazine towards her but at the same instant the father closes it, presses the flat of his hand on Mr Brezhnev's face.

'Write now, write,' he says frowning. 'I've told you what the main article said. Let's not circle around the thing. Say now to Mr Brezhnev: Mr Brezhnev, though we are patriotic South Africans we have long admired the strength of the Soviet Union. The West is lost. In the War – parenthesis, one of us is a veteran – in the War we fought for the values of the West, but the West lost its values and its strength in the very act of trying to protect them.'

121

'Dad, not that.' Hasn't she heard words to this effect night after night on the verandah? She places the Bic's tip lightly on the paper. Her body feels clammy. 'Not so much about the West. Let's think of the Soviets.'

Dear Mr Brezhnev, she writes, *We approach you as two concerned and patriotic citizens of South Africa with a proposal of mutual benefit to our respective countries. We trust that, as the Leader of All the Soviets, there will be much of interest for you in our suggestion.*

Across the morning the father builds the case for his barter plan. He reads out loud the facts and figures he has scratched onto torn-off strips of blotting paper. His bloodless lips work with excitement. From behind his desk he brings a pile of *Elsevier* back-copies, the important pages folded down, lays them on the table in a fan, taps cigarette ash all over them. For each paragraph he speaks, Ella tries to write down a sentence or two.

He says, 'Did I hear you say not to talk so much about the West, Ella? Never deny the West. You are of the West though African-born, proudly African-born. You are if anything hyper-western.' He lights a fresh Rothman's Plain from the one still alight in the ashtray. 'This is how it is, *meid*. During the War the ideals that moved the West were betrayed by the West. We fought hard but got back little. The toll was great. In the world today, the inheritors of the Allied cause have squandered what we once fought for. The Allies fought for solid freedoms, wrongly called negative freedoms – freedom from oppression, freedom from harm, freedoms worth fighting for. But lately these freedoms have mutated. The West's ideals moved elsewhere, here to South Africa. What people in the West now want is the freedom to have everything they want, to say only me-me-me. People have forgotten you need a system: you need law and order to be properly free.'

122

Ella writes: *We admire how your country is run, Mr Brezhnev, especially the firm system of law and order you have. In South Africa, by contrast with other areas of the world, we have a good system of law and order also.*

She reads the lines so far back to him. He pulls his lips tight between his teeth. The moment she says *good system*, he looks suddenly happy. He stands and begins to pace, waving his Rothman's Plain in the air. Falling ash settles on his comb-over.

'There's no freedom without restraint.' His voice rises to a yelp though it's still morning and as far as Ella can tell he's not yet touched the sherry bottle stored with the *Elseviers* behind his desk. 'There are no rights without binding duties. Rights should be earned. Rights and freedom are meaningless where there's no law and order. In this great cesspit of the permissive society, what then do we do? Are we not permitted to seek alternative possibilities? Of course we are!'

Ella has lost the thread of what he's saying but still she matches the twinkle in his eye with her own.

'Consider,' he continues, 'Are we not disgusted at how the military in the Netherlands is permitted to go about with long hair?' Ella nods, twinkles. 'Well, in our disgust, let's turn to countries where the military keep haircuts decently short, like South Africa, of course, but the Soviet Union also, Cuba too. Are we not appalled at how an entire generation of the young is cooking its brains with acid and other drugs?'

Yes, we are, Ella nods.

'Well then,' says the father, 'Let's turn to the Soviet Union again, where drugs are banned and the secret police keep a close eye. I may be an atheist, but the Calvinist views I grew up with have their place. Human beings begin *slecht* and only through hard work become better, like the Calvinists say. And then hardly better. Now, imagine giving a creature as bad and stupid as a human being rights or drugs, rights if they so much as squeak, drugs on demand if they only ask. Give me, give me, they cry. Drugs and more drugs. Well, rubbish, *rotzooi*. The Soviets know that it's wrong. You may as well give people a burning rod with which to put out their eyes.' He spits a gob of grey mucus onto the lawn.

The mother sticks her head around the verandah's French window, produces her camouflage breathing. 'So loud, Har,' she whispers, 'Sounds like you're demanding drugs yourself.'

Ella opens to a fresh sheet of Croxley Cambric. The first one is already full. She adjusts the carbon paper, moves the matt-silver Bic across the page:

On the basis of all that our nations share, let us also, we propose, work together on military preparedness. We will have much to gain, on both sides, from the exchange.

'But the Soviets laugh at us, *meid*. We must capture this, too.' The father flings out his arms, his cigarette butt, as if embracing what she has written. 'Us squealing, holier-than-thou westerners, the Soviets laugh at us and then they go on working. They hoot at how we squander everything we've achieved. They gloat at our political weakness, our moral weakness. We condone an Idi Amin. We permit, no, we welcome in the international halls of power, Houphouet-Boigny, Boukassa, Mobuto Sese Seko. We couldn't possibly turn these clowns away for we mustn't be seen to judge others. We must at all costs grant crazy men their freedoms. If the Soviet Union thinks at all about its strength relative to the West, it need hardly worry, for the weakness here is now endemic. Yet in respect of South Africa alone does the West wag its finger. So why should South Africa listen, when it's in point of fact the world's custodian of law and order, when it has the stability and cleverness to lock these goods into place?'

Across the weekend the heat persists, the father builds his case, Ella nods, twinkles, writes, chews on the ice in his iced coffee, reads out loud. The letter grows by slow inches. First it is three pages long, then six. She scratches out the sentences he dislikes and fits words between the lines. She squeezes in a good opening sentence about surviving in mad Africa. People survive in mad Africa, she writes, by outdoing it at its madness. Isn't this what the father's been saying from the start?

On Sunday morning the father finds an *Elsevier* feature article comparing staple diets across the world. The child with the most food in its belly when it sets out to school lives in Moscow, he cries, cawing like a hadeda, whereas in Holland and similar countries they have cardboard food without substance, *rotzooi*, rubbish American fluff.

'But of course they cannot be denied their rubbish,' he shouts, 'They must be free to choose to eat badly, though the national fibre's degenerating by the day.'

On Sunday evening Ella reads the full draft of the letter to the father. She is in the second rattan chair. He rocks the balls of his feet across the verandah edge.

Mr Brezhnev, there are, in short, multiple ways in which the Soviet Union and South Africa can support one another, she ends. *There is more that unites our two nations than divides us. Quickly the benefits will become manifest, for our economies and the moral fibre of our citizens.*

'That's good, very good, yes, yes,' the father rubs his hands together. 'Our gold and uranium will surely convince them to sit up and take notice. Prime Minister B J will be game, that canny old bird. He knows what our security requires.'

She types a fair copy of the letter on the mother's tall old

Blikman and Sartorius typewriter. She's never typed before but, by the end of the first couple of pages, her two index fingers begin to go like hammers. The pages are squared, folded, and slid into a crisp airmail envelope addressed to the Kremlin in the father's neat bookkeeping hand. He includes the envelope in a letter to his brother Jan in Holland. South Africa and the Soviet Union unfortunately do not have a postal agreement. The lack of the postal agreement, he writes to his brother in a covering note, is one of the obstacles to a relationship between the two countries that the letter to Mr Brezhnev is bound eventually to fix.

It takes three whole 37c airmail stamps to send the letter but the father doesn't complain about the cost.

On Tuesday morning Ella drops the overstuffed envelope into the postbox on the corner of Ridge Road on her way into school. She spends that evening before dinner sitting on her bed. For the first time in days her hands lie idle in her lap. Her mother is cooking their Tuesday meal, fried chicken livers and boiled potatoes. The father is reading his Churchill on the verandah. He hasn't yet checked whether the letter's been dispatched. She wonders when they'll write the companion letter to Mr Vorster. Might it be this weekend? He's said nothing about it. The carbon copies they have taken lie under the glass paperweight in the shape of a dockyard crane on his desk, his retirement gift from Lukes Lines.

She goes to set the table as usual. She senses the father suddenly turn in his chair to face her. Behind his head is the shimmering grey halo of the television screen. The map of southern Africa is sprinkled with flashpoints where over the weekend skirmishes with terrorists took place.

'Look at her,' he says in his loud voice, 'Gawping like some native. Or no, not like a native, a native's too good. Like a woman, a witless woman. Drinking it all in as if there wasn't a brain inside her miscast skull.'

126

What was that? Ella feels her mouth gaping open. She snaps it shut. Run, hide like the mother – almost she wants to. She grips the cutlery tightly in her hands.

'Go on,' he says, 'Finish the table. You think because you helped write a numbskull letter to the Soviets by way of passing the time you suddenly have special privileges to stand there dawdling and goggling? You know how it drives me mad when you goggle. You've no idea how stupid you look.'

With her sleeve Ella wipes his spit off her cheek, the smell of Old Brown Sherry.

'Look at her,' he cries again, suddenly furious, 'The worthless, disrespectful *loeder*. Don't I always say it? Never trust a person who goggles like that. How it contrasts with others we could mention, direct, loving people who looked one in the eye. Still do today. Wherever in the room you stand.'

For nearly an hour that night the father swears and shouts, curses all the women he has ever known – the cold-hearted sluts and *loeders* the gods have inflicted on him, who have let him down all his life; the few warm-hearted women he has met who however abandoned him. Then he moves on to the weak-and-weasel West. 'Yes, don't think I've forgotten you, so-called western world leaders, giving way to each new bully boy on the block, like OPEC now. OPEC has you by the balls . . .'

Ella concentrates on keeping her shoulders square. At some point the mother wordlessly serves the fried livers but takes her own plate back to the kitchen to eat. Faintly Ella hears her sobbing.

'*Godverdomme*,' the father finally says, his voice softer, 'What a cabal of rotters.' He checks his watch, walks over to the television and turns up the volume.

Ella sits on at table, the small grey mound of liver

congealing on her plate. Her hands are tingling. She tries to hold them quiet between her legs. She recites *Chimborazo, Cotopaxi* under her breath but the images she has conjured to match the names fail to appear.

The thought comes from nowhere: she's not the only one. She's not the first to be confronted by him in a rage like this, on her own. She's not the first in her father's life to quail inside like she's doing right now, even though she's making sure to hold each one of her limbs and even her tingling fingers still. The other wife he sometimes mentions on the verandah, her aunt she thinks it must be, after what her mother said, or the woman he says abandoned him, she's not sure, the wife or wives before her aunt, back in Singapore, Edith, Nancy Leong – she, too, every one of them, must have sat like this, trying to keep her shoulders square even as the blowtorch of his anger burned white places in her heart.

The father doesn't refer to the letter to Mr Brezhnev again. A month or so later Uncle Jan in Holland sends a curt air letter saying he can't think what his brother was up to writing to the Kremlin. However, would he please not ever again involve him in such dangerous tomfoolery? Worried about throwing the airmail envelope in the bin, he's had to lock it away in his safe. A vigilant refuse man . . .

But Ella's thoughts don't let go of the letter. She thinks often of the neat look of the typed lines on the Croxley Cambric page. There was something about that weekend project – it wasn't mad, not between the two of them, her Dad and herself. Out on the verandah poring over the Croxley Cambric, it felt good to plan that conversation with Mr Brezhnev.

One day when the father is in the toilet reading, she takes the carbon copies meant for Prime Minister Vorster from his desk. She hides them between the *Anne of Green Gables*

128

books on her bookshelf. He won't spot the disappearance, she suspects, and, if he does, let him come and search, he'll never find them.

At bedtime sometimes she takes out the draft and reads it under the blankets, the good bits especially, the thing about more uniting the two nations than dividing them, the line about surviving in mad Africa by outdoing it at its madness. She remembers how the father nodded at her ideas as if she were a man, a proper grown-up. How his finger jabbed at the Croxley Cambric page to prompt her to type faster, both his words and hers.

One weekend they take a drive to visit Transkei, an independent new nation recently created within the borders of South Africa though no other nation in the world recognizes it. Transkei is the father's fantasy of a country separated from the mainland come true, except that Transkei is a black nation, a nation belonging to the Xhosa people who live there, or so, he says, the Nat goons like everyone to believe.

On television the father and Ella watch the South African flag, this one too, descend its mast and the brown-white-green Transkei flag creep into the sky, as if B J Vorster wanted to make sure that their one-time colonial masters, *die vervloekte Britten*, did not grab all the late imperial razzmatazz for themselves.

His eyes narrowed, the father says he'd like to see what's happening down there in their own local banana republic. They should take a trip. When do they ever take a family trip? For the Boers there must be something in this homeland farce, something clever and cunning, seeing as they're happy to court such negative omens and let their flag run down. Transkei is only three hours' drive away, perfect for a cheap weekend excursion, Saturday morning to Sunday evening. He turns to face Ella: 'Let's have a look at this proof positive of the white goons trying to out-manoeuvre the blacks at their own political game.'

Early that Saturday they set out, the mother stonily silent in the passenger seat. Ella brings the draft of Mr Brezhnev's letter in the pocket of her yellow-check summer dress. At the shiny new border post hut on the Mtamvuna River, the father and Ella present the family's identity papers to the unsmiling official at the boom. The mother refuses to get out of the car.

They stay overnight in a one-star hotel in Umtata, Transkei's capital, and spend most of their time walking the two main streets: one runs north-south, the other east-west. They look at the Cut-Price shops plastered with sales notices for Dri-lon clothes and neon-coloured fruit-squash in multipacks. Hundreds of other window-shoppers, independent Transkeians, are doing just the same as they, ambling the streets with the same kind of aimlessness, kicking at the bloated grass tussocks that fill the cracks in the brick pavement.

They have their lunch, chicken nuggets with ketchup, at a Wimpy bar on the main road out of town, leading back towards Braemar. It's Ella's first Wimpy meal ever and as delicious as she could have imagined. There are no other lunch venues in Umtata, only a second Wimpy, a takeaway on the road west towards Port Elizabeth, with grubbier windows.

'So here you have it, the full farce of homeland independence,' the father says in glee, biting into his nuggets with his strong yellow teeth. 'A vegetative reproduction of nations in our own backyard.'

'The sooner we get home, the better,' the mother says.

In the Wimpy toilet Ella slides the carbon-copy Brezhnev letter out of her dress pocket. Yes, the message is all over the letter, the thing about whites playing at political buffoonery with blacks to outfox them with cunning. Dad knew this all along. So why's he acting so happy, as if his suppositions have only now been confirmed?

For Ella, the highpoint of the weekend, late that Saturday afternoon, is a visit to Umtata's municipal swimming pool. Down a dirt track near the centre of town she and the father and the mother follow the cicada screams of children. They come upon a blue-painted body of water where tens upon tens of young Transkeians are splashing. Ella stands at the entrance gate between her parents and watches the shiny dark bodies bouncing in the sapphire water, the sunlight shimmering green on the agorobo trees. The children all stand concentrated in the shallow end, Ella realizes, because most of them can't swim. They haven't yet had time to learn. When they were part of South Africa, till just yesterday, this municipal swimming pool was out of bounds to blacks.

She doesn't have her swimsuit with her, but the day is warm and the streets dusty. She wants to be in the water. She weighs the short distance between the gate and the pool, sees she can make it in quickly, cover with the moving water her great towering whiteness, this vast length that has now more or less overcome her girth.

'Go,' says the father pushing her shoulder, 'Try it, it's OK, go naked, they are all of them as naked as the day they were born.'

'I button my lip, Har,' says the mother, 'But please give a thought to the piss in that pool, the germs, I don't even want to imagine. The *schuld*'ll be on you if . . .'

'*Hou op.* Let her find out what it's like, Africa proper, being a white in Africa.'

'If you once flew back with us to Nederland, across this terrible continent, you'd experience Africa proper— '

131

Ella walks away from them, across the wide concrete poolside, towards the blue water. The stark hot afternoon light seems to lighten her body, propel it forwards. She chooses a shady place beside the diving board, a good out-of-the-way spot, slides off her dress and places the folded carbon copies under it. In her striped pink knickers and bra she sits hunched on the pool edge for a moment, arms around her knees; then she drops down into the water.

She is the one and only white person swimming but everything's fine, as the father said it would be. No one takes the least notice of her. There are in fact very few people in the deep end and those who are there avoid her. The longer she bobs about treading water, the wider is the circle they leave. She backs into the shadow of the diving board. Here she shows up even less, the sun doesn't expose her luminous white skin. She kicks her legs, flings out her arms and sinks cross-legged to the bottom of the pool. If she could stay down here in this deep blue and silver world long enough, she wonders, for as long as her lungs allow, maybe by the time she comes to the surface her parents would have diffused away, vanished into the bright light. *When I was but fourteen or so ...*

Her swim over, she hangs onto the diving board and once again checks around her. The children are splashing in the shallow end. As if wishes could come true her parents are nowhere to be seen. They must be waiting in the street. It really is the case that no one's looking at her. She gets out and drags her dress over her wet body.

For the rest of the day she carries her damp bra and knickers balled in one fist, the Brezhnev carbon copies folded small in the other. Her soggy hem sticks to her legs.

'Don't blame me, oh, don't blame me,' the mother mutters as they walk back to their hotel. 'If meningitis strikes, or impetigo, or cholera, some bladder infection, you name it— '

On Sunday morning the father drives them out of Umtata. The Volkswagen Beetle strains to hold the tilted camber of the road that leads back to South Africa. Ella leans her head against the back-seat window, closes her eyes, sees again the shiny children jumping in the bright blue pool.

An hour or so later they are drawn up on the side of the road having juice and biscuits. They are not far from the Transkei border post, about halfway home.

'Zo, zo,' the father says, 'Zo – independent Africa, raw and simple, there you have it. Unadulterated Africa.' He rubs his hands together, rasp, rasp, in the way he does when he feels he's won an argument. The mother produces the weighty sigh with which she meets most mentions of Africa, then breaks her shortbread biscuit into pieces.

Ella walks a distance down the main road. A stiff breeze is blowing, flattening the wayside grass and the white and purple cosmos flowers. She opens her mouth to it like a dog. It's a good feeling, the rushing air drying her tongue. There are things about independent Africa she likes, she decides. Walking down the road like this, on her own, with the sun on her arms. The wind smelling of dry grasslands. The children in the swimming pool, them too, and not one of them staring.

The night they return from the Transkei trip, step back through their front door, face their pale reflections in the hallway mirror, Ella sees for the first time how little of Africa is allowed into their house.

To comfort her displaced Dutch heart, the mother has packed their home so full of Holland that, even if it tried, Africa could not get inside. As if the rooms were suitcases primed for departure, each and every one is stuffed full of Dutch things, including the toilet with its Rijksmuseum postcards on the door. In the main bedroom, blue and white

Delft plates in wire brackets cover the walls. On table tops everywhere lie small Persian rugs just as you see in Dutch paintings. On armchair backs the mother has spread the embroidered doilies that she and *her* mother made during the War when the Nazis evacuated them from their happy home in the Hasselsestraat in Scheveningen to the dreary Pippelingstraat in town. The sharp light coming in from the door gives even the satin stitching a shadow. The pale gold colour of the lounge carpet the mother chose because, she says, it matched the velvet upholstery of the couch in the music room back home. That same couch from the Dutch house now stands beside the piano in the South African living room. The carpets, the plates and the furniture, the portrait of Aunt Ella placed like a seal on top, all of it travelled with her, Irene, to Durban when she came out to be married to her sister's widower, packed in slatted crates like rhinos ready for freighting to distant zoos. Her sister by contrast, the mother always says, didn't have the same sense of *ties*: she travelled light.

Dahlia Bed

The mother and the father can no longer ignore the delicate question of hiring someone, a black person, to assist around the property. Hard-working Dutch people though they are, with each new summer Africa's heat, dirt and growth press upon them more closely. All day long the mother dusts her furniture yet the very next morning a new film has spread over the exact same pieces. As for the garden, with the summer rains the lawn grows like sugar cane. One day the grass is scythed flat by the father's diligent mower. The next the blades have stretched back into sharp points. Tough as it may be to admit, now that they are getting older they need help to deal with Africa's encroachment, proper African help, not the cut corners Ella produces when begged – and paid. Why not try for someone like tall Charley back in Durban, a decent boy for outside? The mother by now will have learned to keep her distance.

Ella takes to crossing her fingers behind her back whenever the mother and the father say the words *hulp* and *zwarte* in the same breath. *Black help. If only.* To have someone else around . . . She thinks of Charley standing guard outside her Durban den.

The father's body finally makes the decision for them. One blistering summer's day he mows the lawn without his truss and does something to his hernia. The mother sees him collapse over the lawnmower handle from her watching post at the kitchen door, and rushes to him, calls Ella to follow. 'Don't you two touch me!' he groans.

'I won't come near you,' the mother says, 'But please, Har, agree now about the garden help. Every time you mow that lawn you go purple. Anyone would think you wanted to die in the attempt.'

They hire Phineas, a soft-spoken schoolboy gardener with a guarded expression, taller even than Charley. For some months he has worked next door at the Brickhills'. He comes with excellent references, says the father. Last winter he beautified the flowerbeds around the municipal picnic site: he turns in tip-top work; he gives of his level best. Next year he will sit his matriculation test, the same as Ella, though the Bantu version. This means he is about sixteen, two years older than she.

'Such a nice boy, such a decent face!' The mother can hardly believe their luck. The father narrows his eyes at her.

'Watch, Phineas.' The father drags the lawnmower's handlebar from the teenager's hands the first time the two men mow. He directs the machine vertically up the grassy bank that Phineas had been cutting at an angle. His grey comb-over collapses outwards, his face runs with sweat. 'Watch how I put the effort in. See how close I make the cut.'

Phineas, frowning, folds his arms.

'Har, please, let Phineas do it.' The mother emerges from the kitchen door with a glass of water. 'He's here to help us.'

With the flat of his hand the father pushes the offered glass away. Ella watches from the verandah window. 'No European,' the father mutters, 'shirks good honest work.'

It is Ella's turn to take water out to the father. This afternoon he and Phineas are clearing out the dahlia bed. Now that he has proper help, the father wants to convert

136

the bed and plant roses. Ella brings two glasses. The second one is for Phineas.

The two men are bent over their hoes, breaking up clayey clods of earth. Ella stands waiting for them to turn around and notice her holding the water. Phineas turns first, slowly straightening his back. The father is still bent down. Phineas sees the two glasses in her hands. Then his eyes rise to her face. He holds her gaze, his eyes soft but expressionless.

He is wearing a blue v-necked cotton shirt and grey Terylene trousers. She's close enough to him to smell the moist cut dahlia stems underfoot, the dried sweat on his shirt. They are smart clothes for gardening, she thinks. He must have a mother who looks after him, an elder sister.

His quiet eyes still hold her gaze. For a long while he doesn't blink and she doesn't blink. But then her eyes tear over; she blinks, takes a chance. Just as the father is straightening up, she throws Phineas a quick smile. The smile creases her lips before she can think about it.

At once he drops his eyes but at the same instant the corners of his mouth dent deeper in. He has let a something pass between them, like a furtive nod, a recognition that they're standing here together, two teenagers . . .

A band of heat collars her neck. It may be an airy thing that has passed between them but it's also a wrong thing. If the father spotted them smiling like this, it would be terrible what he'd say, call her out in Dutch for the *loeder* and *slet* he's always suspected she is. Fancy, he'd say, already she can hear him, you, a so-called decent girl, sharing secret smiles with the native garden boy, a servant—

'You be proud,' he tells her later that day. Is he referring to the thing that passed with Phineas? They are sitting out on the verandah in the purple light that floods the hills just past sunset, drinking iced water. Phineas has long gone home. 'Be proud of what you are, *meid*, strong, native-born, an African in effect, not a degenerate European like everyone else in your family . . .'

He surely has seen their smile? Ella looks at her father sideways: the corrugated brow, the bags under his eyes that his black-rimmed spectacles rest on. He gives nothing away. Then, as she leans across to begin clearing the table, he pulls back his glass, the melting ice cubes clunking. He says her name, *Ella. Ella.* When does he ever say her name?

'Ella, wait a minute, I meant it just then. You, the accidental child of your father's old age, unanticipated, uncalled-for, you're a true original, always remember. You're a person for a new country, neither completely African nor completely European. Think about it, face up to it. Whereas I, I'm the last of my line, a European washed up in Africa, a lost cause, a eunuch of history.'

Ella's ice-filled stomach churns; suddenly she feels sick. He's about to declare something she's suspected all along. She's in fact an orphan, a parentless child like the girls in the books she loves, Anne, Heidi, Elnora of the Limberlost? She doesn't belong to the mother and the father. Not one sin of the Dutch fathers . . .

But, no, this isn't his meaning. What he means, he tells her, his eyes fixed on the fading horizon, is that his European line doesn't extend to her, and her mother's European line doesn't extend to her.

'Being born in this new country has cut off the line,' he says. 'Your mother hates the thought but – so what? Born here, Africa claims you. This isn't a bad situation. On the contrary.' He likes the expression *on the contrary*; he makes cutting motions with his hands when he uses it. 'On the contrary, it's good to embrace a new world, a new homeland, this wide-open African world – excuse me, *South* African world. It's good to claim it just as it claims you. You're not a product of war like me, a daughter of war. Yours is a stronger claim, in fact, than a black African's claim, Phineas's say, he's purely African. Remember this. I saw it when we were standing together there in the garden. Phineas only knows the Africa that surrounds him. You, Ella, know the wider world but it's here that you're rooted.

'So be wary of Mam.' Almost he looks straight at her, or anyway just past her left ear. 'Be wary when she claims you back for corrupt Europe. Europe should have no hold on you. Unlike her, unlike me, you're not shackled to your fatherland by a historical ball and chain. God knows how I've wrestled with that ball and chain, all my life. But you, you don't need all that pointless yearning – the indelible taste of pea soup in the gullet, the Wilhelmus anthem, that ridiculous booming about Germanic blood, what a load of old tripe. That separate identity stuff is not for clever people like you, ready to claim a new republic, make it work.'

Ella looks past him. He may be trying to meet her eye, but she won't side with him. He's old, ugly, endlessly cross. Yes, she likes the idea of embracing a new world, she admits it. When she thinks of embracing Africa she remembers flying up and down the continent with her mother; the nights they spent in airport buildings; the sounds of singing and drumming that bore down from all sides. She remembers sucking deep into her lungs the smell of wet vegetation that came seeping through the doors.

But she doesn't want a bad word said about the Netherlands. The Netherlands isn't as he says it is. She remembers dove-grey Oegstgeest and the games on the sand heap; the visits to Oma, the raisins, the ventriloquist in the park . . .

It's true they haven't flown north for several years now,

not since she turned twelve, when the trust fund that covered their travel ran out. The mother addresses her apple-green air letters to the nursing home where Oma has moved. Still, no matter how much time goes by, Ella will never forget the Netherlands, how connected-in she felt.

On Saturday and Sunday afternoons she takes to lying in the sun, her skin basted in cooking oil. Her aim is a proper dark brown *connected-in* African colour, but instead she turns bright red. By the end of the summer her freckles have doubled in size. Her freckle coverage has turned her body half-brown, she calculates, which is better than nothing. By this reckoning, she will every summer go a degree or so browner. She will also go a degree or so thinner. This, too, is her aim. 'If you want to look like me,' says Linda in the school playground, 'Live on flavoured ice-cubes and cucumber.' Linda has grown a metre in a year and is a skeleton in a skin coat. Ella does without the cucumber. Her stomach begins to curve in instead of out.

Yes, she refuses to side with the father, this angry old man in his truss. In her heart she knows where she sides. This is what African birth really means, she knows in her bones. African birth means choosing Africa *every time*, on *every* occasion, Africa over Europe, Africa over South Africa, nine times out of ten, ten times out of ten.

During the last maths period on a Friday afternoon at school, the Independent Learners group in the back row of the classroom is given exercises in formal logic to do as a treat. Since the beginning of this year, Standard 8, Ella has been an Independent Learner.

From their exercises in logic she learns about a pattern called a syllogism, a sum in words that she can play with, that she can manipulate so as to capture situations that at first glance go the other way about, like her relationship to

140

Africa, say, or to the kids in the Transkei swimming pool. Her relationship also to Phineas.

The syllogism goes like this. The first postulate is that, she, Ella, is monstrous, as she has known a long time. She is shifty, late-developed, misshapen, all the way down to her core. 'You, you, you waste-of-space!' the father fuelled by sherry bellows at dinner time whenever she answers him back, as if conjuring some spirit out of her breast.

The first postulate then is that she is a monster.

The second postulate is that blacks are monstrous – that is, if you take white people at their word. The Transkei kids, Charley, Phineas, even Arthur Ashe on television, in fact all black people – they are shifty, untrustworthy, warped. Just simple-minded buffoons, says her father, mere hewers of wood, drawers of water.

And so it follows, runs the syllogism, that as she and the Transkei children, and she and Phineas, plus all the weird toads and locusts in the surrounding hills – as all of them are as one, united in their monstrosity, she is completely and entirely an African too, a black African, her number of freckles regardless. She is flesh of the flesh of all the other African monsters and wild things.

Her syllogism works so well that she enlarges and bends the pattern to make other, equally smart ones. She enjoys the game. She likes how neatly her syllogisms run the world-as-it-is backwards, undo the things people like the father and Prime Minister B J Vorster and the other politicians on television say are right.

Take the way the father calls black people ignorant goons just for being black. This is in itself obviously goon-like because how could *all* black people be ignorant goons? The father knows not one black person, not well. So it's he who's shown up as ignorant as well as goon-like. And if black people are not all ignorant and dumb then she, too, so often called dumb, goggling, et cetera – she can't be just an *idioot* either.

Across the country black schoolchildren are up in arms. There are daily reports in the newspaper, tucked away on page two or six, in the News in Brief section. The children are not in fact armed, other than with bricks and stones, but they are angry. They say they want to choose the language they study in. They also demand huge abstract things Ella knows about mainly from the father's talking – things like freedom and justice. The schoolchildren refuse to go to school because of their lack of freedom and justice.

Ella can't think of a place more free than school; free of her father's voice, her mother's tears. But she remembers the broad-shouldered soldiers she saw all across independent Africa: how their fight for freedom puffed out their chests. She remembers the word *Viva!* chalked on the airport wall in red. *Viva*, she now knows from a dictionary in the school library, is a cry of freedom and also life.

During the school disturbances Phineas stays away from work. Ella misses seeing him around. There's something about their quick, snatched, bitten-back smiles she enjoys. She stands in the garden and stares out in the direction of the African township that lies across the valley, behind the feathery bank of eucalyptus trees. There's more smoke hanging over the township than usual, but it may just be winter mist. She tries to imagine what might be keeping Phineas, but the only picture that comes to her is of her Cuban soldier in his battle-fatigues loping through the township streets.

When the father is out of the dining room Ella switches the Philips radiogram on low, twiddles its short-wave dial, presses her ear to the woven plastic speaker. Between the high-pitched whining noises there are ghostly mutterings and whirrings, sometimes sudden bursts of speech, hard, staccato. But, though she holds her ear as close as she can, there are no words that she can understand, no clear message about what's going on.

Three weeks later Phineas returns, his expression as withdrawn as ever.

'You weren't involved with those rabble-rousers, were you, Phineas?' the father asks at their iced-water break. Ella stands close by with the water glasses. 'Those kids torching the classrooms, ruining the good things given to them by the government, that wouldn't be you, would it? I wouldn't have thought so.'

Phineas gives the father a quick glance, shrugs. 'I had good references, boss,' he says. He doesn't meet Ella's eye but once again his lips dent deeper in.

'So,' says the father once Phineas has gone home, 'Phineas wasn't part of it, *meid*, as I thought. Those schoolkids were egged on by a bunch of troublemakers, Soviet saboteurs, I'd wager, or maybe just ne'er-do-wells, like they say on TV. Individuals are moving in amongst them who mean no good. You be careful, Ella, you're highly susceptible. You steer clear of such people.'

Ella quits reading the newspaper. Nothing in the paper adds up, not in the way you'd expect, where truth means one thing and false means the opposite. She loses interest in her syllogisms. It's too easy construing them when what you read and hear doesn't match what you see around you. The newspapers call the protesting schoolchildren a rabble and a mob, as if they were animals hunting in a pack. But she can see from the one photograph the *Natal Witness* prints that they are teenagers the same as her, wearing school uniform like her own. One or two of the handwritten placards they carry say *Viva!* in wobbly letters – the same letters as she'd make if painting a poster in a hurry.

After a fortnight or so, news of the riots dries up. The police, the television news announces, have imposed law and order. But, Ella puzzles, her father has always maintained this country had law and order from the word go. Why then should it have to be imposed? And that's not all. In bed she hears, till late at night, the wail of police sirens in the direction of the township across the valley. The sounds come faintly yet clearly through the darkness. At school children prone to hay fever cough and splutter through their lessons. It's a particularly dusty winter, say the teachers, but Ella thinks differently. She isn't prone to hay fever yet there's something odd in the air, she too can feel it, something dry and ticklish salts the wind blowing from the township. It stings her eyes, closes her throat.

In place of the newspaper Ella on her towel in the sun reads girls' fiction and teenage romances, any book with a pink spine. She also reads Anne Frank's *Diary*. Her cousin Lieke sent it over for her fourteenth birthday. Ella knows what Anne Frank feels staring at the sky from her attic window, dreaming of escape. Most other books she gives up on, books about Africa or South Africa especially, *Jock of the Bushveld, The Story of an African Farm*. Nothing in these books adds up; nothing corresponds to where they live. The history books in the school library have whole whited-out sections. 'Don't ask me what should be in there,' Mr McDonald says, more gruffly than usual. 'If I told you my guesses I'd lose my job.' The blank pages, Ella thinks, look like plaques on a war memorial yet to be filled with names.

Of the girls' books, Ella so far has read the Heidi, Anne, Katie, and *Little Women* books four, five times over, plus *A Girl of the Limberlost, The Little Lamplighter*. She has read also the Brontës, small dusty Everyman books from the town library. But she liked these books more when she still believed she was an orphan like Anne, Jane and the rest. The only Brontë book she doesn't like is *Wuthering Heights*. Characters like Catherine and Heathcliff who make themselves ill with their tirades put her off. She wants to tell Heathcliff to stop tearing at his clothes and pull himself together. He'll get used to his life without Cathy.

Little by little Ella forsakes questing Jane and the other lonely but courageous girls in scrapes for the beautiful clinging heroines of Mills and Boon, Denise Robbins, Barbara Cartland. In romances nothing at all corresponds to the world she lives in. No one even pretends it does. Everywhere you look there are only English gardens, beautiful English girls with heart-shaped faces finding English love in English gardens.

The weekends of being fourteen and then fifteen pass slowly. Saturday morning to Sunday evening is a sea of time. She draws up timetables, fills each hour with something to do. Bake coconut ice. Read. Make ice-cubes. Sleep. Snip split-ends. Eat ice-cubes.

Whatever she's doing, she keeps a Mills and Boon within reach, propped up beside her recipe book, spread under her head as she enlarges her freckles in the sun. Reading romances while crunching ice-cubes fills up the time like nothing else.

But it's a tough call making time move more quickly. There are weekends when Ella lying on her towel in the sun could yell out loud for something to do. She thinks of crazy impossible things – like painting *Viva!* over and over on her classroom walls; or even walking to the township. She'd like to find out about the place where the strange winds blow. She thinks of locating Phineas's home, knocking at the door, maybe meeting his family, the elder sister she's imagined he has. She might ask to join in with them, *him*, with what they're all doing. 'Let me come on one of your marches,' she could say. 'I've seen these soldiers in Luanda . . .' Isn't she herself an African schoolchild? Couldn't she be counted as one of them?

She thinks of the heroic and forbidden things Anne Frank got up to, sitting with her diary in her cramped Amsterdam attic, hoping for a future. She thinks of Anne's minders, the Dutch people who looked after her family, how it must have been hiding people on the run. Even Tante Suus, the mother says, helped her older brothers in the Resistance shelter Jewish refugees: she opened the door to them at dead of night; let them creep in under her bed to catch an hour's sleep. Even bossy but ordinary Tante Suus. She tries to imagine Tante Suus and her brothers in bed hearing the fugitives stir just beneath them, under the mattress, their quiet but harried breathing. There was more to their lives than lying in the sun reading romances, eating ice-cubes, writing stupid letters into the void.

She thinks of her Aunt Ella and the village trading store she planned to open somewhere on the Lowveld. She sees her in her midnight-blue dress fast-pedalling a bicycle down a tussocky track, her long hem hooked up over her elbow, the tall Blikman and Sartorius typewriter loaded in her front basket. No-nonsense Aunt Ella, always happy to try things out, wouldn't she have done something like this, set out to the local village in order to type up letters for people? There she is, plonking the typewriter down on a tin chest in the dusty street, checking the ribbon, lining up her paper.

So, what's it to be, she looks up at the person standing at the head of the queue, his face like Phineas's, a gleam on his forehead: a greeting to your grandma, a *proposal of mutual benefit* to the Soviets to help the fight for freedom, justice – whatever makes Phineas's eyes cloud over when the father asks why it is he's been away?

Death

The father invites Ella on a drive back to the ravine where Bogey met the lammergeyer. 'There's something important I want to show you,' he says, as they leave the house, testily, as if she might refuse. He repeats himself as they get out of the car at the edge of the pine forest, close to the lip of the ravine. 'It's very important – to safeguard the future. So keep it to yourself. You've reached an age where I must be able to trust you.'

What he wants to show her is not outdoors as she'd thought but in the car itself, the boot that he now opens. He lifts up a notebook-sized item wrapped in a soft beige dust cloth and, without a word, places it in her hands.

The object inside the beige covers is smooth. The dust cloth slides over it. The shape is like a myth, recognisable, unflinching.

'A gun?' she says through a dry throat, her false question echoing strangely. The barrel is already lying along the length of her hand.

'Yes, a Colt 45, more to the point. Royal Navy issue. We all carried one, just in case. I've had it cleaned. One of Tom Watt's friends. Also bought these bullets off him. We'll load it and try it out, give you some shooting practice. To claim the new republic, we must be prepared to stand up for it, defend it. Even the women and girls.'

'Shoot here? Now?' She looks down at the soft blue-black of the gun in her hands, across at the thick weave of forest down in the valley. She remembers lying in the dust there at the ravine's edge, in line with the gogga and the lammergeyer.

'Yes, here, now,' says the father, as if he remembered nothing. 'We fire across the ravine. I'll show you what to do. It's not difficult once you get the hang of it. The important thing is to squeeze the trigger as if it was putty.'

'But . . . what if— ? Are we allowed?'

'Of course it's allowed. There's no one about. It's perfectly safe. The ravine is just empty air. We have a right to defend ourselves, practise self-defence. You never know where a threat to your safely is coming from. As the recent events showed. The black especially, he can turn quickly. Whites, too. But blacks are closer to nature than whites.'

His hands busy themselves with the gun, sliding, knocking back, clicking into place.

'Not everyone turns. Blacks or whites. Phineas wouldn't turn.'

'Don't be so sure,' he looks down the gun barrel across the ravine. 'In blacks the primitive is closer to the surface than in the white.'

She sees him squeeze the trigger but the sound is still a shock, the reverberation clacking around the walls of the ravine.

'Your turn.' The gun is back in her hands. She follows his instruction, remembers his movements. 'That's right, legs a little apart, good and stable, hold the thing out in front of you, straighten your arm. Take aim, that taller tree across the valley. It's a powerful weapon you've got there. Respect it, think seriously when using it. '

He didn't say enough about the kickback. He himself, short as he is, hardly registered the impact. Ella pulls the trigger towards her and the noise seems to knock her sideways, only it was the gun itself, leaping like a live thing in her hands.

148

'Way off course,' says the father. 'Looped into the valley. You've got to keep your eyes open when you take aim. And hold steady. Remember, you're defending yourself, think of that. You're guarding your country, everything it stands for.'

He works his way through the box of bullets, two more for him, the rest, four, for her. By the eighth bullet her arm is aching, her eyes smarting. 'You take it,' she pleads.

'What did I bring you here for? For pleasure? No, this is your lesson, *meid*, your chance to show what you're made of.'

She steps away from him, hauls the gun to eye-level. But the trigger seems to squeeze too soon, before she is rooted and steady. This time the kickback really does throw her off her feet, against the father's thigh. The gun slips out of her hand. He stumbles as he reaches for it, rights himself before she does. Even so, the barrel touches the dust. Straightening up she catches his frown.

'I'm sorry I wasted your time,' she says as they get into the car.

'You wasted my time and all my bullets,' the father says. He rubs the gun with the cloth, then puts it in the glove compartment. 'What a fool I was, thinking a child of your mother could forget its weasel nature. Well, mark my words, the day will come when you'll remember this. When you'll want to stand up and be counted, defend what you believe.'

Oma dies one midwinter's day when it's high summer in Europe. After the father has calculated the funeral expenses he finds there isn't a bean left over, not a *stuiver*, for the mother to fly back. The funeral service was so very tiny, Tante Suus, ailing herself, tells them in a short trunk call. Just the staff from the nursing home, a few nieces, Cousin

Lieke. The mother drops tears into the receiver, strokes Bogey in her lap. The father stands by with his stopwatch, his hand clamped on the telephone's connecting wires. 'So, so sad I couldn't come,' the mother whispers, staring hard at the back of her husband's head.

Over their morning Douwe Egberts on the verandah the mother reflects out loud. Without being able to bid farewell, she says, it's hard to believe her mother's no longer alive. She's missed her these many years now. Well, now this missing feeling'll never end.

Ella lying on her towel can't think of Oma as either dead or alive, maybe somewhere in between. It's long ago that she last saw her. When she remembers Oma she thinks of her bifocals, how they winked in the light when she moved her head. She remembers practising her ventriloquism for her, sinking her voice into her chest and rumbling it, Oma clapping.

The mother takes to reading newspaper obituary columns. She begins with the back pages of *The Natal Witness* and *The Mercury*. The black-lined notices from the Netherlands papers she saves till last. Twice a month an old Vrijeschool friend sends out the papers by surface mail, rolled into parcels like packs of toilet roll. The mother works through the packs methodically. The political commentaries she sets aside for the father.

When it's someone in their teens who has died, a 'beautiful angel', 'snatched from us', whose 'smile will never fade', her voice catches, choked by a hiccup. She computes the young person's age from the dates given in the notice, shakes her head over the bridge suicide, the accidental drowning, the tragic suffocation, the bravely-fought illness. She reads in full the Patience Strong poem about the new star in the sky. She hiccups again. She's seen too much death in her life, she shakes her head, too much. The loss of her beautiful sister aged just thirty-eight. Her father's premature death to pneumonia, a few months after her sister. The long fading of her mother . . .

Her arm crooked over her closed eyes, Ella in the sun imagines the obituary notices streaming from the mother's mouth as if they were the black typewriter ribbon unspooling from her Blikman and Sartorius typewriter. The notices belch from her mouth in an inky knot, tumble over the verandah flags. The father, as far as she can tell, doesn't let the dark stream that unspools at his feet concern him. Now and then she hears him spit his coffee grounds into the grass.

He's especially silent, Ella notices, when the mother mentions her sister. One morning she refers to it directly, the black-lined death notice published in the *Haagsche Courant* in the early 1950s. Ella hears the thin crackle of the Netherlands papers. The *Witness* is made of cheaper, softer newsprint.

'Look, Har, another dead person in their thirties, here, from Delft. Cancer took her too, a woman around her age. A very casual notice, in my opinion. Though we could barely see for grief at least we did a good job with the obituary, all those years ago. Do you remember those lovely lines, from Roland Holst?'

'How could I?' The father's voice sounds deeper than normal though he speaks in Dutch. With the mother during the day he uses Dutch. Ella rolls her head in the direction of the verandah. 'You never sent me the death notice. What I do remember is putting her on a plane back to Nederland to get therapy. Some Indian nursing orderlies here at Louis Botha airport provided a wheelchair to get her from the building to the plane. They conjured that wheelchair out of nowhere.'

'You didn't tell me before,' the mother says softly, the newspaper crisply rustling, 'You never got the notice? I'm sure we sent it.'

'You never asked. Your wonderful family didn't send a letter till after she was dead.'

Her father standing on the rutted runway at Durban airport, Ella tries to picture it, the short, bow-legged man with the angry forehead saying a last goodbye to his wife. How do you say a last goodbye? She and Oma never managed it. She sees him standing there beside the wheelchair, sentinel-straight, his square hand cupped on her shoulder. And she, the woman in the wheelchair – Ella imagines her in her midnight-blue gown – she squints up at him silhouetted against the searing Durban light, her relentless inescapable brown eyes.

They forgot to send him the death notice, so he says. Ella turns this surprising new fact round in her thoughts. The death notice that, when all's said and done, brought the two of them together, the mother and the father – *this* mother, the younger sister, and the father – he didn't ever see it. She watches see-through sun-flecks drift across her vision. And then, a year or so later, she imagines, after the exchange of a few blue air letters, he, the father, the widower, Har, set out back to the Netherlands – is that how it happened? He set out to claim his death notice from his dead wife's family? At which they put him in the way of the younger, pray-to-God-healthier sister instead.

Ella picks up her Mills and Boon. She'd like to find a Mills and Boon in which a hero was consecutively married to two sisters. She'd like to be able to imagine in more detail how it was when her bow-legged father turned up on the doorstep to claim his second bride from the same household. But Mills and Boon doesn't stray that far beyond the beaten track.

Some evenings when the news is dull and there is no roll-call of dead soldiers, the father on his circular walk from the verandah via his desk to the television and back, tells himself a story. Ella hears the Old Brown Sherry bottle out on the verandah begin its rattle, the screw-top lid its scraping. She sees him sidle past Ella's portrait without looking at it. He pretends to read something scratched on the blotting pad lying on his desk. He sidles back past the portrait. He comes over to adjust the placings at table. In front of the television he clears his throat.

'I mean,' he blurts, 'Those lovely chaps, all of them dead. Scandalous, it was, scandalous. That's what I mean.'

No one has said a thing one way or another, but still, several evenings a week at dinner, he must before sitting down say what he means. Ella bends her eyes to her plate. The mother sits upright in her chair, poised for flight, the heels of her hands pressed against the table's edge.

'The treatment our dead received, none of you can understand.' Already he's at top volume. 'Those toffs carrying on about how *relatively small* the sacrifice was, fellows who wouldn't know the arse from the elbow of a gun.' He casts a look at Ella. 'And we, fresh off our beloved *Tjerk Hiddes*, the salt still in our ears, Jan Bakker and I, and dear old Schilperoort, the eternal hanger-on, taking the train straight from the East India Docks to Liverpool Street Station. It was there we saw the rotters sizing up the end-of-war casualty lists. Those lists wallpapered the news kiosks under the arches. I mean it – wallpapered. Pink-cheeked as the day they were born, the rotters were, never saw an hour's military action in their lives.

'Jan and I stood reading for ourselves, peering, the print was so small. "Oh," says the pink one nearest to me, "It's a lot but you'd think there'd be more, after a six-year war." Saying this *lul* to a man he could see from the uniform was fresh back from his own Royal Navy. I felt my fists go up.' The father's fists go up, he punches the air. The mother ducks her head. 'Jan grabbed my arms. So I used the weapon of my best English instead. "You fuck off, you stupid Englander," I said. "What do you know about war, *idioot*? When did you last leave this island of yours to find out? What do you know of the many men who after what they have seen are alive in body, dead in spirit?"

'The pink pair was already backing away, but I couldn't resist a final missile, my most priceless *Nederlands* curse to follow my best English.' The father sits down heavily. '"*Wees gesodomieterd*!" I told them roundly. And translated for good measure. "Be arsefucked, you *klootzakken*, you dirty testicles!"'

'Har, Har!' Mam begins her loud breathing, rattles her knife and fork. 'How will decent society in Nederland ever receive us back if you teach the *kind* language like that?'

'Back, back, always back with you, you fantasist,' the father says more quietly, pushing away his cold plate of food. 'Back to the fatherland, bah! What did my precious fatherland ever give me – for all my loyalty, my service? Once it had used me up my fatherland vomited me out on the trash heap of the world, *gesodomieterd*, without a guilder to my name.'

One evening after the Liverpool Street story, Ella follows the father onto the verandah. 'You and Mam,' she tries to get the words out fast, 'If there's a reason why you always, you know, talk about dying – ?'

A wordless noise. The father opens his mouth in front of her face, corkscrews his finger at the side of his head.

'A reason, *idioot*? Don't you listen? Doesn't it *stand to reason*?'

He turns his back, lights a Rothman's, smokes it in three drags, rolls his heels across the edge of the verandah flags. Then he turns to her again. He pushes her down into one of the rattan chairs. As she sinks back he succeeds somehow in keeping his mouth a constant three-four inches from her eyes. His square hands are braced on the armrests.

'This girl's parents,' he spells out, 'This girl's parents think often about death because death is a fact of life. I tried to teach you this when I gave you shooting practice.'

In front of her face is the *wah-wah-wah* of his lips, the mustard-yellow teeth going up and down, the white threads strung between the thin dry lips. Ella doesn't want to look at these ugly things but it's impossible to shift her eyes away.

This girl is the one life her parents have spawned, he goes on spitting. May the fates forgive them. And this means, mark his words, she needs to think about their deaths. Hasn't she herself said it if ever he in a blue moon attends events at her school? He looks worse than a grandfather, he's a wizened dwarf. And fair enough. He is. So she should bear in mind these two imminent facts-to-be, the father's death, the mother's death, and then what follows. What she'll do after these events have taken place: how to survive.

Lock up the house and go camping in the hills by myself, Ella thinks, still struggling and failing to avoid looking into his mouth, the white threads thinning and thickening as he talks. She tries to think of something else, something happier. She imagines the great gust of freedom she'll feel rushing past her ears on the day when their two deaths – the one preferably straight after the other – when their deaths open a door, letting in the light.

She thinks of taking the car – it would be her car then and she would be able to drive it, she has watched Dad driving long enough. She would take the car and drive north, why not? – zigzag across the continent, see the sights they have swept over on their cross-Africa flights, Okavango's green fingers, the Mountains of the Moon, Kilimanjaro and its eternal snow, the Nile delta's pitchfork shape. She imagines belting out as she drives the song she has heard on the radio, *I want to break free-ee*, shouting the words through the open car windows, the wind shafting through her hair. And when she reached Egypt she wouldn't cross to Europe, no, she's seen Europe, or at least some of it. No, she would cross not to Europe but to Asia. There must be a ferry or something across the Suez Canal, a pontoon. And once she's in Asia, there will be a road leading to the Himalayas, its high snowy peaks, so she imagines, the rosy light of dawn gilding them. In the Himalayas she will pay a visit to the lammergeyers that swoop there, riding the high air currents . . .

With a huffing noise the father turns his back on her and lights another cigarette. Ella gets up slowly, moves towards the verandah door. The door handle creaks as she opens it but he doesn't look round. A blue coil of smoke stretches up over his head and makes a circle around the naked light bulb.

At the end of the winter before Ella begins her school-leaving certificate, the father develops a new health complaint – prostate pains. The condition is benign, in his doctor's opinion, there's no need for concern. But man is a dying animal, how many times has the father not said it? The day after he receives the diagnosis he begins to rehearse an emergency scenario, the choreography of a family crisis. He's thought it all out in advance, what-to-do-when.

He calls Ella to his desk and asks her to stand beside it, straight up.

'When I die – ' he coughs, licks his lips. 'I've been thinking about it, Ella, that question you asked. Why all the talk of death? In a way it was a perfectly fair question. You wanted to be prepared. We all grow a little wiser with age. So, in the spirit of the question, let's look this thing in the eye. Let's think about our deaths as if they soon will happen.'

156

He clicks the Bic in his breast pocket. The pen, its matt-silver surface, grates on her no less than it did in the days they wrote to Mr Brezhnev.

'When I die,' the father begins again, and every time thereafter, around once a week at least, clicking the Bic like a metronome. There's rarely an obvious trigger for his speech, not that Ella can detect. She sniffs surreptitiously but there's no Old Brown Sherry on the air.

'Mind, *meid*, it may happen when you least expect it, when I die,' he says. 'It'll strike like that bird threatened to do with Bogey, suddenly. It won't be like shooting practice. It'll be just you by yourself. So when the news comes, the news that I'm dead, when the call comes from the hospital to your school, and then from the head's office to your classroom through the intercom, this is what you do.'

The intercom – Ella has told him about it, the white box with its plastic grille that sits quietly crackling above the blackboard in every classroom. Since the student riots, government schools across the country have installed intercoms in case of a state of emergency. In Rhodesia they've had intercoms in public buildings since before the border wars.

'When that happens,' the father continues, 'When the teacher calls you to the front, he, what's his name, the thin fellow who runs marathons, yes, Kavanagh, he'll say words to this effect. He'll say, Ella, you're to go to the head's office, there may be bad news. I believe your father, unfortunately, has now died.'

Your father unfortunately has now died, Ella silently repeats the sentence. Each time he works through the story, there is without fail the ugly Dutchified *now* that the Irish Mr Kavanagh would scorn to use. *Jouw vader is nu dood, is nu eindelijk dood*, is the sentence he's thinking of. Your father is now at last dead.

157

'When he says this,' the father presses on, 'You will not cry. This is my order. Mind that you take notice. I will have no tears. True, you may feel no need to cry, this rotter is no great loss to the world, we know that, but, in any case, I order, you will not cry. With all your faults you have some backbone, so you will not imitate your mother, you will not even want to cry. I'll have no useless female tears spilt over me.

'What you do instead is this. First, you take a deep breath and straighten your back, exactly, like that. When straight-backed it's always easier to control the emotions. Next, you go to your desk, pack up the books you've been using and put them neatly in your bag, just as normal. Talk to no one. After a piece of unusual news, talk can unsettle, so you will not talk. Instead you'll nod politely to Kavanagh. He may want to extend a hand, but don't waste a minute, sweep past him with a nod. Remember, it's an unusual occurrence and the whole class will be there watching. Don't give them anything to watch. Sweep by, leave by the door' – how else? Ella thinks – 'and make your way to the headmaster's office, slowly, so as not to get out of breath.

'Then, once there, in the head's office, you call your mother. At this point she may not yet have the news, that I'm now dead, I'm trying to arrange it that way, so you'll have to break it to her. You'll be the message carrier. Once she has the news, your mother will need your help. You know this. She has a backbone like a sponge' – Ella thinks of Mam on the aeroplane floor – 'But she's also a lady, princess on the pea, she can't do without extra support. When her sister Ella died she was a mess. I made my way to Holland to give her extra support. I put her sister's wedding ring on her finger. When I die you must make sure you get to her as soon as possible. Before you say anything, check she has taken her pills. Phone Holland for help if necessary,

Cousin Jan-Kees, Lieke's older brother, the accountant, he'll be happy to assist.' Ella has a vague memory of Jan-Kees, the carefree laugh he produces readily and often, sometimes when there's nothing to laugh about. 'If your mother wishes, let Jan-Kees come out, fetch her home in style. But while you wait for him, play the man, rise to the occasion. Do not whatever you do give way to panic.'

Sourness rises at the back of Ella's throat whenever he reaches this point in the scenario. How small he must believe her heart is, she thinks to herself each time he says these same words, small and hard as a hazelnut, to deal with his death in this way.

But she swallows the sourness, draws her back up even straighter. Well, if that's what he thinks then let him be right. Her starring role in the intercom drama depends on his being off the scene, dead, *now dead*, and on her growing stronger *as a result*. Fine, he's said it, let it be true. She feels little for him, almost next-to-nothing. If it weren't for her night watches she'd feel nothing at all. At this point in his scenario she hates him. In her tiny heart there is only thin air and this little pinch of black dust, of hate.

Quietly, without breathing a word, Ella changes her school-day habits. Now, whenever she enters a classroom, any school room, the laboratories, even the girls' changing room, she runs through her private drill. First she checks the walls to see where the intercom speaker is. It's always over the blackboard, if there is a blackboard, but still she checks, makes sure from the glowing red light that it's operational, this fateful window through which the death-laden future may at any moment burst. She calculates the time it will take to walk from her desk to the door. Then she sizes up the teacher. Will they be happy to let her go, to sweep by without so much as a handshake? They'll have to be. She will be insistent. She straightens her back. These days she keeps her back very straight indeed. If the father only knew how straight, how ready she is to run through his routine, then perhaps he'd see at last how disciplined she really is, what a rational, useful *man* she can be.

In the general hospital down in Durban the father has his prostate removed. What gives grief, he says looking hard at Ella, is better out than in.

The doctor declares the operation successful. It's a new lease on life, the father agrees. The minor embolism on the wound a few days later is unfortunate but easily dealt with. As for the week of radiation therapy the following month, he embraces it. It's as well to be 100% safe. He drives himself down to treatment in the Beetle, cigarette in hand.

Happy as he appears, whistling sometimes through his front teeth, the When-I-Die routine increases in frequency. He speaks the piece sometimes twice a weekend; now and then twice a night. Ella finds a way of looking attentive during the drill without properly listening. As he clears his throat to begin the thing again, 'Now, *meid*, when I die . . .,' she lets her fringe fall over her face.

Sometimes, very occasionally, he breaks off his string of instructions with a sudden shake of his jowls and takes a new direction. 'When I'm dead,' he says, 'think how delighted you'll be.'

Is he testing how hardened she has by now become? He can test away. She's rock-solid, hard as nails.

'Imagine how you and your mother'll be able to go on holiday. There's life insurance put away for that, holidays, the mountains, the beach. As we never go on holiday. Your mother might be tempted to put her lips to a sherry or two.'

Ella feels buoyed by his lightness, forced as it sounds.

'Not holidays only, Dad,' she comes back one summer evening on the verandah, mist settling in the river valley. 'The happiness won't only be having the holidays. When

160

I walk to the headmaster's office, that day when the news comes you are *now* dead, I'll skip. I'll want to jig for joy. I'll know that I'm free when you are dead.'

But this he doesn't like. A shadow moves across his eyes. 'Take care, *kind*,' he says grimly, and downs his tumbler of sherry. 'There's something called Beyond a Joke.'

'But I was saying no more than you ever say,' she flings back. She thinks of the Colt 45, immediately switches the thought off. 'You and Mam, you're the ones who go on, death, death, death, night and day. In other people's homes, Linda's home, believe it or not, there are babies, people talk about the future. Anyone would think, listening to you two, death was the main point.'

'And maybe they'd be right, *meid*, maybe so. For me the path from cradle to grave was never meant to go via another cradle. That was not the plan. It was not your mother's plan. Listen to what I'm telling you here. Your Mam never thought she'd marry. After the war there were few men available, very few decent men. Her sister got the last *nietsnut* down on his luck hunting around for a good Dutch bride. That one, the sister, she had a baby or two, yes, but they came out too early and dead, due to the cancer.'

Ella's breath misses a beat. She looks over at him. Other babies? Another baby or *two*? He doesn't meet her eye but the frown has left his forehead. He's stating these things as plain facts, without sadness, neatly linking them up with the other plain facts of his life.

'There was a war on when I was a young child, rationing, restrictions, you name it, though we were neutral, and then of course another war followed twenty-five years later.' He sips thirstily at his empty tumbler. 'I was in my thirties, best time of a man's life. Me and my generation, we kept death always in mind. As a boy of five or six, the time of the first war, I would sit on the front doorstep of our house in the Koestraat in Leiden and watch the people go by. I remember thinking to myself, I don't know why, in a few years' time these folks will all be dead.'

Ella shifts a leg that has gone numb, ever so gently, to avoid creaking the rattan. But he has come to the end of his flow. Above the pockets of mist in the valley the sky overhead is clear and starry. The distant hills stamp black shapes on the blaze.

She thinks of the unborn siblings her aunt – Aunt Ella – miscarried before she was born, surprising presences she had no idea of till now. She remembers the strange pressure of interest or curiosity she used to feel coming at her from Ella's portrait, after Mam first told her about it. An image steps into her thoughts of the babies lined up, their melty brown eyes like their mother's – a ghostly row of which she makes a part, the only living part, hovering by herself at the back.

Ella and her mother sit at the kitchen table, sorting through a pile of the finger paintings she did back at the Vrijeschool in the Netherlands. Cousin Lieke sent the pictures in the small parcel containing Oma's effects. They'd been stacked in her attic along with the mother's winter coat. Lieke has asked to keep hold of the winter coat.

The mother pulls a messy brown painting out of the pile, an outline of the African continent.

'What muddy colours, Ella. I'm surprised they let you use them. In my day at the Vrijeschool, we only ever painted using yellows and blues, spiritual colours.'

Ella remembers squeezing the lettering into that ear-shape of Africa, how she tried to keep the red paint from running into the brown. 'I like the picture, the shape.'

'Maybe, but the colour's depressing. According to Rudolf Steiner's teaching, you see, everything's imbued with spirit and that's what we reflect in our painting. Lightness, fluidity. We are spirits before we come to this earth. Did you know that, if we believe Steiner, human souls choose their parents before they are born?'

'That's mad.' It's out before she can stop herself. She can hear her father's scorn lacing her words. 'What about unwanted children, unhappy children? Did they choose their parents? Would I've chosen you two if I'd been in my right mind, my unborn right mind?'

Hurt darkens the mother's face like a bruise: '*Hou op nou*, Ella. I don't like to hear you talk that way. Those are bad, cruel words, you know it.'

But Ella cannot stop. Suddenly she's seeing something in a clear, un-muddy way, something about how choices loop up in chains, about how one choice follows another in a continuous unbroken sequence.

'If I chose you two, *if* I did,' she says, 'Maybe it's because *she*, your sister, had already chosen him. And before she chose him, her dead babies, those babies Dad told me about, that you've never mentioned, they chose *them*, the two of them. It has to be that way, their choices shaping my choices, my choices joining up with theirs, else it makes no sense. As for me, I'd rather have my soul staying unborn than the thought of choosing the two of you. Especially him.'

'You watch yourself, *meid*, or you'll end up sounding as cross as he does.' The mother folds her arms. 'You don't speak about your dead aunt's sorrow like that. Anyone's sorrow for that matter. You're not your father. You don't have the war to blame.'

She turns the paintings face down, carefully smooths them flat.

'His blue eyes,' she next says, 'He had beautiful blue eyes. I think my sister Ella chose him for his eyes. You may be right there, she chose him. I didn't choose him. But even now, every morning when he opens his eyes, no matter the night before, they look newly washed.'

'And the red bags under the blue eyes?'

'Ella, I insist you stop.' The mother makes a sound like a suppressed sneeze. 'He read, think of that, think of what that meant to me, to us, us girls from a *beschaafde familie*, a civilised family. He had no formal education beyond school but he had stories to tell. He'd seen the world. His world was bigger than mine.'

That night Ella finds a new perspective on her long-hoped-for but till-now-impossible orphanhood. In fact, she decides, leaning on her sill, staring at the stars, she can still be counted as an orphan, or anyway half an orphan. She is born of one dead mother and one live one. She belongs to Africa, her live mother, like her father says, and she belongs to her aunt, the dead one, the woman who fell in love with her father's blue eyes, the mother-aunt who conceived the other babies and prepared the queue for her to join.

Her so-called parents she can leave out of the picture. Her father himself has said it. Their lines of inheritance to her are cut.

The father has always been a zealous economizer. In all things he contrives to cut costs, close to the bone as he can. He goes to the supermarket by himself in order to hunt down bargains: day-old bread priced down to 5 cents is one favourite; a pack of chicken bits at quarter the price of a pack of chicken breasts of similar weight is another. There's a surprising amount of meat on a chicken wing, in his opinion.

Now, following the prostate operation, his zeal is sharpened. He wants a new challenge – to slice in two the family's spending on non-essentials, the little treats with which the mother sentimentally coats her African life, imported biscuits from Holland, doilies and decorative candles for the house. Let's see how lean life can go. The mother is under instruction to keep a ledger notebook in which non-essential expenses at various shops, the Dutch delicatessen, the continental butcher, Ada's Hair Salon, are recorded in red.

'Can't he see I'd be dead but for these things?' she moans.

'*Hou op*, Irene. Your endless *gezeur*! When, ever, are you denied your pleasures?'

To make savings on family grooming, the father invites Ella to cut his hair. Now that she's so tall, towers over his head when he's seated, she can put scissors to his crop. She can go in any old how, he isn't vain. However she goes in, she'll be cheap. And there's another advantage. Lately he's been suffering pains in his legs and arms, the old complaint, sudden tweaking pains due to bad circulation, nothing to do with the prostate. It's tough to sit for too long in one spot. The *kind* can be made to go faster than a barber.

This fortnightly economy, he calculates, will save the family up to ten rand a month, the price of twenty-five cans of Bully Beef. Bully Beef from Argentina, a taste acquired in his Navy days, is his basic measure of saving. If he lets Phineas go home early, he saves four cans of Bully Beef.

Ella tucks a dish towel into his collar, wets her comb in a glass of water, as she has seen the haircutter at Ada's do.

'Style doesn't matter,' he instructs. 'Just shorten it. Slice your way through.'

She thinks of cutting and sewing cloth in Domestic Science. She knows about bias cut as against basic trim, how back-slicing works in relation to scalloping. She understands the different ways in which skeined materials like hair move under the shifting angles of a blade. But the father's hair is coarse and wavy. And her scissors are paper shears he has sharpened on his grinder.

Taking a breath she scythes into the thick tonsure over his left ear. Then she blunt-cuts her way round. His back quiff springs under her hands like steel wool. The silky comb-over she feathers, then layers and fluffs the edges where it serves as his fringe.

She makes a more or less decent job of it, setting aside a step-cut or two behind the ears. She can tell it's not bad because the father looks her in the eye. Let's see, he says, if you can do it again next time.

For days after the haircut the white tufts of the father's hair blow about the lawn in snowy flurries till, she imagines, the wind distributes the stuff across the town like seeds.

The second time she cuts his hair, two weeks later, she's about to bring the scissors to his head when he comes out with a strange word. What was that? She leans forward. *Atro-piss*? She raises the scissors. *Atro-piss*, he blurts again. This time she didn't mistake it.

Atro-piss? she wants to ask. Is it a medium-intensity Dutch swearword, like *rotzooi*, unlike *sodomieter*? But she keeps quiet. She clips the hair on the back of his neck.

Not long after she finds out more. She finds out the father has granted her a special position, a status all her own. One day during silent reading at school she is paging through a reference book on mythology and, there, the name jumps out at her. Atropos, it says, is the fiendish Greek Fate who severs the thread of life with her abhorred shears. Atropos is a daughter of the night, a shape of gathering doom.

To the names *succubus* and *loeder*, which she shares with the mother, the father now adds this one, *Atropos*, which is entirely hers.

The haircuts become a fortnightly Saturday morning fixture carried out without words after coffee on the verandah, before Phineas shows up for work. The father triggers the event by flourishing the paper shears in the air like a starter gun and snipping them. 'Atropos, Atropos,' he says. Ella runs to get the dish-cloth and the comb.

Late one night following a haircut Ella hears the father stammering to himself in the passage outside her bedroom. There's a thud, the sound of a body slumping. She checks her watch, nearly midnight. It was long ago her mother went to bed.

'What is it?' she whispers through the crack in the door. Silence. She draws her back up straight, grips the door handle tight, cranes into the darkness.

The father is crouched on the passage rug, his left leg splayed awkwardly to the side, as if he has fallen very suddenly to his knees. He is clutching the carousel toaster to his chest, a screwdriver in his hand. He sibilates a word, *Atropos* could it be, or maybe just a Dutch swear word? His voice is very indistinct. She bends down, reaches for the screwdriver, but he pulls it away. Sherry pulses off him in syrupy waves.

At breakfast today the toaster's carousel brackets got jammed. He has, it seems, set out to fix them, but his glasses have slipped down his nose and his eyes stare blue and unfocused at the appliance. Pointlessly he rattles the toaster handle. She sees why his speech is choked. A handkerchief is balled in his mouth.

'Dad, what is it?' she asks again.

He spits the handkerchief into his hand, then suddenly begins to talk, a gargled mix of English and Netherlands. His *moeder*, she thinks he says, the one woman who loved me, today, can you believe it, she would've turned one hundred years old.

Ella leans down towards him, he leans away from her. She pulls back. Touching him isn't a risk worth running. As the closing door puffs a thin column of air onto her cheek, he begins to swear under his breath. 'Heartless *kreng*, ungrateful shit,' she hears him mumble, 'Cruel Atropos.'

This time she's sure. He said *Atropos* and not an unfamiliar swear word. The word came at that instant she closed the door.

At school every student is given a pocket-sized Bible, a special gift from the American Bible Society. *Good News for Modern Man* in a green, wipe-clean plastic cover. 'Look,' Ella extracts the book from her satchel that evening. She stands in front of the television and holds it in front of her father's face. 'Something for nothing. I thought you'd be pleased.'

'That's rubbish for nothing,' he says, and knocks the book out of her grasp. 'You chuck that in a parcel for charity, or in the *pul*. We don't have Bibles in this house, certainly not bad translation Bibles. The cheats and lies of Christianity aren't for us. The King James Bible is the only translation we accept. It's a very fine piece of good English. You put that piece of shit in the *pul*.'

Ella slowly picks up the Bible. She places it on top of a mound of coffee grounds in the kitchen pedal-bin, to protect it from the greasier rubbish lower down. This is a terrible thing to do. The librarian at school teaches them to treat books well. Her father follows her to the bin. She can feel his breath on her neck. His hand comes down on top of hers, presses the Bible deeper in.

Late that evening he calls her to the verandah. For a change, she can see, the Old Brown Sherry has softened his mood. His cigarette quietly smokes in his hand.

'*Meid*,' he says, 'Go to the bookshelf there by my desk, and fetch down my King James Bible, the one I had when I was at sea during the war. It's beside *Mathematics for the Million*. Or the *Roget's Thesaurus*. A plain black book, the gold lettering on the spine nearly worn away. There's a thing in there I want to show you. About how death's syncopated by words, beautiful English words.'

The father's special bookshelf – she's allowed to touch? She swallows her surprise. Didn't he just ask her to put the gift Bible in the bin?

'Go on,' he prompts, his eyes on the hills.

Her hands when she holds the book out to him are shaking, can't help it.

He keeps looking ahead. 'Turn to the fourteenth chapter, Book of Job.'

She leafs through the middle; the pages riffle smoothly. She finds *Ezra, Nehemiah, Esther.*

'Hurry up.' He reaches to take the book from her. 'You should be able to find a page quicker than that.'

She looks up. Here it is.

'Good. Then read. Chapter Fourteen is what we read on board ship, when one of the chaps had fallen. Sometimes it was given even to the Dutch boys like me to read.'

'*Man that is born of a woman is of few days, and full of trouble,*' she reads. '*He cometh forth like a flower, and is cut down; he fleeth also as a shadow, and continueth not.*'

She stops for air. She took that second sentence too fast, on a single breath. Stupid. When he's trying to tell her something she must stay steady. She remembers the story of the Japaner warship, the fallen chaps, the six in their sail-cloth – she's eavesdropped on it a hundred times. But her hands still shake. It's what she just saw, couldn't mistake it. The Colt 45 in its beige cloth tucked there behind the King James Bible on his shelf.

Hearing him shift in his chair she resumes. '*But man dieth, and wasteth away: yea, man giveth up the ghost, and where is he?*'

The father sits like a stone. At the end of the chapter she expects a fresh request, something choked, blurted, but there's nothing. His shoulders are hunched. The bags under his eyes glisten in the verandah light. She leaves the Bible on the table. She doesn't want to put it back. She doesn't want to slide it up against the gun lying snug in its gap behind the books.

For whole weekend afternoons, spring, summer, autumn, after Phineas has gone home, Ella lies on her towel, wherever the verandah's sight lines don't reach her. Her mission to merge her freckles by tanning the spaces in between is proceeding steadily if slowly. She is still pale under her swimsuit. In the early evening, before the municipal baths close, she goes swimming, traces fifty, sixty lengths. Till her tan's complete she won't go swimming with Linda. If Linda sees these freckles she'll tell her to stop damaging her skin.

Across the suburban hedges of Braemar, as she lies sunbathing, the sounds of nearby family lives come drifting. In neighbouring gardens there are games of hide-and-go-seek and rounders, high-pitched calls and a rushing of feet, obscure scufflings in the hedges. Brothers and sisters all over, she can hear from her towel, hit balls to one another, talk and whisper, enjoy a playful butting creatureliness that lies beyond her understanding.

She decides to quit reading Mills and Boon. The stories are all the same; the heroines all look alike; even their declarations of love echo one another. The peak of excitement when the girl finally gets the hero takes too long to arrive and anyway is over after just a few pages.

That final Saturday she borrows five Mills and Boon in one go from the town library, stacks them on her sunbathing towel, looks at each one just for the climax. The fourth offers a good twist in the tale where the hero has sound reason to believe that the girl's dead. The reader is with him in his funk. There's been a terrible accident in

170

the mountains. But then, five pages from the end, sure as eggs is eggs, he has the girl. Through a combination of good luck and ingenuity, she has slithered her way to a safe rocky ledge. Ella hardly looks at the fifth book's ending. That's it for Mills and Boon, as far as she's concerned. That's it for Barbara Cartland also.

In a half-used jotter salvaged from the waste-paper bin in her English classroom Ella begins to write her own story, lying on her belly in the grass. She imagines the story will take up about a hundred pages, this at least is her aim: to write one hundred pages to fill the time that Mills and Boon till now took up. The story will be an adventure, not a romance, she decides. She's had it with romances. The story won't be a novel. *Novel* is a grand word she's only ever seen on a label in the library, marking the shelves of the dusty Everyman books.

In her story a girl named Mali, aged fifteen with melty brown eyes, sets out to swim from Dakar, Senegal to the easternmost point of Brazil, the narrowest part of the Atlantic. The story begins with Mali on a flotsam-strewn beach, surrounded by well-wishers. Through a megaphone she announces she wants to achieve something no one else ever has achieved. Though the sea is choppy she strikes out boldly, her face to the horizon. Ella imagines the waves beyond Gorée Island off Dakar lapping Mali's copper shoulders, her hair floating like a cape. She writes the episode twice through, squeezing adjectives into every sentence.

Ella has an idea Mali might be washed off course to Cuba or else die in her attempt on the Atlantic, weighed down by the long plaits that in her vanity she's refused to cut off. However, she – Ella – will leave that decision till she gets to page 100.

Mali's adventure story comes at the expense of her

notebook. The notebook, Ella finds, has become as repetitive as Mills and Boon. Every day it is the same old moan, the same old scene: the father sitting on his verandah, sometimes talking out loud, sometimes not, these days more and more not. Different from the dawn-to-dusk grind of the notebook, the made-up story gives her liberty. With each paragraph, the scene changes, Ella's mood shifts, Mali pushes further and further into the open green sea.

Passions

In Ella's matriculation year the season of tropical storms begins early, in October. There are nightly blackouts. When the thunder storms pass directly overhead, the light fittings in the house spout blue flames. Even in this area accustomed to the cyclones that churn up from the Mozambique Channel, the storms this year feel needling and harsh. By early December the tin roof over the tool-shed, that Phineas recently mended, is pocked with hailstones. The father's new rose bushes, planted by Phineas, have been flattened to the ground.

During the storms, Ella and her father watch the great antlers of lightning cross and clash in the river valley. One stands to the left of the verandah windows, the other to the right. The mother and Bogey are crouched together under the dining table, keening.

'Come away from the window, I beg you two,' the mother moans.

Ella doesn't bother to reply. She cannot bear to look at the mother there on the floor, on her knees, as she used to be on their air trips, the skin on her face pulled tight by fear.

'Shut up, Irene,' the father occasionally bellows over the noise of the thunder.

On the mother's birthday, not long before Christmas, lightning strikes the deodar in the corner of the garden. The tree is the last and the tallest in the line of six deodars that runs down the length of the garden fence. Though wetted through by the driving rain, it burns up in moments, throwing a long plume of orange flame into the sky. As the fire surges to its full height, its pinnacle feathering, the mother begins screaming so loudly the father turns on her, his hand raised. His hand is raised for several moments but he doesn't touch her. Instead he lands Bogey a kick in the ribs that sends the dog sprawling against the skirting board.

On Christmas Eve the mother, the father and Ella are out at the supermarket when another storm strikes. There's less lightning this time, more wind and hail. In the windowless supermarket they barely notice the storm. It just grows very cold. But back home, wherever they look, damage faces them. The deodar closest to the house has had its top snapped off like a matchstick. The falling debris has brought down a corner of the roof. Hailstones have smashed the verandah windows – the broken shards clasp the air like ruined hands. A white drift of hailstones is piled against the mother's beloved piano, laced with glass.

Even the mother is silent when first they survey the scene. Then she makes a dash to the bathroom for her pills. Only later, when she sees the state of the piano, the stained varnish, the mottled keys, a dreadful raw cry escapes her lips.

'Is there a curse on this house, Har?' She grinds her hands together. 'On this family? How many other homes in our area do you see struck as we are, two strikes in one month?'

The father mumbles something about this particular rim of the African shield, their exposed location. Lightning seeks out seams of iron in the high ground, he's read this somewhere. A man's obliged to pay somehow for the privilege of his view.

'Good that we've decided not to have a proper Christmas this year,' he adds. 'What we save not buying presents we can use to mend the roof.'

174

You decided not to have Christmas this year, Ella says out of earshot but out loud.

Though it's a gift-free Christmas, the mother goes ahead and prepares her traditional festive meal of cold garlic chicken, dill-and-potato salad, chilled pears in red wine. Braemar may not be Durban, but here too it can be sultry on Christmas Day. Unluckily, however, the Christmas weekend is extraordinarily grey and chilly. An icy wind blows off the hills still capped in hail. The cold, moist food laid out in the cut-glass Dutch dishes glints nakedly. The pink pears look flayed.

Without a word the father takes his piled plate to the kitchen. Through the mother's remonstrations he shunts the food into a pan and fries it up with curry spices. She drags on his arm, pleads with him to stop. Can't he see he's insulting her? But he is adamant, unflinching. He will and he shall warm up his food. He will and he shall add a dollop of flavour to that dental paste she is trying to pass off as chicken. Cold putrid muck on Christmas Day isn't his idea of festive cheer. He eats his improvised kedgeree straight out of the pan.

'If only we could've predicted,' the mother says sorrowfully. 'Even without presents, without window glass, we could've had cheerful candles, hot gravy with the chicken. We should've bought candles at the shop.'

After dinner they sit in the living room wrapped in blankets watching Fred Astaire and Ginger Rogers movies on television, their skin as blue-veined as the *décolletage* of Aunt Ella in the portrait. The mother has taped bedsheets over the broken windows. The father pours Old Brown Sherry into Ella's water glass, up to the rim.

'That'll chase down your mother's muck and warm you up inside,' he says.

The mother shakes her head but keeps her mouth

closed. She covers her own water glass with her hand.

'A young person should learn how to hold her drink early, Irene,' the father turns to her, his back to Ella. 'Nothing so embarrassing as a woman drunk, a female who cannot hold her drink. Nothing so boring, so dull, as a female who won't have a drink.'

Ella quietly pours the sherry into the mother's potted ferns.

In the New Year, the year Ella will turn sixteen, her English teacher enters her as a school representative in the annual provincial debating competition. She begs to be withdrawn. Try being an understudy, Ella, you may not be called upon. No, please no, I can't. But you're so good at public speaking. Think of your poetry recitations, the prizes you've won. Maybe, but I'm no good at argument, even pretending to argue. She can't meet the teacher's eyes to say this.

Only when faced with her father, she knows, is she the master of argument. Only opposite him does she rise to the occasion, does her voice grow articulate and purposeful, her logic impeccable, her spirit blazing. On what grounds do you say that? she asks him in cold fury, at first mostly in her thoughts, now more and more to his face. His eyes blaze back, his mouth works. She makes her eyes lock with his, she stares him down. On what grounds do you say I'm a succubus, a *nietsnut*? she yells. How do I drain the life-blood from your veins? No one should be spoken of as you speak of me, without reason. Till the day I'm old enough to leave you I'll shout you down when you say these things.

A veil of quiet has fallen over the country now that the township children have gone back to school. Out on the verandah Ella experimentally sniffs the air but the nose-burning smell that drifted on the winter wind has blown away. Things are, if anything, more peaceful than before.

176

At the time when subversives from outside were daily expected in their midst, people were jumpy, alert to hidden threats. Now they know the hidden threats arrived as predicted but were dealt with. Before communist influences could become entrenched the agitators moving amongst the children were targeted and stamped upon. The Prime Minister's ace Terrorism Act sorted them out.

There still are occasional disturbances but they are of a different nature than before, piecemeal and sporadic. There's sabotage to a railway line, a bomb in an empty restaurant. Now and again terrorists are picked up, the announcements are made on the television news, but that's as it should be, the police are doing their job, Minister of Justice Kruger has smashed down his gauntlet of steel. 'They got that arch rabble-rouser the other day,' the father reports one dinner, 'That clever but dangerous doctor from Durban, what's-his-name, Biko. The shock of the arrest thankfully killed the wimp.'

Ella swallows her grimace when he says the word *wimp*.

Lately the cramps in the father's legs and groin make it difficult for him to sit down for more than short stretches so he no longer spends the hours on the verandah that he used to. The night air, he says, doesn't agree with the gripe in his gut, the small of his back. After dinner he stays indoors, watches television. He brings home a brand-new TV set, a colour one this time. Money saved from the non-Christmas, Ella thinks to herself. He watches his new television by pacing in front of it, looking sideways at the screen.

By now he has read the many volumes of Churchill's *History of the Second World War* twice over as well as all the biographies of the war-leader available in the town library. There are no other books to interest him, he says, not in this library, not in any other library anywhere. He intends to quit reading. Frith Fouché's librarian mother

177

recommends a thin book by a man called Conrad, something about a shipping company line operating in the Far East. But the book looks too cloudy and obscure for his taste, he says, short as it is. Maybe it's the murky dust jacket, the wishy-washy watercolour of a steamship. He borrows the book but doesn't open it.

For his birthday Ko sends him the *Collected Short Stories* of W.S. Maugham in a fat, cheap Heinemann Octopus edition with a note scrawled on the title page: *He got it. Ko*

For a few days the father keeps the book open on the coffee table beside his desk and, with his elbows propped on his knees, reads. Then he closes the book and puts it away. Maugham got it, he says, but the world he talks about is past. Conrad's world is past. The men he knew in the East were not all of them as weak-chinned and soft as these fellows make them out to be. Now can he please spend his time watching television, this is his preference, as much television as he likes, the news especially of course, but pretty much everything besides, at all times of day, and after his own fashion, which is to say, pacing, smoking and commenting as he goes?

Sitting in her chair, the jotter with its story about the swimmer Mali on her knee (written to page 49), Ella watches the father watching television, yelling *klootzak* at public figures near and far – that whining lying Mother Teresa, the retarded Minister of Education who cannot string two articulate English words together, namby-pamby Jimmy Carter, those worthless goons of African politicians. The more she watches, the more she becomes convinced. Her father yells out of pleasure, first and foremost, but also to spread his aggravation around. Each and every evening, she's sure, he has a fixed aim, and that is to test to its limits the tiny dimensions of her hardened heart.

One night there is a news report about a terrorist incident

at a power plant. A homemade bomb was found mounted on the plant's perimeter fence.

'Troublemakers,' the father turns on the would-be saboteur the same attack he once made on the African schoolchildren. 'Ne'er-do-wells. Biting the hand that feeds them.'

'What do you mean *troublemakers*?' She won't let him get away with it. 'That's rubbish. Maybe these amateur bomb-layers think the hand that feeds them is pretty stingy. Africans build this country, after all, they do the real work. What reward do they ever get? Half the time the hand that feeds them turns around and hits them also.'

She's on her way, taking him on, staring him down. 'This country rests on African labour, huh?' The father balls his fists at his sides. 'To whom have you been speaking, *meid*? Better consult the people who know a few things. *You cannot help the wage-earner by pulling down the wage-payer.* Abraham Lincoln. That's another source of wisdom you might be listening to.'

'But the wage-earner should be recognized too. It's obvious. The pittance-earner. African people have made this country with their own hands but they own almost nothing, next to nothing.'

'How you drive pins into my eyeballs! That kind of language – where in God's name do you get it from? *It's obvious. Pittance-earner.* Who plants it in you? No normal child could come out with the things you do unprovoked. The Africans are right to try to blow up a power station. That's what you're saying. What tosh, what rot!'

The redness of his face scares her, the shininess of his nose, but still she can't help it, a sound escapes her lips, a half-laugh, a laugh masking as a cough. He rears in front of her, filling her field of vision, grabs her shoulders, fingers digging in. There's hurt somewhere, maybe in her shoulder blades. He pulls her upright and her teeth smack together.

'Enough!' he roars. 'Another word, another sound, and I'll call your school first thing tomorrow to report this conversation. I should do so anyway. It's my duty. To think that in my old age I'd be fighting the Cold War in my own lounge. You're talking to the wrong people, *schepsel*, you're under bad influence. Someone's feeding you this. Someone's getting seditious material through. It's as if I hear Chairman Mao speaking, listening to your rubbish. I want you to give me the names of who you're talking to.'

You're shouting very loudly, she wants to say. My ears are two inches from your mouth. You're shaking me. Can't you hear my teeth go? But she keeps quiet, her shoulders droop in his hands. She feels all used up, her body trembling. Her heart's the opposite of small. It has grown pulpy and swollen with the rage it has absorbed.

The morning after the quarrel about African trouble-makers, Ella snatches a look at the papers lying on her father's desk. He's out of the house, on his weekly visit to the butcher's, followed by a drop-in with Tom and Nobby at the ratepayers' association. She pushes a few loose cuttings about oil sheiks to one side, some foolscap criss-crossed with sums, workings out, not sure what she's looking for. In set-to after set-to he says more or less the same thing: *I should report this. Give me names.* What does it mean? What's he trying to tell her?

A cold finger suddenly presses into her nape. What's this here, this word *Magistrate* in his clear flowing hand written on the memo-pad under the cuttings? A word on a notepad could be an ordinary, everyday reminder, couldn't it? Go to the magistrate's to renew Bogey's dog licence. Check about the new water rates. But she can't be sure, can't convince herself. The opposite might equally apply, her name might be dobbed in, her school alerted. From the photo-comics she used to read she knows about spying, surveillance, the sifting of records. Already, even as she stands here, maybe the library books she has read are being listed and checked, the Brontës, the Mills and Boons. Did she ever leave traces, write in the margins? Soon, very soon, even now, someone could be put on her tail, to follow her home from school, see who might make contact.

Night after night she wakes sweating from the same shadowy dream. She doesn't remember the unfolding of the dream, only its final moments. She's at the bottom of a concrete stairwell, with damp stains on the walls like in the photo-comics, her jotter pressed to her chest, under her t-shirt. There are security policemen in balaclavas surrounding her. They have no badges but still she knows they're policemen and she knows what they're up to. One has her by the hand and is pulling her towards a white van standing by. Worst of all, she's falling into line; she's letting herself be pushed into the van like a lamb.

She lies wide-eyed in bed and tries to think. Puzzle through what might happen if her bad dream turns real. What'll she do when she's dragged from her bed into the white van, from the white van into court? What'll she say? When she comes before the magistrate, when on the strength of nothing more than her father's testimony they charge her with troublemaking, sedition, sabotage, she must have a defence to hand, a believable story. But the problem is that she has no story. She has only the silly adventure tale about the girl, Mali. She has no confession to make, no outside information to give. 'I worked these things out for myself. I never thought the African schoolchildren were up to no good.' How lame. How can she stand up to cross-questioning when she has no story?

She must make up a defence, have it off by heart. Engrave it on her memory like her Eisteddfod poems.

Yes, that's right, she practises, no one has influenced

me, no one. My father's accusation is wrongful: he's a false witness. I implicate no one but myself. Think of it this way, she recites. If in any situation you were made to feel the underdog, wouldn't you then identify with all underdogs, wherever you found them?

But how useless it sounds! She sees herself standing in the magistrate's court telling her story, a row of fed-up faces staring across a polished table. She knows she will fail to convince them, the magistrate and his secretary, the witnesses. She will be found guilty as charged.

At breakfast the mother runs her thumb along the dark rings under her eyes.

'Why not give it a rest for a while, Ella, all the argumentation? You're getting nowhere with it, either of you. You'll never change his mind.'

She puts her face out of reach of the mother's hand.

'You don't know half of what goes on. He's always the one to start. You're never there to see.'

'I can hear it all, unfortunately. The bedroom is well within earshot, as I'm sure the neighbours know, too. And I see how exhausted he gets. You're wearing him down, you know that, don't you, at a time he needs his strength? He has many problems now, the circulation, the groin, the waterworks. The weak heart's the least of it. I won't have you wearing him down.'

Parsley

Hard and shrunken as Ella's heart now is, there is one place, secret, loamy, where it won't go smaller. A strong force pushes at this place, a green, growing shoot that came up quite suddenly and every day stretches taller. This desire to touch and be touched, this sticky persistent desire – this hunger to be beside, against, another body, it threatens her determination to make her heart small.

Touch, touching, being touched – almost all the time, whatever she's doing, reading on the lawn, sitting at her desk at school, Ella tries to imagine the touch of this other body, this face bent to hers. She imagines the hand on her hand and the warm arm leading up from the hand. And, no, it isn't a nameless hand she imagines, or a faceless body. She can see the hand clearly. She can see the arm leading up to the brown sinewy shoulder. She can almost feel this breathing body here nearby her, beside her, close – so close its presence tightens her stomach like a fist.

These two hands, she doesn't mistake them. These two hands in her daydream are ordinary everyday hands, she knows them well. These hands with their long thin fingers are used to pressing tiny seedlings into the earth. She has seen them often, patting the wetted soil around the slender green stems.

It happened before she properly saw it coming, this strong nameless feeling that has grown between herself and Phineas, this lovely dangerous thing. Phineas is, after all, the gardener, the native, the African garden boy. But she herself is African as well as native – way back she proved it. She is flesh of the flesh of all other African creatures and wild things. She and Phineas are of the same flesh.

On Saturdays, Phineas's day in the garden, the father bans Ella from sunbathing. She contrives other ways of being outside, secretly in his vicinity. With the father keeping more to the house, this is often possible. She hangs about and weeds, clips borders, finds jobs that don't get in his way. She's near enough to him to be able to sense his movements around the garden, spot bits of him coming around corners, his hands on the wheelbarrow's handles, the sharp crease that forms in the back of his knees as he bends, hoes.

The thing between herself and Phineas, Ella knows, doesn't come only from her. It's something between them. It has grown from the look they shared that first day she gave him a glass of water. She sees how he tips his head in her direction when she's outdoors. Even the nape of his neck when she moves about the lawn seems alert to her, as if he's always about to turn around to see her. The look they shared that day planted a seed from which this strong green shoot has sprung.

Phineas asks the father if he can please come to work an extra afternoon, Wednesday as well as Saturday. He wants to earn more money to help his family, he says. Plus the garden can do with some extra assistance. Ella overhears his request, feels herself blush.

First love, she wants to write in her notebook. She puts the story of Mali to one side. She has reached page 71, way over the halfway point. Her notebook comes back into its own. She keeps it under her pillow at night. By day, she slides it in alongside her Mali jotter between the *Anne* books on her bookshelf. *The first sign of my first love*, she writes. *In the garden. The look in the garden. The smile.*

What's she doing? She draws her hand back, scribbles out the words she has written.

But the force driving her hands can't be restrained. *The second sign*, she writes. She really must write this down. She's fed up of being a single solitary cell of a person, a single cell with a tiny constricted heart.

This amazing feeling. When he looked over from his side of the flowerbed, when I looked over from mine.

But no, how can she write these things? These bare naked words, they're asking for trouble, begging to be pried at. She draws her hand back.

A passion for the garden boy. Who'd be so mad as to leave evidence?

Then her hand creeps back to the page. She must write something down.

The second sign. Down at the clinic. In our different queues. This incredible thing.

He looked over from his queue, I from mine, at the same moment. The same place at the same time.

First love, she wants again to write. Her hand doesn't move. Isn't first love about being at the same impossible place at the same unlikely time? Isn't that what those Mills and Boons in their different ways were all saying?

Cholera is reported in the African township, three or four cases, with one fatality. The provincial authorities advise the inoculation of the whole of Braemar including the white inhabitants. The contaminated river touches the communities on both sides, the Europeans on the right bank, the Africans on the left.

The mother invites Phineas to accompany them to the clinic in Braemar. Free inoculations are on offer in the African township like in town, but, you never know, Phineas's family may not allow him to go. Especially now that he's working all his extra time in their garden, there may not be the opportunity.

As soon as they arrive at the clinic however, there is a problem, the obvious problem. The main Braemar clinic normally sees only white people. The mother didn't think. The big-bosomed nurse leans across the dispensary ledge rigged up on the lower half of the clinic's stable door. Loudly and slowly she outlines the delicate situation to the mother, as if she did not know English.

Phineas and Ella wait at the car, each leaning at an end, Phineas at the boot, Ella at the bonnet. She doesn't look over at her mother, won't see her being made to squirm. She watches instead how Phineas is making his shoes yawn by prising the loose sole open along the kerb and then folding it back under his heel. He waggles the sole and gapes it at an acute angle, its yawn stretching into a smile. He makes this shape once, twice. Ella smiles, Phineas for an instant smiles, sucks in his cheeks.

The mother returns. She explains that the clinic has been so kind as to agree to set up an extra queue. The official one, the white one, is over here, lined up at the dispensary door. Phineas's queue, comprising the black clinic workers and Phineas, is over on the other side of the clinic yard. They are creating it only because of the emergency. The makeshift dispensary point is that pile of cardboard boxes topped with a plank.

For an hour they wait their turns in their respective queues. Phineas's queue is short but slow-moving, Ella and the mother's long but relatively fast. The scratchy inoculations seem to take more time when it comes to black people.

As things work out, Ella and Phineas reach the inoculation point at the same time. She'll write it in her notebook. *Destiny plaiting us together. The second sign. This incredible amazing feeling.* She looks over at him at the same instant he looks over at her, then they both step forwards. He closes one eye, a slow wink, a sign of solidarity. She's aware of the inoculation going in, the tiny scrubbing brush of serum pressed into her skin, but the sensation is at a distance. At the instant the pain flares up her arm she thinks of Phineas's wink.

Now that Phineas works extra time, the rule about Ella reading on the lawn applies also to Wednesdays. She conjures another way around the father's rule that still means being around Phineas. She thinks up a garden project, something that will legitimately allow her to be outside. She clears a strip of red earth along the side of the house and sets about making a herb garden, a small one that won't require too much digging. The seedlings she buys at the vegetable stall in town, sage, rosemary, thyme, a mixed box, using her haircutting money.

She digs out the patch one Sunday afternoon when she's alone in the garden. The delivery time for the seedlings however she can do nothing about. A garden supplies truck drops them off the following Wednesday before she gets home from school. She finds Phineas already in her patch of opened ground, mulching compost into the clods of soil, the boxes of seedlings laid out in a neat row on the grass. He has followed her train of thought, she's sure of it: he gets the pretext of the garden-within-the-garden. She can't help smiling at him, directly into his face.

From then on, every afternoon that he works, Phineas gives some of his time to the herb garden. The father and the mother notice nothing of this. The cleared patch is in a good, out-of-sight position. And Phineas's work elsewhere in the garden never falls short.

Once, after a bout of rain, locusts attack the sage plants. Ella stands plucking the voracious bodies off the already skeletal leaves and Phineas is suddenly beside her, shaking his head, clicking his tongue in sympathy. He shows her how to pinch the damaged growing points with her thumb-nail. Another time she finds him thinning out the parsley seedlings that have grown tall and bushy because of the storms. Whenever she comes upon him in the herb patch he is hard at work. His hands invite her to join in, demonstrate with firm gestures what to do. As they work, the two of them don't speak. There's no need to speak. Speaking will only draw attention. His arm's alongside her arm, their hands dug into the very same soil.

In her notebook Ella records the stage-by-stage development of the herb garden, but without writing Phineas's name. *Planting*, she writes, alongside the date, then *thinning, sprouting, weeding*, each time alongside the date. Careful, be careful. She wishes she could show him the notes, so he could see how much they've been together, how much they've done. But the book never goes outside with her. A notebook outside would only invite questions.

Something is between them, something is definitely between them. Sitting at her notebook she draws capital letter *P* in bubble script at the top of each page, then scribbles the letters out. She transforms the scribbles into cloud patterns, inky bunches of balloons, so inky you cannot read what lies beneath. The danger she's running is very great, she almost can't imagine how great. But the feeling can't be put away. All the time it presses at her, this hunger to be close to Phineas, to involve him in herself. She squats down and watches him rake between the rows of plants they have just weeded. The green shoot sprouting under her ribs unfurls and stretches up to her neck. She takes the watering can from him and wets the borage they have put in to replace the savaged sage plants. The green shoot drives its roots down through her groin to her knees.

The third sign of my love, she writes. *His gifts.*

Parsley

My love gives me gifts.
Sunshine. Oranges.

These words she doesn't scratch out. So what? she says to her reader on the sly, your suspicions reflect badly on you alone. Who can find me out from what I've written? Who can name my love?

Walking into work from the township Phineas likes to pick up the bits of dried orange peel he finds in the road. Orange peel dropped on the tarmac in the hot summer sun within hours makes dried-up orange chips. By the time he gets to their house he has collected a palm-full, now and then a pocketful.

During breaks from weeding, he digs into his pocket and shares out his orange peel. The pieces of orange lie curled on his palm, each with its papery underlay of pith.

She picks up a piece of peel with the tips of her fingers, taking care not to touch him. If she touched him – she can't imagine . . . The green shoot would run into her brain and bump up against her skull.

There must be a huge amount of this stuff lying about on the streets of Braemar, she says, looking down, You manage to find so much. Children must peel and eat oranges as they go about.

They don't know about the treat they leaving for others, says Phineas, else they will collect what they drop and take it home.

He shows her how best to eat the peel. He puts an orange chip to his lips, waits until she copies him. Then he nibbles the edges of the peel, wetting it, moving it round till all the edges are wetted.

At last, when the peel is soft he pops the whole thing in his mouth and sucks it like a peppermint. She does the same. It's the most surprising treat. The chip floods her mouth with orange pulp sweet as juice.

189

Now that they're talking a little her courage swells.

Phineas, she says, what's your real name, your Zulu name? You must have a Zulu name. He smiles, shakes his head. No, he says, no Zulu name, I don't have a Zulu name. My name is Phineas. You must do, she says, what is it? What do they call you at home? They call me Phineas he says, you know, Phineas from the Bible. Who was with the prophet.

On Sundays Ella takes her notebook with her to sunbathe on the grass, looks at the many new words and lines scattered across its recent pages, the special inky cloud patterns that steam up from them. She loves writing the words, even if she scribbles them out later. Writing, she notices, fuels her courage, dulls her sense of danger.

On her towel she daydreams sometimes about Phineas being here, what he might do if by apparent mistake he turned up to work on a Sunday. She imagines him creeping up behind her to give her a surprise, putting his hands playfully over her eyes like she has seen Aileen the girl-next-door do with her boyfriend. She hears him reading out the words she has written, even the scratched-out ones. *My first love*, he reads. Am I really your first love? She sees him smiling into her eyes. 'Course you are, she whispers, so why don't you tell me your real name?

As far as Ella knows, she has succeeded so far in keeping one of her true physical defects hidden, even from the mother. The *Winkler Prins* encyclopaedia calls it a tongue-tie, a *gebonden tong*. A thread of flesh winged by a thin membrane attaches her tongue to the floor of her mouth.

Till now, the tongue-tie hasn't bothered her much. With some English words it has even helped. To make difficult sounds like *th* her tongue has already been in position, laid fatly across her mouth behind her teeth. But lately, shouting at the father, the tongue-tie has been strained. The pointy bit rooted to the floor of her mouth feels thinned and pulled.

She tries poking around her tongue-tie with some nail scissors. The membrane is very fine. Wounds in the mouth heal fast, people say. But it's no good. It's difficult to grab hold of the slippery tongue. Whenever she does have it caught, pressed to the side of her mouth, the scissors get moist, slide out of her grasp. She makes a tiny nick close to the tie. The place bleeds like a tap.

Could I have the tie looked at? she asks the mother in the kitchen, then the father at table. A loose tongue never suited a respectable woman, he says darkly.

Getting rid of the tongue-tie, she decides, is part and parcel of her project to shrink her heart into a ball. Without the tether on her tongue she will have to work harder to contain her feelings. She will have to be even tougher on her tiny heart.

The throat specialist who examines the tongue-tie forms his mouth into a small round rosebud *o*. His surprised bifocals wink in the light like Oma's used to do.

A very tight tongue-tie indeed, he seems to shake and nod his head at the same time. He advises a routine severing procedure as soon as possible, yes, on Medical Aid, requiring the basic payment only.

The procedure is carried out under local anaesthetic. Ella watches the specialist's lenses dip and wink in the bright light as he works. There is a crunchy tying-up of stitches but no pain. A clot of blood gathers at the back of her throat. She spits it into a white basin, a modern one, running pink water, fitted into the armrest of the operating chair.

She likes her new, freed tongue. In the car on the way home, though its underside is bristling with stitches, she practices reaching her tongue up to her nose, curling it over and under, making clicks. She can try to speak Zulu now, she thinks, she'll ask Phineas for tips. She'll begin by asking him again about his Zulu name, his family name this time. What is the name they call in registration at school?

After a few days the stitches dissolve and leave behind a small scar, a short plait of thickened tissue under her tongue. She likes this, too, the tingling but tender itch when she runs the scar across her teeth.

It is the Sunday morning after the operation, late summer. The white light has robbed the trees and other standing things of their contours. The shimmering fields and hills are drawn on the sky in metallic ink. Ella and her father sit together looking out of the verandah's invisible fourth wall. She's aware of the open door at her back, the breeze blowing through it.

'I called you from your endless inane sunbathing to tell you something,' the father says. He barely releases his lips to speak. 'Been meaning to a while.'

'Yes?' Just right. As deadpan as she wanted.

'You're aware, *kind*, many things are changing for you right now. You're growing up fast. Things'll keep changing rapidly for a while.'

'Well,' she says. 'So?'

'Despite appearances you're a clever girl or, anyway, your school reports tell me so, clever, definitely, but also, like I often say, disobedient, unruly, always against the grain, always. You get good marks even so, even in the subjects that matter, Maths, Science. You get good marks in my beloved English, too, but English doesn't matter, not for life.'

Of course I do well, she responds silently. In her imagination she forms her lips into a *duh* shape, something the *Brady Bunch* kids do on television. Since when did an absence of stupidity equate with following the rules? *Of course* she gets good marks, she wants to say out loud. But she won't help him explain himself. She won't say that if she didn't do well she might as well lie down and cut open her veins with a kitchen knife. Doing well is the way things are; it makes the world steady. No amount of character weakness can take it away.

But the world, according to him, is soon to grow less steady.

'Till now, *meid*, these successes of yours have come naturally.' He moves in his chair. 'What I want you to think about today is – be warned. The situation won't last. Soon, very soon, you'll start to slip backwards. The signs are already clear.'

'What do you mean?' Too late she bites her loosened tongue.

'I mean that soon, in the not-too-distant future, with you growing up, as obstreperous and rebellious as you are, the boys will start to overtake you, in almost everything. You'll no longer do as well as them.'

'Overtake?' The word's out before she has time to stop it. What's wrong with her? She doesn't have to talk to him. Remember the memo-pad. Why's she bothering to reply?

'Law of nature, Ella. Girls at your age, changes happen, they grow more inward. It's not the same for men. At this stage, boys, young men, they come into their powers, they open to the world. Contrary to girls, they see the value of work. Work shapes the world so they devote themselves to it. They start taking over. It's what nature dictates. Women begin to concentrate on the things that come more naturally. The boys, the men, succeed instead.'

Ella can feel her cheeks and mouth stretch, adjust, trying to find a camouflage, an expression of exaggerated surprise.

'I'm serious, my girl,' he shakes his cheeks at her. 'I'm

giving you advice to bear in mind. Mark my words, as boys grow up, their brains better their bodies, overcome them. For girls it's the other way about.'

But brains have nothing to do with changing bodies, she wants to say, cleverness is inbuilt. She has a man's head on her shoulders, a reasoning brain, her father himself has said it.

'So from now on, be on your guard, but give way.' His mouth pulls into a discouraged line. 'This is what my ripe old age teaches me. The boys'll overtake you.'

Ella's nails dig into her palms, her bare toes grip the earthen flags. She knows she should leave the verandah now, right now. The breeze of the open door flows over her back. But no, she cannot leave. She must hit back. Every bone in her body rejects his advice. She must settle for second-best? She's a girl, that's all she can expect? Is he trying to goad her somehow? Is this, God forbid, a jibe about doing the garden with Phineas? But, no, his face is an unmoving mask.

'Why are you telling me this?' she asks, her voice low.

'Why am I telling you this? I'm telling you this because I want you to be forewarned. I want you not to give up all of a sudden when the boys surge forwards, as nature dictates.'

'You think I'll give up because I'm *only* a girl?' Still the words spring into her mouth from nowhere. 'Is that why you don't ever tell me things, because I'm *only* a daughter? Those stories about the war I hear from my bedroom window – yes, I do hear them. You don't entrust me with them because I'm a girl?'

He waits a while before speaking. She gets up, then can't move from the spot. Standing up to him – yet again it took something from her. She struggles to catch her breath, feels the blood whining through her pulses.

'*Kind*, no, that's not true. To whom do I tell my stories –

a few old friends? If I don't tell you my stories, it's because you're— ' He pauses a long while. 'Because they're not for you,' he finally says. 'They're not your world. How many times have I told you my world is closed to you? It's over, and thank God. My stories have nothing to do with the advice I'm patiently trying to give you.'

'But they have everything to do with it, everything!' Her ears ring with the sound of her own voice, high-pitched and screeching. 'You tell more than just your old friends your stories. You tell your new Braemar friends. I've heard you. You write your monthly letters to your brother, though you won't talk to him on the phone. You want to put things on record for Jan, you say. But not for me.'

'*Meid*, listen to yourself. Who'd want to share private matters with you, when you talk to people like this? Truly, your perversity is extensive, it runs in every direction. I'm telling you to rein it in. You only demonstrate the value of my advice. Don't denature yourself, that's what I'm telling you. Act the young woman. Perversity isn't attractive. Splitting hairs, scoring points, and then in that horrible chainsaw voice, it's not attractive. Don't be an unnatural woman, hard and unforgiving, like many women in your mother's family. Don't go resenting men for the qualities that make us who we are.'

Something snaps in her mouth, she feels it go, a stitch, but no, her stitches have already melted. 'Perverse!' she manages to get out, 'Unnatural!' Her tongue contorts to breaking point. Another word, two, three, she's got to spit them out, refute him, but then a bubble of blood, warm and salty, wells from her mouth.

The father reaches across, presses his hand to the side of her face, pushes her to the door. The blood runs over her chin.

'Get inside,' he hisses, pushing, 'You're soiling the floor.

Go, clean yourself up. How are you my daughter? At times like now, who'd want anything to do with you? You're an ungrateful *loeder*, as I've always said. It exhausts me, your infinite waywardness. You're beyond my help.'

'Who needs your help?' she gargles. '*I* don't. I don't need your help.'

He releases her face, flicks his hand and wipes it on his trousers.

'If I'm not your daughter,' she breaks out again, 'then you're not my father. So why don't you just go and die properly, like you always say you will? Then I can show how little I need your help.'

The father pushes her a second time – a harder push, to her arm, held, sustained. She staggers a little, gets over the threshold. The verandah door closes behind her, the glass panes rattling.

For a second she feels deflated. Through the silver sunlight searing the glass in the door she sees him standing, only an arm's length away, his back turned to the house. Against the shimmering hills he looks insubstantial, as if you could break him up with a single breath like a dande-lion clock. But so what? She hates him. His smallness is deceptive. Because of him the screeching demon comes and jumps into her mouth.

A steam train runs three times a day along the branch line that snakes through the green hills connecting Braemar to the surrounding Midlands towns. The branch-line serves the local condensed milk factory. The last train every day transports shiny crates of condensed milk to Durban, the tins stamped with bright blue pictures of fat Friesland cows.

For something to do during the school holidays, Ella and Linda travel with Linda's mother into Maritzburg, the largest of the neighbouring towns. Linda's mother works in John Orr's department store on Church Street. The girls while away the morning looking at the clothes shops, the accessories mainly; the accessories are cheapest. Sometimes they use their pocket money to buy 7-inch singles from the record shop, Boney M, Diana Ross, Gerry Rafferty, Billy Joel. They sample sweets from the clear plastic tubs with hinge lids at the Pic-'n'-Mix counter in OK Bazaars. At the chemist they use the nail varnish testers to paint their nails, each nail a different colour. Linda carries nail polish remover in her small wet-look plastic handbag, so they can remove the colour before they arrive home.

Around noon, they make their way to the railway station. At the bottle store on the station corner they pool their money to buy a 59c bottle of sweet Virginia wine, each time the same bottle with a screw-top just like Old Brown Sherry.

'Watch here,' Ella boasts to Linda as she takes the first slug on the pavement outside. 'This is how my dad tanks it down.'

The wine sloshing noisily in their empty stomachs, the girls buy single tickets for the 12.30 steam-train back to Braemar, then sit and wait on the dusty concrete platform. The train is often late. The Maritzburg platform is wide and long and for some reason is meant to be famous, maybe because it's so wide and long. The wind here is always blowing, eddying discarded plastic bags into the air and twisting them about.

The second time the girls take the train they cadge a cigarette from the group of hollow-eyed white men who sit on the brown platform benches, waiting aimlessly for a train that never seems to arrive, at least not for them. After this they always try to cadge a cigarette. The men offer them the lit cigarettes they are smoking, not cigarettes from the packs in their pockets, but the girls aren't fussy.

197

Hoisting themselves into the puffing train, their high heels chafing, the burning cigarettes held between their brightly manicured fingers, they feel grown-up, carefree, on top of the world. If ever the waiting men try to get closer, give them a leg-up, follow them in, they dash to the nearest empty carriage, their legs fast, strong. They snib the door latch shut, collapse into the soft cracked seats, giggle fit to burst at their so-easy escape.

'Don't you wish there were a couple of guys for us here, though, Ella, some nice guys, not always these old geezers?' Linda one day says.

Ella looks up surprised, mid-giggle, suddenly lost for a reply. Funny how she hadn't noticed before. How they never meet boys their age. But she hadn't noticed of course because there's only one boy she thinks of, only one. Not in a hundred years though, not in a thousand, could she tell Linda his name.

The train begins to blow steam. The disappointed men come knocking at the window, make disgusting shapes with their mouths. But Ella and Linda turn their heads away, still giggling, drain their wine bottle, share the last of the cadged cigarettes. They are so carefree, so independent and rebellious! As the train begins to move, Ella turns back, puts out her new loose tongue at the now-running men.

Beyond the station, around where the houses disappear, they open the carriage windows and hang their heads out, Linda from the front window facing backwards, Ella the other way about. Laura beats time against the glass and they sing in chorus, as loud as they can, 'I want to break free, oh how I want to bre-eak free!' Ella closes her eyes against the wind and tries to make-believe it's Phineas here in the carriage with her, hanging out of the opposite window. *Let's escape somewhere together*, she imagines whispering to him. Would she have the courage, if he was here? She has

198

the courage to stand up to the father, doesn't she? She sees the two of them, Phineas, Ella, tracing together the escape route across Africa she's already traced for herself, across Okavango, the Mountains of the Moon, Kilimanjaro. They're in the Volkswagen Beetle and from the back trails a banner saying something powerful – *Freedom*, perhaps; maybe even *Viva!*

'Do you really want to break free, Ella?' Linda cuts into her thoughts. Ella opens her eyes. Market gardens, dark green bush, sugar cane fields skim past behind Linda's head. 'Oh, yes, I want to break free,' Ella cries back. 'How I want to break free!'

They pull themselves back into the carriage, close the windows, shake the soot from their hair. 'One day I'll do it, I *will* break free,' Ella nods earnestly at Linda.

''Course you will, 'course,' says Linda. 'And so will I. After this year we can leave school, we'll be free. But right now I'm thirsty. Why didn't grown-ups ever say wine makes you thirsty? And tastes bad?'

When Ella gets back from her steam-train trips, her father and mother are often not at home. The father is seeing a dermatologist in Durban who specializes in after-radiation skin treatments and other therapies. He drives himself down twice a week, the mother accompanying him. The father calls the dermatologist the lady doctor though in fact she isn't a trained doctor. He says she has capable hands and honest eyes, features many so-called real doctors do not have. Those hands of hers will bring relief from the full-body itches that now afflict him, he has no doubt. Every visit she puts him through deep-pressure body massages that, for a day or so at least, keep the discomfort at bay.

On their Durban visits, the mother tries to make other appointments, with other specialists, see what might be done about the continuing pains in the father's groin and more recently in his back and kidneys, the many ailments that have broken out since his prostate operation and the radiation treatment that followed. The lady dermatologist believes some of the veins in his legs have collapsed, hence the itches, hence also the extreme cold he suffers, the purple mottled skin.

Each and every time however, an hour or so before they are due to set out for Durban, the father tells the mother to cancel. 'Enough, let them go. Those stupid quacks you like do nothing for me.'

Ella times her steam-train outings to coincide with their absences. She looks forward to the moment she lets herself into the empty house, closes the front door behind her and listens out. Already she knows there'll be no one at home but still it's good to lean against the closed door and feel the silence spread around her like a cool sheet. The rooms are empty, the verandah vacated. There are no voices, no sounds at all.

She goes to change her clothes and brush her teeth. In the bathroom she studies her face in the mirror, surprised each time at how bloodshot the cigarette smoke has turned her eyes, that and hanging out of the train in the wind. The wine makes her groggy but also puts a gloss in her cheeks. She feels warm inside, cheerful, she even looks cheerful. She brings her face closer to the glass. She wonders what Phineas sees when he glances over at her across the herb patch. Would he think she'd look better looking cheerful? Closer up, she sees, the distorting effect of her skew-whiff jaw is less evident. Has he noticed her crookedness? she wonders. What might his idea of a good-looking girl be?

She goes to stand in the narrow gravel passageway that runs between the garage and the boundary hedge separating their property from the Brickhills'. It is her new favourite spot, secluded, out of sight of any window in the house, even the tiny slit windows in the garage wall. Phineas knows the place, too, thinks it safe. He leaves his tools standing here, his rake, his hoe, his spade, leant up in parallel against the mud-spattered wall.

Standing by herself in the passageway Ella swings on the bit of storm-water guttering that slants down from the garage roof at the passage corner. The wine loosens her limbs so she can swing in a bigger arc than usual. Sometimes she rolls her skirt up and tucks it into her pants. She likes how the breeze that always blows along the passage touches the top of her legs. Other times she stands by Phineas's rack of tools and runs her fingers across the handles, the places he has held, the spade, the rake handle, its wood darkened by his sweat.

Not long ago, around the time she began taking train trips with Linda, she tried smoking here in the passageway, practising with a Bic pen holder stuffed with tea leaves. The instant she lit up the father appeared out of nowhere.

'Forget that rubbish, it stinks,' he said, drawing a cigarette from the Rothman's Plain box always standing up straight in his breast pocket beside his Bic. 'Try the real thing. A woman who can't handle her cigarette is as bad as a woman who can't hold her drink.'

It would be good to meet up with Phineas here in the passageway someday, Ella thinks to herself. It would be good and it would be easy. Cross paths with him as if by accident. Watch him go for his tools, then circle the house, walk in from the other end. If he were here with her now, if he were here – she tries to imagine. If he were here they'd smile at each other probably. They always smile. If he were here the narrowness of the passage would force them to stand close together. They'd face each other but not touch, not quite. She thinks of leaning towards him, of him leaning in closer. She thinks of her tongue, her new loose grown-up

201

tongue with its crinkly plait of scar tissue. She thinks of the tip of it, how it might be to touch him with it ever so lightly, say on the cheek. As she thinks this, a powerful current surges from her middle, drives down into her feet.

Then one Saturday she does bump into Phineas in the passageway, genuinely by accident. He's fetching one of his garden tools, she comes walking in from the other end. There was some reason for taking this way around the house but she no longer knows what it is, and it no longer matters.

He straightens up. To go further she must turn her body sideways, sidle past him. She misses the Virginia wine loosening her legs, making their movement smooth. She can either swivel towards him or away from him. She swivels towards him. As she turns towards him he half leans towards her or at least he seems to. His head looms in front of her face, large, bony. She sees his hairline, his close-cut hair, the shiny patch in the middle of his forehead – her eyes close. She can't remember being this near to a boy, a boy's body, ever before. She knows he won't kiss her, it's dangerous, far, far too dangerous – but if she leans towards him? if they are a finger's breadth apart . . . might their noses, their cheeks— ? Her eyes still closed, she imagines his skin, that gleam on it, the tiny raised hairs on his skin, the gooseflesh. He must have gooseflesh because she herself has gooseflesh, sky-high gooseflesh, bringing her in closer . . .

Something will happen to her lungs unless they move. Her chest will cave in, her legs buckle. And then they move. She opens her eyes. She has gone past him. He has leant back against the wall to make room to let her pass. He doesn't look at her but she's sure – she wants to be sure – his lips have dented into a smile.

The story in Ella's jotter about the swimmer Mali crossing the Atlantic has petered out completely. The foam-frilled waves lapping over Mali's drenched plaits as she strikes out stalwartly across yet another choppy mile – they're too many. She's no longer interested in impossible adventures like Mali's. She wants to write about love, properly, truly, about love. The green shoot. The scribbled-out words in her notebook depress her. She turns to other people's lines instead, to find feelings that fit in with her own.

At the town library she leafs through a dog-eared copy of Palgrave's *Golden Treasury*, the only anthology of poems they have. Hardened strips of glue scatter from the spine of the book as she reads. Her notebook is in her pocket. When she finds a line she likes she drops down onto the cork-tiled floor and writes it down in her best handwriting.

But there aren't that many satisfying poems around, not for a girl thinking of a boy. The ones that sound good are mainly desperate and mainly by men. The man in the poem is moaning and sighing about a woman who stands at a distance from him, on a height; he's like Heathcliff throwing his wild cries across the distance. Whereas, with Phineas and herself, well, there's no distance, or at least not that kind of distance. She and Phineas mulch side by side in the garden, they are so close her gooseflesh nearly touches him. She makes-believe she can feel the warmth of the glow coming off his skin.

Five of Shakespeare's sonnets are prescribed as a set text for the matriculation exam in English. Ella reads the poems so many times over she has them off-by-heart. There's a good love-energy powering through the lines though it doesn't work for her, a girl. She can't imagine speaking them to someone. Even if she said *thou art more lovely and more temperate* very softly to herself while squatting beside Phineas in the herb garden, she'd sound a fool, a true *idioot*. If she said the words aloud, he'd probably click his tongue in worry. The problem wouldn't be the Shakespeare, it would be her, speaking that way, in her Eisteddfod voice. Phineas knows about Shakespeare. He's studying *Julius Caesar* for his school-leaving certificate. 'Y'know, I like Mark Antony,' he says. 'I like his power.' She thinks he uses *Y'know* instead of her name.

Ella tries to write her own love poem, but it turns somehow into a poem more about death than about love. She begins at the back of her notebook. Despite her efforts to switch the poem round it follows its own path, presses forward with its own theme. It even insists on being in Dutch, not English. Maybe the solid dark Dutch words work better with the theme. She calls the poem 'Strand', Shore.

'Strand' has two verses and ends on a tail of repeated words. In the first verse a girl, a young woman maybe, is walking along a beach, her footsteps tracing the lacy waterline. She is meant to be thinking about love, the man she loves, but he is not with her and he does not arrive. In the second verse – according to Ella's plan – she sees the man she loves coming towards her, his tall, grey shape enlarging through the sea-haze.

But as things now fall out, the eye of the poem in the second verse takes a different direction. Instead of following the young woman's point of view the poem pans away from her. Suddenly she's seen from high up, as if by a seagull. She is walking the shore, a tiny figure, walking and walking, the waves fanning on the sands in front of her, the waves fanning behind, waves following waves, erasing her footprints in the sand.

Weg

Weg

Weg . . .

the poem closes – the footprints are rubbed away, away, away.

204

Ella ends up liking her headstrong poem, more or less, but puts it to one side. She still wants to write about love. She squints sideways at the scribble patterns in the front of her notebook, unravels some of the words and lines she has written there and joins them together. A poem, a kind of haiku, begins to fall into place.

First love.
In the garden, the gift.
Parsley, sage, thyme, orange peel.
The cool shade along the hedgerow.

The poem's no good but still it captures everything. She doesn't scratch it out. Time spent with Phineas encrypted in word-pictures. Every letter of his name contained within the lines – and, more, every letter of her name embraced also, both in *parsley* and in *orange peel*. The two names jumbled up and mixed together and then fattened with black ink. She must be going soft in the head with love though, because every time she reads the poem she feels weepy. Her heart, after all her efforts, has not grown very small.

Bonfire

The father stockpiles his winter bonfire in secret. When Ella comes round the corner of the house that day, he is standing on the earthen mound in the back garden adding the finishing touches to a tall wigwam of firewood and kindling mounted on a base of bricks, a cigarette stuck between two fingers. Beside him, in spite of the oil shortage, are three large cans of the petrol normally used to fill the lawnmower. It's a Sunday afternoon, the time when the mother takes a long nap. Spotting Ella, the father raises a slack hand, as if giving the signal for a Guy Fawkes show, that doesn't much excite him, to begin.

She approaches slowly, ready at any minute to be warned off, but the warning doesn't come. Alongside the basic bonfire ingredients, she sees he's made a pile of his photograph albums, the ones with black pages in brown leather-look cardboard covers successively entitled *Har B: Singapore, I, II. Har B: Tjerk Hiddes I, II.* The four albums, as far as she last knew, were standing in numerical order alongside *Mathematics for the Million* on the bookshelf near his desk.

'Not for you, no, not yet, maybe never,' he said years ago, one day when she reached up to touch them.

The albums are balanced on top of a large Old Brown Sherry box crammed full of paper junk, ledger books, old newspapers, cardboard folders in faded colours marked with the looped initials *GB*, *G* for Gerhardus, Har. Out of a corner of the box juts a green Chinese paper lampshade. 'Enough kindling for a good blaze,' is the first thing he says when she faces him across the firewood. His gnarled knuckle taps the screw-top of a petrol can. He must've poured about a can-full over the wood already. The air's acrid with the smell. Mysteriously he now switches into Dutch, 'You've come at the right moment.'

It's an invitation to a conspiracy, that's obvious. She has stumbled upon his covert operation, so he has no choice, must invite her on board. She says nothing, only stands up straighter.

He takes a match from the Lion matchbox in his shirt pocket, the box poking out like a pot belly beside the pack of Rothman's Plain. With a thumb pressed to the base of the match, he strikes it, bends forwards, throws it from waist-level onto the wood.

The match catches the kindling almost at once, but still he follows it with several more, until the rising flames begin to dance around his hands.

'Look how it burns!' he laughs out loud, in English, his body still bent.

She points at the Old Brown Sherry box. 'You want to put that on?'

His finger is at his fleshless lips: not yet. 'The fire is hottest when it's mainly grey coals.'

A white column of woodsmoke stretches up from the fire into the windless air. Something about the thickening of the column gives him the signal to begin. He squints up at the rising smoke, checks around the garden, then reaches for the album at the top of his pile. He opens to one of the pages he has marked with neat spindles of newspaper. Swiftly, methodically, he begins to pluck photographs from the triangular white fasteners fixed at their corners, then throws them into the fire in bunches. There's no mistaking his desire to see them reduced to ash, these 2×3 inch black and white windows onto places with palm trees where, as far as Ella can make out from this angle, everyone wears starched ironed cotton, sharply etched pleats. She watches them whisk past, pictures of men in boxy suits posed beside chunky 1930s cars, women in pale tea-dresses standing in groups of two and three on a crowded marine parade.

Who were they, she wonders staring, these cheerful young men and their female companions, presumably friends and colleagues of the young Har B? What future were they looking ahead to as they stared into Har's chunky Kodak with their pale forthright eyes? Whatever they thought then though, today they are posing in vain. Their time is over. A running ribbon of ash crumbles the edges of their fine colonial outfitter suits.

'Dead, all dead,' the father says, his hand winnowing, chucking, winnowing. 'All gone, all gone.' He tosses the denuded album carelessly to the ground, as if the memory of how he kept it for decades sitting on its shelf has been blotted out.

A rogue photo drifts to the edge of the embers, close to Ella's feet. It shows a glossy-haired woman by herself at a café, wearing a panama hat too big for her, pitched half over her left eye. Ella makes to edge the toe of her shoe over the photo but the father suddenly starts, glances across. She freezes. With her foot she shoves the photo into the base of the fire.

He turns now to the faded folders marked with his initials, upends one over the middle of the fire, lets its contents spill out.

'All gone, all gone,' he repeats, 'No use to anyone. All dead, all gone.'

'Ko isn't gone, you aren't gone.'

'Gone in all but body, *meid*, and the body'll soon follow.'

Bonfire

Updrafts scatter some of the blackened photographs onto the grass. Pale ovals of faces stare up from half-incinerated pictures. The father takes a rake and roughly pulls the fragments back towards the flames.

'Come,' he says, poking her side with the spine of a fresh album, 'Lend a hand. Don't stand there goggling. You know how I hate it when you goggle. Everything must burn, the marked sections especially. Tear the whole page out if necessary, tear chunks of pages.'

He pours more petrol. The flames sizzle lower, flare again.

Ella rips at her first album, *Singapore II*. A fistful of paper and photographs comes away in her hand. She doesn't bother about the marked pages. There's a satisfying give and tear as the seam along the album's spine splits open. She sees more palm-lined streets, more people in groups dwarfed by dense banks of vegetation, tall trees, creepers, flowering shrubs, a large open green. There are pictures of docks and pictures on board ship, many pictures on board ship, snapped from various angles on deck, on the gangplank. She sees three women in wide skirts sitting on the wooden barrier to a paved esplanade, two are European, one is Chinese or Chinese-looking. They are all three waving. The Chinese-looking woman might be the person in the picture with the Panama hat. She has the same wide smile.

'All this?' she asks, holding the album open at the photograph of the women.

'All of it,' the father says without looking. 'Don't throw from up high, will you, don't let things scatter. Make sure it burns. All of it must burn.'

He feeds the contents of a second folder into the fire. The stack of opened green and blue air letters fans wide as it descends, one style of handwriting unfurling from the next. Straightaway the bonfire doubles in size. The heat is tremendous. She keeps on with the photograph albums; the father sticks to the folders. Most of the folders are filled with letters, she sees looking across. One folder is stuffed with newspaper cuttings, from Australian papers, it seems, the *West Australian*, the *Northern Territory News*. Out of the corner of her eye she sees the familiar words *Tjerk Hiddes* and then also Fremantle, Geraldton, Darwin, Carpentaria, East Timor. She wants to say, Look! but then it is too late. The folder's in flames. A brown mirage billows at eye level. The late sun's glow backlights the rising heat.

The face of a woman with crimped hair and pencilled eyebrows falls from her hand, whooshes high into the air, wafts back down. Caught in the fire's heat, her glossy smile crumples in an instant, as if she were suddenly in tears. Who was that? Ella wonders. It was a different face from the one in the Panama hat. Was it perhaps the wife before Aunt Ella, the first or the second, if she's not mistaken, Edith the English rose? It wasn't the woman in the portrait.

But there's no time to think. As the photograph dissolves in mid-air the father hoots out loud, a weird, feverish sound. It sets them both off. With renewed energy they swoop at the diminishing load of paper junk in the Old Brown Sherry box, ram the fire with their offerings, hoot, yodel. The father quits his pretence of trying to be quiet. Keep watch, Ella reminds herself, be careful. The times when he's exuberant things can quickly go bad.

From the back of the last photo-album she's shaking over the fire falls a single thin leaf of paper, a pale blue air letter. It wafts down so slowly she can read the printed-on stamp, 1950 something. She could pluck it from the air without him even noticing. Her eyes meet the back of his head bent over his box, his hand on the Chinese lampshade. She holds her breath, quickly takes the air letter, shoves it up her sleeve.

210

At some point deep into the burning she sees the father's To Do memo-pad curve its way into the blue flames. The pad must've been at the bottom of the box. Though the mirage over the fire warps her vision, she'd spot the shape of it anywhere, that plastic ring-binding turning through the air. For an instant she allows herself a silent whoop of freedom, as if caught on an updraft like one of the drifting photographs. But then she catches the father's look. In the glare of the mirage he seems to cock his head and wink, not directly at her, but at someone standing behind her, as if to say to this third party, Take care, we're not alone. It's the same when he looks in the direction of Aunt Ella's portrait, yet not quite at it, to the side. Or when, after a night of rowing, he smiles into the distance over the top of the carousel toaster at breakfast. Everything's meant to be all right again but at the same time nothing is.

'Burn, baby, burn,' she now says loudly. She must put away somehow the sight of that odd wink. 'Dad, wait, a second, there's something – ' she steps away from the fire, darts to the kitchen door. Within moments she's back from her bedroom, her notebook with its fattened scribbles tucked under her shirt, folded into a newspaper for camouflage. 'Just a bit more kindling,' she shouts, holds her arms up high, drops the loaded newspaper into the heart of the fire, where the coals are dark orange. She agrees with her father. Let it all go up in flames. What better place to safeguard her secrets? 'Dad, can we do this every Sunday?' And then she sees. *Oh no.* As the burning newspaper curls back and chars, it's the recycled jotter with Mali's story in the back she finds burning, not her ink-blotted notebook. In her hurry she pulled the wrong book off her bookshelf, stuffed it into the newspaper without looking. She feels suddenly dizzy. A swirl of smoke sears her eyes.

'It's not every Sunday we'd have this much good stuff

to burn,' her father says. 'But you've done well, *kind*, for a change, you've been an excellent help. You're too wilful for your own good, perverse in the extreme, but today it was of use. I want you to take care to step in and help at other times too, when I'm no longer around to assist you.'

Ella feels her hot cheeks flush up redder.

The bonfire takes nearly three hours to work its way through the father's photographs and papers. At the end, capitalizing on the fine blaze, he adds the skeletons of the ripped albums. A white medallion forms on the burnt ground, shiny with melted glue. The charred frame of the Chinese lampshade pokes up from the ashes like a skeletal top hat.

'This afternoon I took the opportunity of using those hedge-cuttings Phineas did to burn some waste,' the father says lightly at the dinner table that evening. His face is clear, his eyes unblurred.

The mother nods but makes no other reply. Her eyelids are still swollen from her nap.

Later under the bedcovers Ella reads through the air letter she secretly plucked from the bonfire. She takes her bedside lamp in with her. Several times she pushes back the covers to listen out, check no one's coming. There are two different kinds of handwriting on the air letter – she holds it close to her face. There is the letter proper which is in a fine sloping hand; then a few lines in a darker ink dashed across the bottom right-hand corner. The careful, awkward phrases of the formal letter take up only half the page. A friend in Singapore has heard of Har's loss, his dear wife's death from cancer. That he could not be with her at the end, it's such a great sorrow. The signature is two Chinese characters, two complicated nets.

The darker scrawl across the bottom of the page says more. The Durban address on the air letter has been written in the same heavy irregular hand. It's someone who seems to know Har well, one of the Far Eastern *makkers*. The friend writes that just the other day, at the start of his holiday in their dear old Singapore, he bumped of all people into Nancy Leong. He was wandering across the *padang* Har'll remember so well, nothing doing, and there she suddenly was, just as if she'd been shadowing him, the splendid Nancy with her fine Chinese eyes, remember, how she presided over the trellised verandah of the Great World? We always did wonder what'd happened to her, after the War. Well, here she was, in the flesh, looking much as she ever did, and very sorry to hear your news.

Why not write to her, Har? The scrawl ends on a question. She really did still seem to feel for the old days, and, God, that incomparable voice of hers, like whipped cream. Only her hair was different, shingled like a European's, a little like that style you find in Durban, you know, the women at your club. It made her look familiar, if you get my drift, with the dark eyes, short hair, the waves set close to her face. You'll allow me to say it, she looked not unlike . . .

Ella pushes the covers down to her waist, scrunches up the air letter in her hand. The name scrawled at the bottom of the paper is indecipherable. Her cheeks are once again red-hot. Why did she take the letter? She shouldn't have read it. She should've let it go into the fire along with the rest, her father's things, those drifting photographs, her jotter . . . Her incriminating notebook, too, that should have gone, though here it still is, she can feel it, its flat hardness right here under her pillow.

She lies staring at the ceiling, eyes wide-open. Whenever she closes her eyes she sees again the brand of the bonfire behind her lids. She hears the mother stir softly in the main bedroom, her father go to bed at last. She waits another hour, then puts on socks, tiptoes to the living room. Tonight the light below the portrait is off. She resists looking across at its blue rectangle. In the darkness she pats her way along the wall, reaches her father's bookshelf. Yes, here are the gaps where the photo albums always stood. She locates the fatness of the King James Bible. She pulls the book out and it's as she suspected. The Colt 45 in its cloth is gone from its hiding place. It can't have joined the files in the bonfire, she's almost sure. How can you burn a gun? But the weapon has left the house, of that she's certain. The bonfire is tied up somehow with its going.

The next morning Ella borrows Linda's matches on the way into school and burns the air letter in the scummy girls' toilets beyond the science labs, where no one ever goes. Her notebook she leaves in its usual hiding place. She will have to think more carefully about how to deal with it. It'll need a proper fire like her father's to reduce it to ash.

The father's bonfire gives Ella the idea to have a clean-up of her own. She will strip away her accumulated stuff around the house, the dusty bits and pieces she no longer has a use for. She asks if Phineas might help her with the job, a half-hour each Saturday for maybe a couple of weeks. She wants to clear out the storage area at the back of the garage, she explains, where the cardboard boxes of unused kitchen-ware from Holland are stacked, the croquette maker, the Frisian potato masher. First, though, she wants to deal with the thing that takes up the most room, her old doll's house under its dust sheet. She hasn't played with it in years.

The bonfire has brought a new fixed look to her father's eyes, as if the mirage had cooked them. At her question about the doll's house the look briefly sharpens, but still he agrees. Yes, it'll be good to have more room in the garage. Phineas can help her, yes, though not for long. This time of year, with winter coming on, there's a lot of clearing—

Alone with Phineas, she thinks to herself. *Alone*. Between four walls. With her Dad's permission. It's a treat he doesn't even know he's giving. She goes to the garage to take a look at the doll's house.

Years ago, for her eighth birthday, the year after the Remedial Class, the father made her this big single-storey doll's house. He'd spotted a pile of off-cut masonite on sale at Big Dave's, Braemar's hardware shop. It recalled to him that carpentry course he did after the war, during the slow time after demobilization, when there was no work in his fatherland to be had—

The doll's house became his early retirement project. Every feature and detail of the thing he set about designing and then sanding, planing, dovetailing and painting, even the furniture. Using perspex and tiny pulleys he constructed sash windows for the bedrooms. He made a separate bathroom with a wooden bath; he carved a toilet. He used pipe cleaners to make a hatstand, a trouser-press. It was the first trouser-press Ella had ever seen. She had to ask what it was. All the doors he gave handles, round handles to match the handles on the chests of drawers which he also made.

But the best feature he designed, in his view, was the elevation of the house. He called it the perspective. The doll's house was a bungalow, just as all good houses in South Africa were bungalows. Their square Durban bungalow could have been its template. So instead of opening at the front like a cupboard, as in a traditional doll's house, this doll's house opened from the top. The roof lifted right off and was as realistic a roof as could be imagined, with a double chimney and cardboard roof tiles, each separately painted and pasted on in a staggered pattern, as on a proper roof.

On the morning of her eighth birthday the father helped Ella lift first the dust sheet and then the roof off her new doll's house. She stood by speechless, lost for something to say, looking at the tiny, tidy rooms, the perfect miniature furniture. She didn't dare touch. What if she spoiled something by mistake? Her hands were large, clumsy, her arms huge. She might squash the furniture just by holding it.

'Bend down to it,' the father said at last, 'And mind I see you play with it. I worked on that more hours than I want to remember. It was a big graft.'

But he hadn't thought that this best-designed of the house's features, the pitched roof, was also the thing that made it most difficult to play with. The pitched roof was too heavy and too wide for Ella easily to lift by herself. Each time she wanted to play with her doll's house she had to ask for help to remove the roof. Before long the roof was never off the house. Then the cover sheet was put back on. The father didn't want to be reminded of his design flaw. 'Come, let's store the thing in the garage. I don't like to see it staring at me.'

This will be *her* big graft, Ella says to herself, pulling the dust sheet to one side, peering into the small sash windows: the redistribution of the doll's house and its contents so that other children will be able to play with it. She will hand out the furniture in stages, this is her plan, the chests of drawers, wire lamp-stands, bathroom fittings, trouser-press. She has collected used cardboard boxes for the purpose. She will keep the things in their separate room categories. Bit by bit she will take the house apart, see if the walls come away, the sash windows, the doors on their little hinges. She will add the matching walls and windows to each shoebox lot. Then, one by one, this is the second stage of her plan, Phineas will carry the boxes filled with doll's house pieces back to the township. She will ask him to do this. He can't say no to such an excellent idea. She will tell him to hand out the things lot by lot, the bedroom then the kitchen then the living room, share them amongst his family and friends, till everything's given away.

Phineas today is taking his time joining in, however. She asked him to help at least an hour ago; he has only now pitched up. Here he is, standing in the garage entrance blocking out the light. She can hear him shifting his weight from one foot to another, chipping at a mark on the wall with his fingernail. Something doesn't feel right to him, she can tell. The sight of the doll's house with its dust sheet removed seems to put him off. She stops herself from looking round to see his face.

They must lift the roof together, she gestures. It still is awkward for her to lift on her own, not too heavy now but still too wide for her arms. The roof sails through the air. Phineas has got hold of it unassisted, walks outside with it. She hears him lay it on the grass, a soft thump. He's out there a while. She begins to put some of the smaller bits of living room furniture into an empty box, the lamp-stands, the stools made from wooden beads. But her curiosity defeats her. What's he up to out there in the sunshine? She finds him kneeling in the grass beside the doll's house roof, bent over it, no, poring over it, his nose almost stuck to the painted roof tiles.

He holds balanced on a fingertip a tile that has come loose. Your father made these, he paint these? She shrugs a yes. For some reason she can't meet his eye.

In the shady mouth of the garage he rejoins her, his tall shape once again standing against the light. She finishes clearing the living room of furniture, then tests the room's dividing walls. They come away smoothly, which is one obstacle less to deal with. Her father has made them so that they fit into narrow grooves cut into the main frame of the house and this means that dismantling the structure won't damage it. The whole doll's house, or at least the rooms and wall minus the roof, could be folded away like a Jacob's ladder into the pieces of masonite it was originally made of.

Phineas comes closer. He's standing right behind her, still, unmoving. For some reason he doesn't want to help her, that's obvious. Well, she's not going to say anything; she's not going to look up. If he has better things to do he should go and do them. It's his decision. The job's anyway not as big as she'd imagined. And they have next Saturday. Next Saturday they can make a fresh start, work together like before.

Keep them, Phineas suddenly says. He picks up the shoebox standing beside the one she has already filled. So far she has put just a few things in it, the wire-built kitchen sink, the stuck-together matchboxes painted to look like a fridge. He lays the box in her lap, presses down on it. Keep them, your father made them, they're not to give away.

But no one uses them now, no one plays with them. She returns the box to the ground. It's better for them to be played with. See, your father made them, he says again. Is better you keep them. No, no, she tries to laugh it off, is better other children play with them. Children in the township, he shakes his head, when have they seen a house like this, with four rooms, when do they see furniture like this? They don't know what to do with this, don't know how to play with it. Well, they can see it now, enjoy it now, when you give it to them. They can find ways of playing with it. No, no, no, he's shaking his head again. All will be separated. How can any one child enjoy? So it's better here. Keep it together. Your father, he made it, he made everything. Don't give it away.

Ella draws herself up, looks into his face. He looks straight back.

What do you mean my father made it? What's so special? It's years ago now.

218

Phineas's eyes come in closer. It *is* special, yes, he could not make them now. He's too tired now, he's sick now.

Phineas fits the dividing wall Ella removed back into its groove. Then he goes out to fetch the roof. Without a word he places it back on the house. He shakes out the dust sheet, covers the roof with it. He puts the lids on the two shoeboxes containing furniture. The one with the kitchen fittings he gives back to her. The filled-up box he places beside the school blazer he always leaves lying folded at the garage door. He straightens up, the light in the garage shifts, he is gone.

Ella goes to wash her dusty hands at the kitchen sink. Out of the window she sees Phineas raking dead leaves in the old dahlia patch. The sharp crease in the back of his knees as he bends, how it makes her breath catch in her throat.

The following Saturday Phineas stands waiting for her at the garage door when she comes out of the house. The moment she sees him he begins to walk towards the passageway where he leaves his tools. He looks back once over his shoulder, expecting her to follow. At the storm-water guttering he waits. She comes to stand in front of him and without a word he takes her by the wrist. *Skin on my skin*. She forces her hand to droop, see if his hand will slide downwards, but his grip is too tight for her to nudge him. The sweat in his palm, she feels its wetness, the rub of the dirt on his fingers.

You like me too much, he loud-whispers, glancing over her shoulder towards the house. Don't. Don't keep coming around me, liking me.

What do you mean?

It can't – Not possible. Not good. He glances again.

For me, it's good.

He shakes his head fiercely. No, not good. Y'know what is better, an open fight with a clear enemy.

Better than what?

Than trouble.

What trouble?

We submit or we fight. His chin makes a circle in the direction of the house. For me, I go somewhere away— The township, my people there. We – no good. Your father doesn't like it.

My father doesn't like much. He doesn't much like me.

He is your father. There is work. His hand drops her wrist and suddenly he averts his face. She has to step back. Something about the movement of his head makes her do it. If we— he breaks off, moves into the passageway. I will be in gaol, shot like a dog. I cannot work for my people.

His tools, she suddenly notices, are no longer lined up against the mud-spattered passageway wall as they always were before. In fact they are nowhere to be seen.

The father is not very well. It must be so, because for the first time he's saying it. 'No, I'm not feeling too good,' he says. Most of the time he's bent over in a right-angle, his fingers dug into his groin. According to his doctor, the one he chose years ago for being undemonstrative, 'minor settlement issues' have belatedly arisen following the prostate operation. The father should make sure to take more exercise, he advises, stretch and ease his lower half. The mother encourages him to go on short walks around Braemar. Ella should go along, keep him company.

The walks are not a success. The father sets out reluctantly, Ella dawdles a short distance behind. If he can't see her, she calculates, he'll be less intent on barking out instructions: Make yourself useful, Pick up those plastic bags.

From the first outing it's clear that the walks are too demanding. Sometimes at the first corner, always by the end of Ridge Road, cramp grips his legs. He bends over, studies the pavement grass in front of his feet, rubs his thighs. But this bent position isn't good for him. Suddenly it's as if he is caught in the clutches of evil urchins. His insides make terrible noises. He holds his backside, moans, twists from side to side. Several times he's taken by such urgency he must drag down his shorts and squat where he stands, as close to a tree or a bush as he can make it. Ella standing sentinel can barely breathe for embarrassment.

Back in their garden, she helps him clean himself up. He stands in his boxer shorts facing the lemon tree in its sheltered sunny corner, turns the garden hose to full strength, hands it to her. It's her job to use the hard adze of its stream to scour the dirt off his purple legs. For good measure she soaks the seat of his boxer shorts also.

She tries to keep her eyes averted but still she can't help noticing how very black the matter is that runs down his legs into the grass, strong-smelling, too, but not in the way you'd expect. More like raw nicotine than anything, a dirty ashtray.

She passes none of this on. If the father wants to complain, that's his business. But he doesn't want to complain. When he hands her the garden hose he puts his finger to his lips. *Shhh*, let's not worry your mother. Ella finds no reason to disagree.

She becomes aware that the mother is often on the telephone in the bedroom, whispering. The bedroom door is closed, the whisper is at a strange high pitch. This isn't as it should be. International telephone calls these days go by satellite but they still cost money. Even local calls cost money. Their telephone isn't used unless absolutely necessary.

Passing the door she hears her mother saying the name Ko. She stops, listens harder. Ko, Ko, Ko, her mother

221

says. This is even less as it should be. Ko is the father's occasional visitor, the long-time, long-distance friend who writes from faraway addresses, Haarlem, Singapore, Perth, Madagascar. Ko doesn't phone, he doesn't talk on the telephone to the mother.

But here the mother is saying Ko, Ko, Ko. 'Ko, everything seems to be coming out of him, the moods, rages, everything. There's no stopping it, Ko. It's as if there's an internal sickness, not the prostate, but something else, forcing its way out.'

Ko tries to say something back but the line to Madagascar or wherever must be crackly. 'What was that you said, Ko?' she shouts. 'Old before our time, is that what you said? Old, was it, or sold?'

In the window of Big Dave's the father sees a second-hand fibreglass motorboat on sale, R 50 only. He buys it on the spot.

'Nothing like burning up some petrol,' he says to no one in particular at dinner time. 'Nothing like being on a boat on a bit of water.'

The motorboat is a smart little vessel, white, lightweight and portable, with a single cross plank for its lone skipper and perhaps one passenger squeezed up beside him.

Big Dave takes the boat out to Victory Dam in his truck and leaves it in the free concrete area to the side of the marina 'for your convenience'. So Mr B can go and use his new boat whenever he feels like it.

The outboard motor for the motorboat however is extra. In fact it costs ten times as much as the motorboat, and must be picked up at a later date from Big Dave's second cousin's husband's motor workshop. This is something which the *For Sale* sign in the window didn't enlarge on, but the father pretends to ignore the discrepancy. If he's been done out of a bargain, whether by Big Dave or anyone, he'd be the last man in the world to let on.

'Can't wait to have that swell and rock of the water under my feet,' he says the Sunday they drive out, the mother, the father, Ella and Bogey, to unite the motor with the motorboat.

It doesn't suit him to act cheerful, Ella thinks sourly in the backseat, Bogey panting wetly into her face. Pretending to be cheerful the father only ever ends up sounding displeased. Why'd she come on this mad trip? – only because the mother begged. The boat's a mad idea, in her opinion. Sit up in it anything less than straight and it'll capsize. And the father these days doesn't sit up straight.

En route they fill the outboard motor at the BP station with one-and-a-half cans of lawnmower petrol. The sunlight smashes down on their bent backs. It's a hot winter's day. A searing wind is blowing off the hills.

'It'll be like burning hell out on the water,' says the mother. 'Don't kill yourself with this boat, Har. Please spare me that.'

Like the lawnmower, the outboard motor is started using a ripcord. But for over a year now the father hasn't been able to start the lawnmower on his own. He has relied on Phineas. Some able-bodied man at the marina, he'd hoped, buying the boat, might be able to lend a hand launching it. Till today however he hadn't bargained for the fact that the boat is in every way a solo affair. It comfortably seats only one person. And that means the motorboat's operator must be inside the boat sitting on the transverse plank to start it.

Ella offers to place the boat in the water at the jetty. Her sandals are already off. Isn't it fibreglass, light as a feather? The mother holding Bogey in her lap watches from the car, her hands occasionally raised in exclamation marks of exasperation. See, Ella points out, you hold it steady, Dad, and I get it going. Then I jump out into the water, hand it over to you.

But the father is unconvinced. He doesn't want her to go shooting off on her own across the dam like an *idioot*. It's not the risk of losing the boat but the danger to others out on the water. 'A boat like this, any boat in fact, it's for people with experience.' His shoes are still firmly on.

The following Saturday the father and Ella take Phineas with them to the Victory Dam marina. The mother stays at home with Bogey. Phineas no sooner took off his school blazer this morning and laid it folded by the garage door than the invitation popped from the father's mouth. Since the day they wrote the letter to Mr Brezhnev Ella can't remember him looking so bemused.

On the way to the dam Phineas sits in the backseat of the car, in Ella's place. She's in the passenger seat. The whole way no one says a word but every minute of the journey she can sense him there behind her, his height blocking the light of the back window, his bony knees digging into the back of her seat. At the BP station they stop and collect an extra can of petrol. The petrol they bought last weekend sloshes untouched in the outboard tank. Again no one says a word. Again the sun beats down. When they get back into the car it's very warm. Ella thinks she can feel the heat spreading out from Phineas's body.

'That's just our garden help,' the father thumbs over his shoulder at the entrance-gate to the dam. 'Come to help with a difficult engine.'

The uniformed black man at the boom throws a gloomy frown at Phineas, waves them through.

Phineas has probably never been to Victory Dam before, or any watersports resort for that matter, Ella guesses. However he embraces the experience as if he's never done anything in his life other than launch small unseaworthy boats in dams. They park at the free area beside the marina, he spots their motorboat straightaway, the small flat one. He points, looks at the father for confirmation, swings the outboard motor out of the boot.

'That's my boy.' The father emerges from the car at a 90 degree angle, his fingers grasping his sides.

Phineas carries the boat into the water, his trousers rolled to the knee. He examines the steering stick, checks the starter mechanism. Ella stands at the water's edge shading her eyes, her bare toes in the mud. The snide thought comes from nowhere, taking her by surprise. How he manages it, she thinks, pretending he's in charge when he probably can't even swim.

She sees Phineas turn back to the shore, his hand resting on the motor. She waves, he doesn't. His eyes aren't looking for her. He finds the father standing on the jetty watching him, the water just wetting his shoes, the extra can of petrol in his hand. Phineas raises his arm, then leaves the boat dobbing by itself, strides through the water, bodily picks up the father, strides out again, plants him on the motorboat seat still holding the petrol can. There and back in an instant. Then, lightly, so lightly the boat hardly rocks, he vaults up, levers himself in behind him. He is sitting in the bottom of the boat, his head and shoulders just visible, the peaks of his knees.

To start the outboard motor, the ripcord must be pulled out to its fullest extent, again and again. The father could never have done it by himself. Phineas twists back, then leans far forwards like a rower, twice, three, four times. Finally, with a throaty cough, as if recovering itself, the boat shoots out across the dam, its comical round stern lifted out of the waves, pointed to the surrounding hills, the shirts of the two skippers billowing like spinnakers.

For an hour Ella watches the two of them, the father

and Phineas, trace white circles on the glittery surface of Victory Dam, a few widening loops in one direction and then a figure of eight and a few loops in the other direction. Round and round they go as if it was the best lark in the world, as if there were two and not just one teenage boy in the boat acting silly. Once she sees them stop for Phineas to refill the outboard tank. The boat rocks crazily. The second time they stop it is dead close to the shore, the petrol's all used up.

She waits for the waves to push them far enough in, then wades out to drag them to the jetty. The father looks about as windswept and pleased with himself as Phineas. He's experiencing discomfort, she can tell, he's white about the eyes, but his lips aren't tightly pulled. As for Phineas, she glances at him only long enough to check that it's exactly as she thought – he has eyes only for her father.

At the jetty Ella leaves the two men to bring in the boat. She waits for them in the car. The whole way home she doesn't speak. The father talks to Phineas about outboard engines. As they draw up at the house Phineas's knees dig deeper into her back. Does he lean forward, as if wanting her attention? She keeps her eyes fixed on her lap. She will show him, she tells herself. He has turned away, sided with her father. Well, let him find out what that's like, what a cosy place that is. She will be closed to him now, utterly closed. She will clam herself shut against him.

It is the father's first and the last excursion on the motor-boat; Phineas's, too.

'The thing uses too much petrol,' the father says out of the blue a few days later. 'It's a waste of time and money. I'm selling it back to Big Dave. I can't be taking Phineas out to Victory Dam every time with the excuse about a difficult engine. The men on the gate will start to object.'

226

Poort

Something around the father is seriously off, Ella is sure. The off-thing taints his eye-whites, which are yellow and glassy. He has no lips whatsoever; they're permanently pulled in behind his teeth. He sinks a bottle of Old Brown Sherry a night but four times out of five it does no more than reduce him to silence. The intercom drill is a long way in the past. The stories on the verandah are so far off it's hard to think they once happened, that she didn't make them up. He plays music on the Philips gramophone, American jazz, creaking groaning songs to which he tunelessly sings along, until the mother begs him to stop.

Things have become a lot less noisy than at any time Ella can remember, but she doesn't like it. Though she has no particular goal in mind she begins to cross off the days on Ada's Hairdressing calendar in the kitchen. At some point soon this'll all be over, she tells herself, this long-drawn-out winter season, this feeling of things out of place. June with its chilly evenings has already turned into brisk July. The winter may be dragging its feet, but it's moving on.

She sends her poem 'Strand' to a literary magazine called *Poort* run out of the University of Pretoria. Till now she had not the vaguest notion of what a literary magazine might be but her new Afrikaans teacher Miss Wispansky, a tiny Polish divorcée, puts her on to the idea.

Miss Wispansky is the only teacher at the school who has a university degree. She's the first person Ella has met,

227

apart from her headmasters, who has had an education beyond the teacher-training certificate. She's also the first person she's met who only ever wears black. From Miss Wispansky's classroom door trails a silky tail of Chanel No. 5 perfume. On her noticeboard are pinned postcards of the many foreign places she has visited: Paris, where she says she met her first husband; Amsterdam, where she met her second; Zanzibar, where she went on her most recent holiday. It's possible to lose in Zanzibar even a heart kept under lock and key, says Miss Wispansky mysteriously. Ella begins to look forward for the first time in her school life to compulsory Afrikaans.

Till recently she spent Afrikaans lessons reading under her desk the few children's books in Dutch there are in the school library, but Miss Wispansky's arrival has changed this. Miss Wispansky adores languages, including choky old Dutch, including even mixed-up pidgin Afrikaans. She says she collects them like other people collect stamps or butterflies. Her degree from the University of Pretoria was in both Afrikaans and Netherlands. The course structure recognized that the younger language stood on the shoulders of the older. At her second husband's expense she studied the two for the price of one. I was happy to humour him a while, my blond Boer, she says, I was happy to take on his language as well as its mother.

The day Miss Wispansky finds Ella reading Netherlands books under her desk in Afrikaans class, far from being put out, she claps her hands with enthusiasm. Would you like to write your finals in High Dutch? she asks: it's still possible, far as she knows. She begins to set Ella Dutch grammar exercises and comprehension tests. There'll be creative writing exercises to follow, she promises, as a reward, provided she gets her answers right.

Ella brings her notebook to school, the one in which she

wrote her poem 'Strand'. The pages with bubble-writing about Phineas she tears out and burns just like the air letter in the scummy girls' toilets using Linda's matches. For her first exercise in creative writing she rules a line under the final *weg*, then begins notes towards a new poem, something about a doll's house maybe, mending or dismantling a doll's house. Miss Wispansky walking the rows of desks catches sight of what's already there at the top of her page.

Try *Poort*, she suggests. A special schools issue of *Poort* is coming up. Ella should consider sending in a couple of poems like that one. She'll help her if she likes, type them up. Catching Ella's look Miss Wispansky explains how a literary magazine works, how anyone at all can send in material, even unpublished writers, it doesn't matter how young or inexperienced. She herself once had something in *Poort*, a translation of a short piece by Tolstoy. Yes, that's right, did she not say before? – she knows a bit of Russian, too.

Ella's issue of *Poort* – the one with 'Strand' in it – arrives in the post in the second week in July, the first Tuesday of the winter break. She crosses off the days in the kitchen calendar. *Poort* is a handsome sixteen-page production printed on ivory paper with a dark grey mottled paper cover. The print is sans serif: Ella knows about font styles from Miss Wispansky. Against the ivory paper the lettering looks slightly blue.

She opens to the title page, *Poort*, then reads through the Table of Contents. 'Strand' is by itself on an odd-numbered page towards the end of the booklet. She leafs her way slowly towards it and there it is, standing on a page by itself, the whole poem, with her very own name at the bottom.

weg
weg
weg

is set out in an indented column. At a squint – the thought comes to her for the first time – the words look like a line of footsteps in the sand.

The pleasure of seeing her very own words in print grabs her by the collarbones and pulls her upright. She stands a while taking it in, the independent look of the writing on the page, all detached from the notebook it once came from. She closes the booklet, opens it again. The words are still there. She slides the booklet in and out of its brown envelope. Over and over she strokes the ivory smoothness of the page, the surface of the poem, *her* poem. She sniffs its coolness. Does anyone ever get used to this amazing, braced-up feeling? She wishes she could speak to Miss Wispansky, that she could tell someone, anyone, that here, in this booklet, strange but true, is her poem, her very own words set out here on this page.

In the absence of Miss Wispansky she takes *Poort* to show to the mother and the father. She hears them talking in the living room. The mother at least will recognize it as a piece of craft.

She finds the two bent over the television, the father tapping the screen with a puzzled finger. Just his darned luck for the thing to go fuzzy, when for a change, it being a World Cup year, there's something on TV to watch. The Netherlands team this time is doing well. Already they have beaten Iran, Austria, Italy. Against his better judgment he's now following their successes. Degraded though the Netherlands nation is nowadays, when it does succeed at something, when the old fighting spirit of the intrepid Dutch comes out, the spirit that built the old fort at Trinco, he's happy to cheer along.

Ella approaches with *Poort* tucked up high under her arm, almost hidden, in case at the last minute she decides not to bring it out. She looks from her mother to her father.

Then something takes over, her elbow crooks, her hand reaches for the booklet under her arm.

'Look,' she says, her voice clanging raucously in the air, 'I have a poem, here in this book, I've had a poem published.'

'What was that?' the father brings his eyes close to the television screen, as if the pattern of dust on its grey surface might tell him what the matter is. He switches the set on, then off again, on, off. The mother stoops behind him, peering also.

Ella tries to open to the page. She should've marked the special spot just like the father marked his photo-albums, with a spindle of paper. She turns on too far, turns back again. Her poem was fourth from the end, no, fifth.

'Here it is.' She rotates the page round, holds it out, points to the *weg weg weg* tail. The mother takes the booklet but Ella keeps her hand on it. She slants it so that the father, still standing bent, can see the page also.

'Is that a poem? By you? When did you do that?'

'It's my own work. I had a poem published. My teacher sent it in for me.'

'But it's in Nederlands, Ella, why's it in Nederlands?' the mother asks in Nederlands, peering closer. 'I thought you were good at English, not Nederlands.'

'In Dutch you say? A poem in Dutch? What rot is that?' The father grabs the book and his glasses drop down his nose. He brings the page up to his face but cannot read it. 'Is this what you get up to when you hang about goggling on your towel? This is what you produce, these few words? Poetry in Dutch? What rot, I say. What double rot.'

'It's not rot, it's something I did.' She can hear her voice begin to rise. Hit back, she thinks. How badly she wants to hit back. 'You shouldn't say rot. Say sorry for saying rot.'

Suddenly she sees how her hand might ram the father's glasses up onto the bridge of his nose, her fingers crushing the glasses, his eyes behind the glasses. Make him see. She snatches the book back so hard his arm jerks.

'Ella, Ella,' the mother pushes her away from him. 'Your father, look, he has many things on his mind. I want you to be kinder.'

'Kinder? Who must be kind? All I can hear is that man telling me off for writing rot.'

'Exactly so,' the father bursts out, 'Rot, just rot. Quite right this man is telling you off. Poetry is rot, in whatever language. It's rot that you're bothering with poetry, also with politics. It's pure bloody Chairman Mao I hear from you. You do maths, you do science, you do right by your family. You don't go behind our backs, wasting time with rot.'

The pulse of hate in her is stronger, denser than any she has felt before. It swells like burning oil down her arms, into her hands. If she could, she wouldn't only crush his face, she'd flatten his head against the wall, she'd flatten his stupid mouth, his stupid words. She doesn't care how ill he is. Her head trembles on her neck, her skull feels as if it might burst. She's standing on a thin and fragile edge. On one side of this thin edge is a clear, open track. Walking this track she knows means tucking the book under her arm as before, turning her back, leaving them to the television. It means walking out of the room with a measured gait. Of course she didn't expect the father to like her poem, she'll say to herself as she goes. Why would it please him? He has never read a poem in his life. Who in his view ever published writing who is respectable and decent other than Winston Churchill, and he had a good excuse?

On the other side of the thin edge though is a tempting softness. Her head trembles on her neck. On this other side everything is giving, it's giving up, giving way at last. Yes, she's the rotter he takes her to be. Let her act the rotter.

On this side she can already feel under her fingers the soft givingness of pressing his head to the wall, bringing the glass paperweight in the shape of a dockyard crane there on his desk against his cheek; the even greater givingness of laying her hands around his throat, of squeezing his gulping Adam's apple inwards –

The father is suddenly yelling. His hands grab at his neck.

'Look at her, Irene, you're my witness, did you see, the fire in her eyes, how she raised her hands? Oh she did, yes she did. *Loeder*, to rise up at your own father— Who'd want to be your father? To feel that serpent's look— '

The blow comes hard to the side of Ella's face, jolts her lower jaw sideways. *Poort* falls to the floor.

'You two, no more, I won't have it.' The mother has the father by the waist.

Who did the blow come from – the father or the mother? Ella stands looking at them, her left ear ringing. The mother's on her left, the blow seemed to come from the left. Then she sees the father's face. He's crimson. The hand he's nursing on his knee is crimson. He stands bent over, glaring.

Again her hands itch to move, grapple him down properly this time, take that shouting throat down. She wants to tell him, 'Listen, *listen*, for once— ' Then she sees the expression in his eyes and suddenly she has nothing left to shout.

The angry light in the father's eyes is as blue and cold as ever, but it is also dull, dulled, almost out.

The same instant the fight drains out of her muscles. The stinging in her cheek has already faded. There's no point striking him, there's nothing in him to strike at. When she wanted to grab him just then she wanted to crush out of him what she hates. But what she hates adds up to nothing, or next to nothing. His rage has turned into a small creeping thing that can only say rot, rot, rot.

Poort is lying face-down on the floor. She picks it up. Its fall has ironed a deep crease into the page with her poem on it. She closes the magazine, takes it to her bedroom. She doesn't want to open it again. The damage to the perfect page is too difficult to look at.

When the father's dying finally comes it comes quickly, this show they have been rehearsing for so long.

After all that was said about the intercom at school it is the mother and not the daughter who takes the call from the hospital that Wednesday morning during the mid-July school break. Earlier in the day the father drove himself down to Durban for new tests. Something still the matter with the waterworks, he mumbled at breakfast, grimacing.

The mother's face as she turns from the phone is ghastly. The tumour lies like a stone in his bladder, she says, the kidneys are riddled. Days not weeks, they say, just days.

But Ella doesn't believe it. Though a cold claw fastens on her neck, she shrugs it off. Can't be true. Things don't always turn out as you hope they will. The father will get through this, he always does. He'll outfox them; he'll smash his fist on a desk somewhere and shout his way through. It can't be true that she'll be rid of him, well and truly and forever rid.

She makes a vow to herself. Here and now: at this moment. Vow. At this moment that she's running from the phone to the bathroom to fetch her mother's tranquillizers – never forget. Never go back on this, she vows to herself, this moment when he's after all still alive. Even when he's dead, do not let a veil of forgetting drop over this. Never forget how bad it's been, that being rid of him can only

Poort

bring better things. Never forget that for years you looked forward to his death; counted the days; could not wait. Never forget that looking forward, or regret it.

Late that afternoon the father arrives home in the back of an ambulance car, attached to a morphine drip. The mother goes out to meet him. They walk slowly into the house, he leaning on her arm, a nurse just behind them carrying the drip-stand. Ella watches from the front door. As he steps over the threshold she thinks of saying something, Welcome back, Sorry ... But then the moment's gone. She says nothing. Because she isn't sorry; she doesn't welcome him back.

In the hallway he waves the nurse away.

'You have other patients,' he tells her, 'You have a home to go back to. Those little footballers to feed.'

'Well, if you're sure, Mr B?'

'I'm sure, I'm sure. Of course, as you'll know' – and he winks, Ella's sure he winks – 'I'd feel a lot more cheerful, it would help greatly with my state of affairs, if Argentina weren't doing quite so well at this World Cup. Still, all things considered, for tonight I'm not complaining. I'll bear in mind we had a very nice chat in the car, we made our peace.'

Ella frowns at the mother. The mother shrugs back.

The nurse is Argentinian, she herself explains as they walk her back to the ambulance car. She and her husband are both nurses, they have brought their family out to South Africa for a year's joint training. She and the father discussed the finer details of the predicted Holland-Argentina World Cup final all the way from Durban.

'He's a tough guy,' she says, pulling the car door to. 'A real charmer.'

Unbelievable, Ella thinks, watching the ambulance car reverse out of the gate, that lightness she heard in the

235

father's voice, a lift and glide of emphasis so playful the nurse sparkled when she answered him.

Two days later the call comes early from the hospital. The father has been booked in for an emergency operation to *address* his tumour, the urologist's word. I will make a final attempt to address the tumour. Both nights at home he spends on the yellow velvet couch in the living room under the portrait of his former wife, a corner of a blanket stuffed in his mouth. From her bedroom Ella hears the couch creaking as he turns, or at least imagines she can. It creaks nearly all night long. On the second morning he has detached himself from the morphine drip. It looks used up. He receives the urologist's phone call braced against the door jamb.

For the mother and the father the news about the operation comes as a lifeline. She moves with quickened steps, he gives himself his first shave in days. He calls his town-planner friend, Nobby Clark, 'to look after a few matters in my absence. Vital to keep our discussions about law and order going.' Ella is not so sanguine. She will not yet hope against hope, which is to say, her own particular hope. She will not jump to conclusions. There still is something in the air, some unpleasant off-thing. Bad omens dog their path from the moment they get into the car.

To begin with, the father is no longer able to drive. For the first time it isn't physically possible. His belly is now so distended he can't fit behind the wheel. For the first time, when he gets in the car, adjusting the passenger seat as far back as it will go, he doesn't light a cigarette. The mother, sitting bolt upright, her eyes wide-open, makes her maiden drive to Durban.

Then there are the Indian mynahs. Screaming mynahs dive-bomb the car all the way out of Braemar, as if the family's going has offended them and they are trying to hold them back at the town gates. There's also Phineas. On Wednesday, hearing the father's news, Phineas said he'd look in some time on Friday, see how the boss was doing. On Saturday however he can't unfortunately come. There's a family get-together, his aunts, his grandmother . . . He's vague. Phineas is on his school holidays, like Ella.

'I'm sure he'll be here early, he always is,' the father says anxiously from the passenger seat, scanning the road. 'I'd like to see Phineas.'

But though they scout slowly down the township road to the very edge of Braemar, Phineas is nowhere to be seen.

All the way down to Durban the father keep his arms spread wide on the dashboard, planting a clear reflection of his white arms in the windscreen. Now and then he spits into the handkerchief he holds mashed in his fist.

The mother drives the car up to the hospital's main entrance. The father by now is ashen, looks half-asleep. There is no one at the reception desk. Help, Ella says into the two-way intercom. Quickly, please, a wheelchair. A cleaner in a pink-stripe seersucker uniform brings a wheelchair but there's no orderly available to push it. There's also a sheaf of forms to fill in. Ella pulls, tugs, drags the father from his stiffened position in the passenger seat into the wheelchair. The mother surrenders the car keys to a porter and sits down in the reception office to fill in the forms. After a few minutes, a nurse appears out of the vanishing point of a long grey corridor, plunges a syringe into the father's arm, then melts back into the distance.

The hospital has a large, square entrance foyer. Ella stands in the middle of it, the father in his wheelchair beside her. The foyer's blue linoleum floor is highly polished, gleaming, stretching away to the walls like the surface of an ice rink. She experimentally gives the wheelchair a push. It skims like an ice-block on warm steel. As he skims, the father twists his head back, glances up at her, his feverish eyes suddenly lively. She remembers how he looked at the Argentinian nurse. She holds back an instant but, no, he won't let her pause. He has caught her idea, likes the game. He strikes down on the wheels with his hands and at the same time, what the hell, she pushes, the wheelchair flies across the floor. She sets the wheels at an angle, the father slams down, she pushes. The wheelchair traces a loop halfway round the foyer, comes up short at the opposite wall.

So they carry on, pushing, striking, looping, each time making a slightly larger curve. The father begins to chuckle to himself in the back of his throat. It's like the pattern made by the motorboat that day Phineas took the father out on Victory Dam, Ella thinks, whorls within whorls, like in an ear. Each time he circles back round to her he looks as he did that day on the water, his head lolling to one side, that wide, hugely pleased smile on his face.

'More, Ella, more,' he pants when it looks like she might stop. 'Drive it again, please, one more time.'

Which Ella does he think he's talking to? she wonders. The lady in the midnight-blue dress? It's so rare he calls her Ella. But he won't let her pause and think.

'Again, Ella, again,' he says in his hoarse whisper, his hands striking down on the wheels.

The operation takes place at six that evening. The father is back in the intensive care ward within the hour. It all turns out exactly as everyone had feared – everyone, that is, except for Ella. It turns out exactly as she was hoping, considering the omens. The tumour was larger than even the urologist had suspected. There's no further point addressing it.

That night she falls asleep with the sound of the sea in her ears for the first time in years. They stay over at a

Poort

two-star hotel across the road from the hospital. From the hotel's windows the Indian Ocean is visible in thin blue strips between the tall buildings lining the Esplanade.

The next day they sit with the father in shifts: now the mother and Ella together, now the mother. Twice Ella sits with him by herself. His belaboured breathing fills the room. It's difficult to do anything but listen to it. Sometimes he pulls alarmingly at the tubes coming out of his wound but mostly his fingers work at the sheet, kneading the seam. His right index finger traces clockwise circles around a slub in the fabric.

At some point a dark bird, a pigeon or a mynah, thuds into the closed window, makes her jump. The father in the bed gives no reaction. She gets up and peers into the hospital courtyard below, to see if the bird has hurt itself and fallen, but her view is obstructed by the windowsill. She can't lean out. The window frame is gleamy with fresh paint, the latch stuck shut.

The second time she sits with the father he once opens his eyes and seems to gaze around the room. She tries not to look directly at him. Why would she? She's hoping against hope. Still she can't help noticing how very blue his eyes are in his sunken white face. How white the face is against the starched white pillow.

'Ella,' he suddenly says, his blue gaze fixed on the ceiling. Though his lips struggle to form the word it can't be mistaken. Just once, the name Ella, though this time she's completely sure it isn't her he's calling. Always she's stood in the other one's way.

She thinks about taking his hand, stilling the fingers' restless movements, but her hands stay folded in her lap. What'll she do, she wonders, once he's dead, with this iron lock on her hands, her heart? But she can't yet let herself think this – can't allow herself to think of him as dead.

239

The air conditioning hums. His turning finger rasps on the sheet. His eyelids fall closed. Then, just as she is getting up to leave, he speaks.

'Ella, stop,' he says, 'Talk to me. Won't you drive that wheel again? In the Great World, there on Finlayson Green. Your whipped-cream voice. I've never forgotten. Go on, please, drive that roulette wheel again.'

Ella and the mother take their breaks from the father's bedside in the hospital coffee shop, the Red Gingham. The nurse on duty in intensive care has its extension number. At each of her breaks the mother orders a coffee with whipped cream. She lingers over the drink, spooning up the soft white peaks. Ella chooses from the range of beverages, now orange juice, now Coca-cola, now and again tea. She has spent long enough here, longer than the mother, to discover that the hot drinks all come out lukewarm, taste more or less the same.

During the times the mother's with the father, she reads W. S. Maugham's *Collected Stories*, the fat purple collection that was a gift from Ko. It's an uncomfortable and faraway world, that Ko says Maugham got. She can't work out why he and the father missed it like they say they did, this atmosphere of testy suspicion that weighs on each one of the stories. Late in the afternoon she leaves the book open on the table to step out onto the coffee shop balcony for some air. When she returns the book has disappeared. The waitress on the till has seen no one come or go, other than Ella herself. She sits and waits but the book is not returned.

At five that evening, the phone on the counter throws out a soft pirrup. The mother and Ella are at a table drinking tea. Neither of them gets up. You should go at once, says the waitress, he's on his way.

240

Not true, Ella says to herself skating her flip-flops back to the ward, can't be true. She's hoping against hope. But the room tells her something different, the hollowness, she feels it at the door. Someone has already taken leave. The mother goes in ahead of her. She hears her cry as if from a distance, 'How can it be, that we've missed him?'

There is a very still white hand lying on the sheet, the usual square hand but with the moving fingers now bent into a claw. The mother takes the hand. Ella stands beside her. She looks around at the dusty pink walls, all the details. The drip-stand no longer hooked up to the bed, the two flies on the windowsill she hadn't noticed before, the fuzzy patch on the glass where the bird hit it. Then, at last, when she has looked at everything else, she looks at him down there, this short, narrow parcel of a person, the mouth slightly agape, the finger indentations in the pale chin where the nurses have tried to push it closed.

The mother is led away by a nurse. Ella sits down in the chair she vacated just an hour or so ago. She doesn't take her eyes off the parcel in the bed. He will stir shortly, there's no doubt. He will open his thin lips quite suddenly to speak, as he did earlier, talking about the Great World, taking her by surprise, like the ventriloquist's doll in the park used to do. It's always this way with him: important to guard against bad surprises.

But nothing happens. Time passes. For the first time he fits in with what's expected. It's all over – like you always said it would be, she thinks at last. The parcel in the bed gives no response. There's no life in him, there really is no life. She has hoped against hope. All around she can feel the hollowness, an expanding circle of silence that is stitched to the world at its outer edges by the sound of rush hour traffic on the nearby street.

At the crematorium Ella leaves the formalities early,

241

almost as soon as they've started, and steps outside into the yellow late-winter light. No one looks up or appears to mind. The formalities, she knows, are planned to be brief. A man from the Durban Missions to Seamen is due to say a few words about the father's charity work. There will be nothing about God or the afterlife – just as the father wanted it. Ko promised to fly in for the service, perhaps to recount one of the adventures from the old days, but he doesn't show up. Present at the funeral are the mother, the Missions to Seaman representative, the undertaker, the father's doctor looking shifty, Tom Watt and Nobby Clark standing close together, staring at their feet – and the daughter. The paunchy undertaker keeps checking his watch. At the point that Ella steps outside, the Missions to Seaman speaker is already puttering to a halt.

Ella walks along a tarmac pathway leading to a memorial wall at the lower end of the crematorium garden. The wall is inset with alcoves, some sealed, some open, filled with dry leaves. Halfway down the pathway is a concrete bench with a good view of the crematorium's two chimneys, the heat mirage dancing over them. To sit she has to yank down the tight underarms of her blue velvet dress but still it rides up at the back. It's her one good dress, bought years ago, at the time of the last Eisteddfod.

Now that he's gone, nothing of him must remain – this she's making sure of. She fixes her eyes on the chimney. He must be reduced to dust, crushed to powder – cremulated is the word, she's looked it up. She's better off without even the memory of him. Unless she has a clear picture of the crematorium furnace doing what it's meant to do, she will not be easy in her mind; part of her won't believe that he's gone. At 850 degrees Celsius the human body is reduced to ashes in about an hour, says the *Winkler Prins* encyclopaedia. So while the mother talks to the funeral guests out in the sunshine – Tom and Nobby off to the side, Tom blowing out smoke – she'll sit here and watch the mirage over the chimney.

When I die, don't mind it, he said. Well, look at her now, not minding. Even more than not minding, making sure. See the mother wringing her hands – I should've done this, he might've done that – raking over things: all of it is pointless. He's dead and they have shot of him: his voice, the heavy push of his hands, his hatefulness, it's all gone. He doesn't warrant raking over. He wouldn't have wanted it either, but that's not her concern. Nothing about him concerns her any longer, nothing about him matters. She owes him nothing. She was no more than a mark in the margin of his life – well, what of it? That life's now over, she can throw away the page.

The world is all before her, she's read this somewhere. She likes the sound of it. The world is all before her, there's no need to look back. For a long time she was burdened but now she's free, freed, unexpectedly free. Freer than any time before in her life. To the mirage over the crematorium chimney she says: There you go, past tense, silent at last. I can follow my own interests now and your hatefulness won't prevent me.

Till the end of the winter holiday Ella sits up watching late-night television. There is no one to tell her to go to bed, to stop drinking the father's Old Brown Sherry in slugs straight from the bottle. The mother has doubled her tranquillizer dosage, she sleeps a great deal. Give me just a few weeks, she says, till I feel less awful about everything that's happened, less guilty. That she didn't *see* how ill he was, for so long . . . what a stoic he was . . . What a tyrant, Ella thinks. She sits out on the verandah in the second rattan chair, Ko's, the one facing the father's. The house at her back feels empty and peaceful. The odd off-thing that weighed on the atmosphere has evaporated away. The interference on their television set has miraculously cleared also.

Phineas has given notice. The Saturday following the father's death, a cousin almost as tall and gangling as Phineas dropped off a scrawled note on a muddy piece of torn-off jotter paper. *I am very busy with my matric.* He hasn't shown up since. The Brickhills say he's also given notice there. Will he know about the father? Ella imagines so. The cousin will have said.

Phineas's torn-off jotter paper Ella folds into the back of her poetry notebook. From time to time she takes it out to study the looping handwriting, the tall letters pointing in all directions. Not exactly a testimonial for a potential boyfriend of steady character, she imagines the father's voice saying, then feels ashamed. On the second or third examination she finds on the back of the paper a single word written faintly in pencil, *Solomon.* Could that be Phineas's real name? she wonders. Has he perhaps tried to send her a message? His real name wasn't Zulu after all?

She's not sure why she keeps the note. To remind herself she's better off without him around, those movements of his mouth you never knew were proper smiles? To assure her that, yes, everything's turning out for the best?

Phineas's departure stretches her feeling of freedom wide. She sits on the verandah without worrying about bumping into him, how to fix her eyes, her legs. The garden is vacant, the verandah is quiet. There's no need to take account of anyone at all.

Yes, let's face it, she thinks, looking out across the lawn, since that day in the garage, when he decided to be the father's right-hand man and tell her what to do, or that following Saturday, when he grabbed her by the wrist yet warned her to come no closer – the zest went out of being with Phineas. Those two Saturdays showed what's now confirmed. Though she loved him he threw in his lot with her father. Despite occasional appearances he didn't love her as much as she dreamed.

Wherever they may meet in the future, she thinks, even if it's far away from the house, still the father and his rules will be there, standing between them. At the beginning, when first they exchanged looks, when she plotted going over to the township to join in with his friends, his marches, there was enough of whatever it was between them to ignore this. But that time passed. In those distant days she had dreams about helping Cuban soldiers, copying her relatives in the Dutch Resistance, sheltering people on the run. What was she thinking of? The father, everything he stood for, would always be in the way. Phineas himself said it that day outside the garage. He confirmed it out on the water at Victory Dam.

On the surface of course, if they met somewhere in the future, somewhere else, say, far away from South Africa and its laws, it might feel like just the two of them. They might talk properly for the first time. He might explain about his work back in the township. He might tell her at last his real name. She might ask him to say hers, which he never did. He never called her by her name.

But still the father would be there, the third in their conversation. He has thrown them on their guard for ever. Even if she ran into Phineas now – say he came back to pick up the grey school jumper he has left behind in the garage, folded like his blazer always was – if he came she'd have to talk about the father, she'd have to compose a sad face. She pushes the thought away, somehow it's very tiring. She wants to sit here in Ko's chair, quietly by herself, free of ghosts, the memory of a photograph dancing in the updraft over a bonfire, the feeling of the empty space at the back of the bookshelf where the Colt 45 once lay.

It is her responsibility now to mow the lawn, weed the flower beds. Working here and there in the leafy, overgrown corners of the garden, she finds white tufts of the father's hair, the blown leavings of the past year's haircuts gleaming half-luminous in the early dusk.

She combs through the garden, collecting every bit of hair she can find. Mixed in with leaves and dirt, there is almost enough to fill a Spar bag. The first weaver-birds of the spring have not been thorough in building their nests. Where does all the cut hair in the world go? she wonders, holding the bag up to the sunlight, the greyish clutch of hair inside. Imagine, if everyone had a lifetime's burden of hair blowing about the world . . . It's not a comfortable thought. All that scattered hair means she can't ever be certain he's gone, the earth's cleansed of him.

Behind the mound where they stoked the bonfire she digs a hole, not a deep hole, it just needs to be a hole, and buries the bag of hair. In subsequent days, mulching, weeding, she confirms she did a good enough clearing job. There are, as far as she can see, no more bright white hairs blowing about the garden.

The father, the organized bookkeeper, died at a good, efficient time, during the school winter-break, the recess before the matriculation exams. Ella did not have to take time off either for his final illness or for the funeral. The day before school re-opens Mr Kessler the headmaster telephones to speak to her mother.

'She is indisposed,' Ella says, 'I'm happy to talk.'

The head wishes to put an offer to her. She need not come back to school immediately. Should she wish to cite her bereavement, her matriculation exams can be delayed till January, even next June.

She has never heard anything so stupid, though she doesn't say so.

'Think about it, Ella. It's worth waiting until you feel ready to take the trophy results that have always lain within your reach.'

'Thanks, but no thanks,' she says firmly.

Of course she will be back to school tomorrow. Indignation fires her cheeks. Of course she will be writing her exams. They are in four weeks' time? Fine, she knew that already. She has been planning to write them all along.

'Your dear father would have wished it, I'm sure,' says Mr Kessler.

'No, I wish it,' she says. 'I don't think he cared one way or another.'

Canada

That new spring Ella enters an international scholarship competition. If she wins, the scholarship will take her to another country within the English-speaking world for an extra year of schooling, a bridge to university, or, at least, the great universe of grown-up life. The first stage of the competition is to write an essay on the topic, *The Effect on me of X*, where X is either a film or your favourite book.

During the dead days between her matriculation exams, she writes her essay. She describes how she was saved from being a Valium-addicted loner by the never-say-die spirit of Anne Shirley in the *Anne of Green Gables* series. Though the story is mainly made up it's surprising how real it sounds. She sails through this stage of the competition. Her essay, the acceptance letter says, though it had its eccentricities, was suitable and deserving.

Interviews follow, rank upon rank of interviews, first in a white-washed Tudor-look country hotel outside Braemar, then in the Imperial Hotel, Durban, then in a very grand beach hotel outside Durban, in Umhlanga Rocks. There are also written tests, an aptitude test, a language test. These she writes at school, in the hot, empty days leading up to Christmas.

At each step of her interview path experts with differently sized glasses peer at her over clipboards held at a secretive angle close to their chests. The set-up is all too familiar. She's back in Dr Fry's consulting room, back with the foot

248

specialist in Durban. She knows she'll be found wanting. It has happened before. Essay writing is one thing, scrutiny by experts is another.

But by some miracle she clears the hurdles they set. The day before Christmas Eve a call comes. Her mother is once again in bed. A Scottish voice at the other end of the line puts a wonderful question. Would she like to spend her scholarship year in the land of Anne of Green Gables?

Ella asks the voice to repeat the question, though she had no difficulty understanding it the first time. She just wants to hear the thing said all over again.

The mother takes the long-delayed decision to return to her motherland. With her dear husband gone, her daughter in transit, there's nothing to keep her on this benighted continent, this lightning-prone ridge. She'll take her sister's portrait back to where she, Ella, always really belonged, where the light and the temperature won't corrode the paint.

The house is sold, a cash sale. Nothing is said about the Braemar property's vulnerability to lightning strikes. The charred tree trunks were long ago cleared away. The sale raises enough to buy a second-floor apartment in what the mother calls a good area in The Hague, not far from various concert halls, close to a leafy park.

Bogey goes to the Brickhills next door, a happy arrangement for all parties. The Brickhills lost their old fat dog to a heart attack a month or so before the father's death. Only a hedge's breadth away from his old haunts Bogey will feel right at home. One afternoon the Brickhills' maid Eunice comes to take away the doll's house. She has four children at home who'll like to play with it, she tells Ella, and that's not counting her late sister's two she also looks after. She carries the house away on her head, the dust sheet folded on her crown as support, the furniture rattling about inside.

The roof she holds in her big muscular arms, squeezed to her chest, Phineas's grey school jumper draped over the eaves.

Now that the house is sold the mother sets about packing up the furniture. Every stick of it that she brought out with her will now travel back as it came, in wooden chests like zoo animals, the painting of her sister in its own special slatted box. The father's few bits, the table he made on his carpentry course, the Chinese lamp-stand with its kitsch jade glaze (that somehow has lost its lampshade), the ugly tea-chest from Singapore, the horrible saggy rattan furniture – these things she will leave behind. Cheap-looking stuff like that will not look right in the Hague apartment with its picture windows.

She writes home that it's not necessary for Cousin Jan-Kees to come and help her. The father may once have insisted on this, she tells Ella, but he didn't reckon on her pride. She has too much pride to lean on family charity. Nor does she need to. She'll manage everything fine, even the flight. The new tranquillizers the hospital doctor prescribed are excellent, they knock you right out. The whole journey through the sky she won't be aware of a thing.

Ella helps the mother pack up the house. Her responsibility is the father's things plus her own bits. His clothes she packs in empty melon jam cartons and lines the filled boxes at the gate, four of them, with his one smart jacket laid on the top, his Royal Netherlands Navy uniform folded underneath it, for Eunice to carry away that evening after she finishes work. Apart from the clothes, there's little else of the father's to tidy up. Funny, the mother says puzzled, looking at the lined-up boxes, I could've sworn Har had more than that, a chess set maybe, those photo-albums of his, the ones with brown covers?

Her own things Ella puts in a square tin chest bought at

Big Dave's for R 50, the price of the father's motorboat. Her notebooks and the carbon copy of the letter to Brezhnev she spreads in the bottom as lining. She tells herself she will buy fresh notebooks in Canada. She adds her pair of built-up leather shoes and the father's beetle-bored chess set, which she has kept hidden under her bed, the chess set his brother Jan gave him when he set out for Singapore. Beside the chess set she places his sherry glass, unwashed, the sticky lip-marks still on it, and the Wilhelmina Cross for War Service in the Royal Netherlands Navy she unpinned from his uniform.

Linda's father offers to store the chest in his garden shed, to wait until such time as she will return to South Africa. The day she hands over the chest he grabs her chin and makes her look into his face. 'You'll be back, won't you, young Ella? You're our ambassador now, you know that.' She cannot nod because of his hold on her chin.

But she will come back, she knows. She isn't lying. She's nothing if not an African. The father said she was, more or less. He sealed her destiny, her African genealogy. You stand at the start of a new line, he said, or words to that effect. It was one area where they saw eye to eye.

In Canada, in the leafy suburb of Toronto to which the scholarship board assigns Ella, it is like being born anew. She lives in a two-storey wooden house on a maple-lined street with a family: two soft-spoken people, the manager of the local petrol station and his wife, whose son and daughter are both at college. Ella becomes their ward, their live-in on-loan child. During the weeks she is an only child just as before, but at the weekend she has two borrowed siblings: George, an engineering student with grime under his fingernails who restores old cars; Emma-Leigh who's at drama school but unsure about continuing.

The Shouting in the Dark

Here in Canada, in north Toronto where the gardens have no fences, Ella feels free to be whoever she likes. However, she prefers to keep things simple, so she chooses the most straightforward way to be. She will be just a teenager. She will be a teenager in jeans with over-plucked eyebrows, looking like most Canadian girls her age, but one who has the outstanding talent, so her new Canadian schoolmates tell her, of speaking the Queen's English. It's perfect being this way. Everywhere she goes, she's taken at face value, as an ordinary Canadian girl who speaks copybook English.

With the stamp of ordinariness safely upon her, she risks a few less-than-ordinary things. She joins an evening poetry group organized by the Attic, the local bookshop on Main Street. Her poem the group most likes, called 'Haiku', is about a black and white photograph melting in the updraft from a bonfire. She also enters recitation competitions across Ontario. She travels from east to west across the vast province, from Thunder Bay through North Bay to Ottawa, with her declamation of 'Kubla Khan'.

Using slides donated by the South African Tourist Board she develops a slide show that she takes around schools and debating societies in southern Ontario. The slide show stuns its audiences with ten minutes of spectacular landscape photographs marinaded in golden sunshine. She clicks her way rapidly around the carousel, with minimal commentary: see the purple hills, the towering mineshafts, the river valleys clotted with poplars, the wide white beaches. Then she switches on the light and tells her blinking audience: 'That's the dream the Tourist Board wants you to believe, but the reality is different. The reality is hatred and here are the details. During the student riots two years ago, to give just one example, the police used so much tear gas that, a few miles distant, your eyes smarted and ran. My eyes smarted and ran. The police fired on unarmed schoolchildren, boys and girls my age, one of them I knew— '

After her slide shows people break out clapping, raise eyebrows at her courage, or is it her foolhardiness? How will she ever return to South Africa? they ask. Shouldn't she take more care?

Ella shakes her head firmly, thanks everyone for their support. Like at the Eisteddfods, she enjoys lifting her voice for an audience, seeing the lights in their eyes shift, brighten. The difference is that now she's talking not of England and tree-fringed country lanes, as at the Eisteddfods, but of South Africa, anger, resistance, 'freedom one day soon'. The soldiers in free Africa, they were the boldest people she had ever seen. Telling her tear gas stories, she thinks of them. She thinks sometimes of Phineas. The thing he said that last time. We submit or we fight.

Following her talk at the golf club in Barrie, a stooped woman in a Toronto Maple Leaves shirt and shiny trainers intercepts her at the door. 'I can't help asking myself, my dear,' she whispers, 'what background are you? Jewish? You must have something ancestral. Why, otherwise, would you be so furious?'

At her north Toronto high school Ella is enrolled into the Ontario Grade 13, for which three subjects are required. She takes four, Mathematics, Further Math, English, Greek Philosophy. Greek Philosophy is an extra but she likes it almost as much as she likes Math. Greek Philosophy is made up of straightforward observations about the world linked into logical chains she can agree with completely, the taken-for-granted things that back in Braemar she wrote in her notebook and thought she had worked out all by herself. Everything is water, everything flows. You never step in the same river twice. Life proceeds by number, in patterns. If x is y and y is z then z is x. All things are linked and proportionate to all other things.

She earns pocket money by cutting her school friends' hair and tutoring English grammar and maths after school to children in younger classes. Some of her pupils are Vietnamese boat people who have no English at all. With the first dollars she earns she buys at the Attic Bookshop a book whose title calls to her from the shelf: *White Man, We Want to Talk to You*. The book is banned in South Africa, the cover says, though it's all about the country. It has some good ideas about how the place might be improved. When barriers exist between people like they do in South Africa, the author Mr Herbstein says, you must pull them down before you talk. She believed nothing different before she ever read the book, and is happy for Mr Herbstein to agree with her. His book makes good plain sense, unlike *Lady Chatterley's Lover*, which is the second book she buys with her pocket money. *Lady Chatterley's Lover* is also banned in South Africa but its agitation and blather puts her on her guard.

Not long after she finishes reading *White Man, We Want to Talk to You* she joins the three-day Fast Against Apartheid campaign organized by the local United Nations group operating out of Wantage County Hall not far from her school. She finds it's not so difficult living on fruit juices and flavoured ice-cubes. After all, she has had the practice.

At the break-the-fast meal, she falls into conversation with a tall African-looking boy called Ivor Dearlove whom she knows from Further Math. Ivor, it turns out, is originally from Cape Town. In the year of the school riots his father, a headmaster in a Coloured high school, openly gave his support to the striking students. He had to take his family into exile in Canada to avoid arrest. Ivor says this matter-of-factly, as if it had cost them nothing: they pulled up their roots and shook off the clinging soil and now are happily settled in Ontario. His older sister has had a baby here. Recently he won the position of first trumpeter in the school orchestra.

She and Ivor see Bette Midler in *The Rose* together at the local movie house and have a milkshake afterwards. It's her first proper date with a boy; it'll also be her last date with Ivor. Looking at Ivor's face across the rim of her milkshake glass she can't help thinking of Phineas, comparing Ivor and Phineas. She can't help remembering how smoothly Phineas's skin stretched over his cheeks, how his bones glowed through his skin. Ivor's skin isn't smooth and his shave is uneven. How her breath caught, how that charge travelled down from her throat to her feet, she remembers, when the gleam of Phineas's smile came up from under his brow.

But the story of Ivor's family gives her a boost, it backs her up. It's good to look to the future, to turn from the past. Ivor's family has done it. The world lies all before them, before her. Things that were once important and real are now far-away, the deep blue Indian Ocean, the stars of the Southern sky. The craggy grey stone of Upper Canada has come in place of the African shield's red rock. But she knows that these faraway things, though she sometimes misses them, have not vanished. Only the smaller things, the things that were sad or difficult, those *are* gone forever. That scorched medallion of sticky earth at the back of the house in Braemar. The white hairs blowing about the garden. The hand on her face, pressing. Things she doesn't ever want to think about again but that sometimes, though more and more rarely, crop up uninvited in her thoughts.

Looking ahead, not back – it isn't a rule she needs to impose. Tomorrow stretches wide before her. There's so much to be done in it. There's so much more to be done with every new day now that she doesn't have to go about clenched like a fist, ready at every moment to take up arms, do battle with her adversary. Her hate-fuelled fight is now over: Daughter versus Monster, *Schepsel* versus Father, a fiercer bout every time. The fighter who was created by that fight has died in her, or at least has crept to a place where she no longer hears it stirring.

As for her one-time opponent, she doesn't think of him. The weekly letters from her mother she stuffs unread into the brown cardboard suitcase she came with to Toronto. The letters will only remind her of what she wants to forget. Now that her mother's safely back in the Netherlands, she likes to hark back to Africa, to reminisce about everything she didn't properly appreciate when she lived there, more's the pity, *wat een zonde*, the pine forest walks, the breath-taking views, the bracing air. Her monthly phone calls are full of this kind of talk. 'Sitting on the verandah of our house, drinking in that view,' she says in Netherlands, 'You felt you owned the world, didn't you think, Ella?' 'No,' Ella says, 'No. I didn't feel that. And besides you didn't ever spend much time on the verandah.'

If she is asked in passing, at the primary schools she visits, the evening classes she gives, how she got here to Toronto, so young, without her parents, she has on hand a few set-piece stories to explain. Her mother has always lived in Holland, she tells people. She, Ella, was drawn to Canada because she loved L.M. Montgomery's *Anne of Green Gables* and because Canadian forces liberated Holland in 1945 – this story is the true one. Her father was a rolling-stone type, she says, a bit of an entertainer, a raconteur, a wanderer, a blagger. He rolled his way around the sultry ports of the Indian Ocean; he died years and years ago. He had four wives, and a daughter almost by accident. This second story has some truth in it. Holland is where her heart belongs, she says, and Africa is a big and interesting place where she once spent time, collected and ate fried locusts, every morning drank fresh ostrich blood, lived in a thatched Zulu hut.

She repeats the stories so often, in bus queues, at recitation events, though not at school, not with her host family, that they become a manner of speaking, a habit. As she runs them through, as her mouth moves, she thinks about something else.

The world is all before her, but time, as the Greeks have told her, doesn't always run forwards in the smooth way you might expect. Unanticipated reminders can bring sudden loopbacks, interrupting the plain surface of things. Knotholes surface in the wood; one story fails to branch into another.

For the summer holidays Emma-Leigh proposes a cycling trip to Prince Edward Island, the home of L.M. Montgomery. They can take the train through Montreal to New Brunswick, then cycle the road through the pine forests from Amherst to the PEI ferry. 'I never read those books,' Emma-Leigh smiles, 'but I'm keen to have a look round our smallest province. They say the weather off the Atlantic makes the trees grow sideways, almost bent to the ground. They also say Lucy Maud herself was a weather vane, now up, now down, nothing like sunny Anne. In her diary she kept writing *I want freedom and a friend.* Looks like she didn't know which one was better.'

Ella wastes no time falling in with Emma-Leigh's plan. Though the summer is several months away, she signs herself out of school for the day and makes all the arrangements. She books the train tickets to Amherst at Toronto's Union Station and buys a second-hand bicycle, a boy's racer. She borrows all the *Anne* books from the school library, reads to the end of the first book and then stops, with Anne still carefree and irrepressible. The next week she also takes out *The Diary of Anne Frank* and skims through it in an evening. Funny, she notices, she hadn't spotted before: how much Anne Frank is like Anne Shirley. Anne Frank also lacked freedom and yearned for a friend.

On the first official day of spring, the snow still thick on the ground, a journalist from the local paper comes to interview Ella during her morning break at school. The following Saturday he meets her at the local ice rink, takes a picture of her skating clad in an orange ski-jacket, arms awkwardly akimbo, the unusual sight of a Dutchwoman unfamiliar with ice. The story and the photograph appear in the paper the following Monday but bar a few friendly glances from the staff at the newsagent where she buys it, it attracts little attention. *My aim is to get over to Prince Edward Island this summer*, the serif Times New Roman by-line announces. 'Way to go, girl,' says the woman at the till. 'At your age I still loved those *Anne* books, too.'

A month or so later the *Gazette* forwards her a letter. Someone has written in response to the article. She props the letter beside the phone in the hallway, reluctant to open it. The letter, she knows, will hark back whereas she is moving forwards. All letters hark back. That air letter signed in Chinese characters by the woman with the Panama hat. The *Gazette*'s article already feels as if it was about another person, a newcomer she no longer resembles. She has gone skating many times since the day she was photographed. She made sure she did. Nowadays she can skate backwards, more or less; she can make the occasional figure-of-eight. The PEI trip with Emma-Leigh is just around the corner. Everything is ready. George has taught them how to mend punctured tyres and fix bike chains. In the evenings they go running, sometimes even skating, to get fit. Emma-Leigh tells Ella she'll make a final decision about drama school while they are on their journey.

For several days Ella leaves the *Gazette*'s letter where it lies. As with the stuffed envelopes that come from the mother in Holland, she has grown used to leaving letters lying. Then Curt, the same journalist who wrote the article, calls to ask about the letter. When readers do write in, he says, we're always keen to gauge what they like to respond to. In this case, was it the photograph in the ice rink, the story— ?

She tears open the letter with Curt still on the line. *Wim Vermeer*, she reads the name signed in a large sloping hand across the bottom. It sounds distantly familiar, maybe because it's Dutch? She'd thought to read the letter out but, as it's only a few lines long and all in Nederlands, summarizes instead. The whole thing pivots on a question of names. In the context of the Dutch connections mentioned in the article, the letter writer Mr Wim Vermeer has recognized something about her name. Many years ago, he says, he served on a Royal Netherlands Navy N-class destroyer with the British Eastern Fleet alongside another officer bearing her family name. True, the ages don't quite compute, she seems quite young to be this man Har B's daughter, but the name – he'd recognize it anywhere. He'd wager it's related to his old friend.

If any of this rings true to her, the letter concludes, could they meet? He gathers from the article that her father is no longer alive. Still, he'd appreciate hearing news of him and, in return, he can perhaps give her, Har's daughter, a story or two about the old days. He includes a phone number, a west Toronto address.

For a while after Curt's call, Ella, still at the phone table, stares at the signature. *Wim Vermeer*. Then it jumps into focus. The *Van Galen*, Wim Vermeer. She hears the father's voice speaking the name out on the verandah, the clink of his tumbler on the glass-topped table. Wim Vermeer, the fellow officer trained in Trinco, transferred after time spent on the N-class sister ship the *Van Galen* back to the *Tjerk Hiddes*.

She arranges to meet Mr Wim Vermeer in a downtown café off Bloor Street not far from the Royal Ontario Museum. The café, suggested by Curt, is called the Red Gingham. Is the name unlucky or only vaguely inauspicious? There's no point worrying about it. She sets out early.

On her way down Bloor Street she passes the University of Toronto Student Union building, the big noticeboard wired to the gate. A bright yellow poster with green and red lettering catches her eye. *Waging the Armed Struggle inside the Police State*. Police state? – with those kinds of colours, that can be one place in the world only. She goes up to the poster, bends down to the small-print biography of the speaker at the bottom, and feels suddenly dizzy. Comrade M is an ex-guerrilla fighter, the poster says, a campaigner for justice in his home country, South Africa, now seeking asylum in Canada. He first left his home township aged sixteen, at the time of the student riots. He studied at the Solomon Mahlangu Freedom College in Tanzania, a school for black children on the run, named after the first protesting student to die. He's gone back across the border several times carrying armaments and supplies.

Ella looks at the blurry black-and-white photograph printed beside the biography. A young man in a woollen hat, his face half-averted. A round chin, a fleeting smile.

Solomon Mahlangu, she asks herself straightening up slowly, where has she seen that name before? *Solomon?* She pictures looping handwriting. The name on the muddy note Phineas sent, that's it, the name she thought was his other name. Solomon. Was he trying to send her a special

260

message after all? She leans against the noticeboard to still her trembling. Did he intend the word as a secret sign? This is where I'm headed, is that what he was trying to tell her? This is my work. What I must tell you is more than just about your father.

But what does it matter? She checks the date. She can't attend this talk by the ex-guerilla Comrade M who isn't Phineas, doesn't have his smile. The talk's this time tomorrow. It'll be a bind to come into the city centre two days in a row, sign out of classes yet again. When, after all, she wants to be free of ghosts.

In the Red Gingham café Ella sits at a corner table with a cup of instant coffee, the cheapest coffee on the menu. Picture stencils of fruit salads make a wavering line around the walls. Curt has arranged to call by in an hour and a half to make sure the conversation is proceeding okay. If it turns out Mr Vermeer *did* know her father he might even take a picture, write up something. It's a great small-world story: how the war despite its cruel sunderings forged contacts across continents.

And Wim Vermeer *did* of course know her father Har B on the *Tjerk Hiddes*, it's confirmed the minute he shakes her hand and sits across from her, this tall, well-preserved man in his late sixties with his quiff of good white hair and light Canadian accent who however says the words *Tjerk Hiddes* with the same intonation that her father used to use. It's further confirmed when he at once begins sifting through details and pictures she thought she'd never encounter again but now flash up as clearly as on the day she first heard them, peering through the curtains. The green and blue harbour at Trinco shaped like a human hand. The nugget bricks of Fort Frederick. Old Schilperoort and his bitter rum-and-chocolate drinks called *kaai*. The Grote Oude Hoer, the courtyard bar full of scavenging crows.

The happy ship; the happy happy ship. How happy was he, Wim, to be transferred from the *Van Galen* to the beautiful solidarity of the *Tjerk*.

Quickly she perceives that Wim Vermeer like her father is far more interested in his own stories than in others'. He talks and he talks some more. It's just as well, because, as she informs him as soon as he sits down, she has no stories of her father's to tell, he never told her his stories. Never? Wim's white eyebrows lift. No, never, though here and there, admittedly, she overheard stuff, picked up a few scraps. Then let me know what you'd like to hear. You'll know, surely, of our destroyer's finest hour? The time you sank the Japanese cruiser on the way to Suez? she suggests. Or the fight to the death in the North Atlantic? No, not those, I heard about those, but by then, as I can tell you, I'd already left the *Tjerk Hiddes* and the war at sea.

'It happened like this.' Wim bends himself over his cup of filter coffee, rubs his hands as if to gather his thoughts. 'What a time it was,' he finally says. 'It changed us totally. After that, none of us would ever be the same again.

'By early 1942, you see, the Japanese empire had thrown its arm across the whole Indonesian archipelago, where the one-time Netherlands Empire had seemingly hastened to make room for it. In the east of the island of Timor, at the very end of this great arm, at the fingers if you like, pockets of Australian and Netherlands Indies guerrillas, once of the Sparrow force, continued to the end of the year to put up a plucky resistance. But even they finally conceded that the game was up. The locals were turning them into the Japanese authorities wherever they found them. Evacuation had become urgent, by Christmas if possible.

'It would be the trickiest and most dangerous of operations, as you might imagine. Only the most reliable of war vessels would be able to undertake it. Who to turn to but the *Tjerk Hiddes*? The ship of happy heroes that for some months already had been patrolling Australian waters, plying between Port Hedland and Fremantle, watching out for Japaners, the ship that moreover had experience evacuating troops from Flores under the guidance of the deft Klaas Sluijter? We were the victims of our own great reputation for courage under pressure, at least in the opinion of this yellow-livered officer. We were to be skewered by our own success. Our instructions, you see, were enough to chill the blood of the very bravest war hero.'

Ella looks out of the window. Hard to believe it's the city of Toronto out there, the sharply angled high-rises, the rush hour traffic streaming by – that, if she focused a little harder, it wouldn't be two rattan chairs she'd see, and smoke-rings rising.

'The evacuation the *Tjerk Hiddes* would have to undertake at East Timor would be entirely on her own,' Wim Vermeer continues, 'Under the cover of darkness. In early December that year there was no moon. And our charts for the straits around Timor were incomplete. We'd be approaching an uncharted shore in utter darkness. To increase our speed and hence our efficiency we therefore relieved ourselves of our heaviest armaments, all our torpedos and our 14.7 inch anti-aircraft guns. It was with significantly reduced protection we'd encounter any Japanese bombers who came our way.

'But who were we to reason why? as the saying goes. We were only two hours out of Darwin steering due north to throw the Japanese off the Timor scent when, as if to test the sincerity of our intentions, their bombers suddenly sought us out. Ten bombers at first, then what looked like another ten. Hell-fire broke out not just from the skies, but immediately overhead as the guns we still had on board did their best to blast back. And from that moment till sundown our good ship was attacked without let-up, in relays of bombers and dive-bombers, they just kept on coming. And from that moment till sundown our Captain had us on Emergency Full Ahead, taking the zigzag course for which he by then was famous, though that day he had to maintain his zigzag for longer than ever before, or than anyone thought possible. It saved the day though, how he grimly hung there, blackened by smoke, that and the rapid action of the guns. By a miracle we survived, more or less intact, with just a few nerves rattled and one man dead. An accident with our own guns.

'Sometimes I get flashes from that nightmarish day, see it again as if it was yesterday. Klaas Sluijter up in the rigging. The dive-bombers swooping, looking like every next one might be a kamikaze. And Har your father there beside the X-installation guns, what a figure he cut, short, bow-legged, with his thick glasses. He was well known for drinking everyone under the table but he stood out because of the glasses. Obviously it wasn't an everyday occurrence to find a Navy officer manning the guns with poor eyesight like his. It certainly wasn't an everyday occurrence to find that same officer up with the 12.5 cannons whenever we met with enemy fire. Crommelin our chief artillery officer, see, he was often ill with something, nerves perhaps. So your Dad took over. He was always there, his glasses winking in the sunlight. During that attack on the Timor crossing, in fact, I remember it clearly, his glasses were cracked by the kickback during a salvo. Both lenses. Could hardly see a thing, poor fellow, but still he stayed up there, shouting *Fire!* long after the other officer on the job went hoarse.

'It took three trips, each two days apart, all between the hours of midnight and four in the morning, when the night is blackest, to evacuate over a thousand people including women and children off Timor to Darwin. The *Tjerk*

Hiddes made all three crossings without once stopping or refuelling. Throughout, she was entirely on her own, unassisted, almost without firepower, sliding like a ghost across a sea so black the stars overhead were reflected in it.

'It was one of the unsung heroic actions of the war, that rescue, the first trip in particular when we were attacked. I'm surprised your father didn't tell you about it. You write yourself, the newspaper said. I'd say put down this story, get it about. Let others know.'

As if to prompt her he draws a pen from his shirt pocket and lays it on the table. The pen is not a Bic, she's almost surprised to see. Probably he just wants to take her telephone number, but still she shakes her head.

'I don't think I can, Mr Vermeer.' Her hair flies about her face. 'It's not possible. Seeing as he told me nothing himself. When he talked about the war, he talked to his friends and was mostly angry. He said he'd been done wrong by the war, the West. By the whole of history. He was going to rebuild the white republic. Every man he met he tried to recruit, I now think. Those stories were a heavy load for him to carry. For my part, I want to be rid of that load. I write poetry, not stories. I don't want to re-live his war or shoulder his burden.'

But in spite of what she has said she finds herself taking a napkin, picking up the pen. Wim Vermeer's eyes follow her writing hand. She writes the word *Verandah* along the napkin's red gingham border.

'It's a funny thing,' he says, 'That the story of the evacuation of East Timor is one you say you never heard. Whereas it's a story I never stop telling. It follows me like death. It was the point where the war and I parted company.

'You see, when we finally returned to Port Darwin after Timor I took my leave of the happy ship *Tjerk Hiddes*. For good. Had to. I was ashamed to seem to give up, but I'd had it. Shock. The doctor signed me off. War at sea is strictly for heroes, hell-bent heroes. Stuck on the face of the waters like a sitting duck, begging for the enemy's planes to seek you out, as we were during that Timor jaunt – it was too much for me. Eventually I found an office job in Fremantle, stayed there till the end of the war. Insurance – some of it to do with shipping. Dutch work in a way though no longer in the Navy proper. In '45 the company transferred me to Canada, Oakville, west of here on Lake Ontario.

'Walking through Darwin the day I left our happy ship I bumped, as it happened, into your Dad Har B on his way to having his glasses fixed. I embraced him like a brother. It was my chance to say goodbye, ask the question that had been troubling my head since that terrible night. I looked into his eyes through those two cracked lenses and popped it out point-blank. How did you do it, Har? I said. How did you stick it out? I'm finished and I wasn't even on the guns.

'Here's what he said in reply, "Shat myself, then carried on." Excuse my language but he meant it literally. That was his way. "Looked up at Klaas Sluijter there in the mast shitting himself, and carried on. Thought of the ship." He was braver than I, Har B. Braver or more foolhardy, I'm not sure. I couldn't have lasted till the end of the war as he did, in that tiny unsung rump of a Netherlands Navy, first in the East, then on the North Atlantic convoys, no less. Not under any circs. Impossible. I was a nervous wreck. The whole beautiful solidarity thing didn't impress me in the same way. But it did Har and he survived to tell the tale, it seems. Or not to tell the tale, as you say . . .'

From the doorway of the Red Gingham Ella watches Wim Vermeer's nest of white hair drift away through the late afternoon crowd flowing along Bloor Street. He is moving steadily though quite slowly. There's still time to call him back, she tells herself. When he turned from her just then he looked suddenly lost, uncertain. She and Wim, strange to think, spent less than an hour and a half together talking. Curt's still nowhere to be seen. But what's the point of continuing? He has given her after all his main story. Anything else is just detail. If she called him back, what would she ask him? On board ship, was her father always angry, or did that only happen after the war? Did he shout out to himself on deck as he did at home, spitting and swearing, even when there were no guns to fire? She suspects she knows what Wim would reply.

Once Wim turns and raises his hand and she raises her hand. But she doesn't call him back, she won't ask him her questions. She wonders whether she'll tell Curt Wim's story when he arrives, as she knows he hopes she will, or whether she'll make something up, as she thinks she might. She squints out across the crowd. Wim's quiff is still there in the distance, though smaller now, further away, steadily receding. The grey evening light makes of its whiteness a bright dot.

The nights she stood at her bedroom window in Braemar squinting into the darkness, looking for the invisible stranger who would step out of the shadows to decode her father's stories: the scene surges into memory. Has that stranger now at last appeared to her, she wonders, in the shape of Wim Vermeer? Is the secret now at last laid bare, the louring secret she has so long watched out for, the secret that there was in fact no secret, no hidden shame, there was in truth nothing to unravel? The secret that – unlike Wim Vermeer – her father was haunted by no spectre: he simply stayed with his ship. He was the solid but myopic officer in a tight spot. The secret that he had nothing to hide, no shame, no funk, nothing other than his war wounds, and those, at least till the war had ended, he kept under tight wraps. The secret that no matter the terrors he spat at the night sky, he always maintained his watch. Staring out from the verandah as if on board ship, he sat ready for whatever the horizon might throw at him.

She looks out across the crowd. The white dot that was Wim Vermeer has vanished. She walks back to her table in the café. At her place the napkin with the word *Verandah* written on it still lies. Beside it is Wim's pen, which she sees is engraved with his name. Did he mean to leave it behind? she wonders. Should she return it to him or keep it? She thinks she will keep it.

She folds the napkin small, in half, in quarters, in eighths, till it makes a tiny pillow, and shoves it into her empty coffee cup. Then she takes a fresh napkin and with Wim's pen writes another word, *Solomon*. That second sign she received today, a secret she never expected to have decoded. As she writes a tension she did not know she harboured flows out through her hand. The final stroke of the *n* makes a black gash in the tissue paper.

So, she asks herself, has she faced him down, the unsung hero her father firing at the enemy through cracked spectacles? Has he gone from her now? She can't tell for sure. All she knows is – she can keep on. In spite of him, because of him, she will keep on. He kept on, during all those incidents at sea. Phineas did, too, after his own fashion, as she now strongly suspects. She remembers the loops within loops on the surface of Victory Dam. Keeping on. On the napkin she writes under *Solomon* the words *Bonfire*, Poort, *Canada*, *Zigzag* . . . Then she gets up, folds the napkin into her pocket and sets forth – out of the café door, up the street, one foot in front of the other, one word after another, tacking this way and that through the late afternoon crowd.

Ella waits at the University Union's side-door for Comrade M the ex-guerrilla speaker to finish. The door is open. She watches his woollen hat, the same as in the photo, encircled by jostling, clamouring students. She had to leave school at the normal time today but still caught the talk's closing. She heard Comrade M describe seeing a friend fall to police guns in a township. On a map he traced his escape route across the South African border through liberated Mozambique to Tanzania and freedom. Help me bring that same freedom to my country, he ended. Donate generously, we exiles need funds.

Ella steps out in front of him as he approaches the door. Hello, she says, goes straight to the point, I want to do more than give money. He smiles at her accent. You're from home. She wants to say she has no home, but she nods. Go back, he says without hesitating. Lie low but go back. We need people on the ground like you, to fight low-key but with energy, give support, provide safe houses. We need ordinary white householders with the courage to leave their back windows open at night, so that people on the run can gain access, find a place to rest. Become a maker of our new future. Stand and be counted.

Where has she heard words like that before?

He gives her his card, writes a number on the back, an office in Toronto, the date of a next meeting. It's the day before she and Emma-Leigh go to PEI. Don't tell anyone you're coming, he says. Take a route downtown you wouldn't normally take. We'll look forward to seeing you.

Just one more thing. Ella opens her mouth to speak. At your Freedom College, did you ever meet . . .? But he's already moving away from her. *Phin-e-as*, she begins to sound. His eyes fix on her lips, then flip away. 'Call us,' he waves, 'We'll be expecting you.'

Zigzag

Ella pulls herself upright in the armchair in the Dutch apartment and stretches. Her bones creak. The sky paling to grey behind the trees in the park picks out the two documents, the pale photocopy of the Volksregister's *blank page, the grey official letter, still lying here on the window sill. With the growing light her reflection in the window has receded. A ghostly outline flickers against the green of the beeches opposite.*

She moves to the kitchenette and lights the gas for coffee, watches the blue flame dance under the kettle. Wim Vermeer's naval adventure featuring her father the stalwart gunner, the good man in a tight spot – for years the story pointed to a new side of him, a different angle to think about. Now she's once again left puzzling. Is there something else again the story is saying?

She walks back to the window with her coffee cup, leans against the glass, gazes out across the park. A chain of puffy cloud is touched by a faint pink light from a still-invisible sun. Thinking back, she wonders if she has misconstrued, looked out for the wrong things? In her stories, after all, her father's always the antagonist, always shouting at the night. Wim Vermeer's adventure tale: that, too, fits the pattern: see her heroic but hell-bent father, peering through cracked glasses beside the X-installation guns.

But is there a different way of seeing the story, another way of telling it? Even the gap in the Volksregister,

270

thoughtless and mean as it looks, what else might it be showing? What was it her father used to say? Born here in Africa, Africa claims you. Watch out for rival claims. Be part of where you stand. Is this why he refused to acknowledge her as his own? To give her a new beginning, cut off from the past: not just a war veteran's daughter, the child of a eunuch of history? Ella can hear his voice in her memory. Beware those blank spaces in the Volksregister *lying in wait for you like traps.*

And hasn't she, in point of fact, fallen in with his logic these last many years? What has she done but lived out his instructions, on some levels, in certain ways. Defend where you belong. You'll have no more than this ever. Stand up for what you claim. Less than two years after she heard Comrade M speak in Toronto she was back teaching English in the townships around humid Durban – KwaMashu, Inanda, Umhlanga. She knew what it was to learn English from the outside. She set up her safe house for political fugitives on the run, building it contact by slow contact, one small node in a vast network that still blankets the country. For years now she's done this: smuggling people with hats pulled low over their faces into the space under her bed late at night. She spends the hours till dawn listening to a stranger's breathing beneath her head, watches the crack in the curtains for the creeping blue light of the police. The people she shelters are mostly young, mostly male and scared, but she's trained not to pick up on the individual details. She never hears their voices, never knows their names. Yet each time without fail, as the first light breaks and she prepares to wake them and set them on the road, buttered bread wrapped in foil already to hand, she cranes down to check their faces. One day, you see, you just never know, it might be him.

Lying awake in bed she remembers back sometimes to

her Durban den, the iridescent sunflies winking between the hydrangea flowers, and it feels as if her whole life has pointed only in this direction. Except these days she is – or was – the cover not the coquerer. The fact that she's good at night watches, staying awake till first light – how lucky this has turned out to be.

In the corner of her left eye Ella's aware of a patch of white, the sheet she last night hung over the portrait on the wall, catching the brightening light. She walks across, steps up onto a chair, lifts the folds of the sheet off the frame, lets the sheet drop. Here again are the portrait's eyes. The tiny flakes of dry blue-white oil paint that make up the eye-whites glister in the sunshine. In spite of all her worry, the mother didn't get round to having the painting restored. When she returned to the Netherlands from South Africa, nothing of her old life, her life with her mother, father, sister, was restored to her.

Ella steps down from the chair but the eyes remain fixed on her eyes. The picture beside her father's desk all those years, she thinks, in Durban, in Braemar, his face bathed every day in her Aunt Ella's detached gaze. You, Ella, she says out loud, woman whom my father loved, whom did you see when you stared out of your gilded frame? Him, always him. There he is, sitting every day in your company, saying my name yet dreaming of another.

Life proceeds by number, said the Greeks, in patterns. What if her father's story fits into a different pattern than one of antagonism and hate: his hate, her own hate? She thinks of Captain Klaas Sluijter plotting a zigzag course across the blue ocean. Her father and Phineas in the boat on Victory Dam, laughing together like carefree boys. Different patterns: zigzags, circles, continuations; not warring opposites. The long line of fugitives sliding in under her bed. She remembers her father's stubby fingers

272

gripping the white loop of the telephone wire, the day of the trunk call, when first he spoke to the other Ella in her hearing. How tightly he squeezed the wire so that Ella's sister Irene might have an uninterrupted line of connection to the old world he despised.

The lawyer's call at ten o'clock is expected, yet still it makes Ella jump. He does not waste time on greetings. 'Ella, Chris here, it's as we expected. Your bid to remain this time has failed. You must prepare to leave the country, at least for a while. However, the story's not yet over, believe me. I plan to plead against the decision.'

Ella holds the telephone between her shoulder and her chin and picks up the sheet she just let drop. As the lawyer talks she gets back on the chair. With one hand she hooks the sheet over the right-hand corner of the portrait.

'You yourself have given me the lead,' the lawyer is saying. 'That thing you were telling me yesterday, about your work giving refuge, on that basis we can mount a case for asylum. Refuge granted for refuge given. A question now not of your father's oversight but your own hard work. Your fight, in short, is by no means over.'